PRAISE FOR
SILENCE

"Park Tracey, the author of *The Bereaved* (2023), is a remarkable writer, and this book is another triumph. The character of Silence is a wonderful creation who endures a life suffering, doubt, and blazing anger, and readers will be invested in her fate. The archaic language and fine detail relate what it was like to live in a typical household of the time, all the household practices of everyday life, and how, for example, to prepare for long winters: 'Withal, the apples have been cut and dried, the apple-butter crocked, the cider pressed. Crane-berries and wild grape are gathered and dried.'

A historically astute and compelling must read."

—*Kirkus Reviews, Starred Review*

* * *

"Julia Park Tracey's *Silence* is a powerful, lyrical marvel of a novel. The challenges that Silence Marsh faces and the questions that she struggles with after she has been sentenced to a year of silence by her Separatist community not only create a vivid and authentic picture of Puritan New England, but also resonate in meaningful ways with our own times. Silence's story is both haunting and inspiring, and I am grateful to Julia Park Tracey for having given her such a captivating voice."

—Jean Hegland, author of *Into the Forest*

* * *

"I'm a huge fan of Julia Park Tracey. Her new novel *Silence* is a moving, transcendent novel in the vein of Groff's *Matrix* and Toews's *Women Talking*. Historical fiction, yes, but more importantly, an inquiry into female agency and power in a world that takes the breaking of the spirit as its right. Beautiful."

—Christian Kiefer, author of *The Heart Of It All*

"*Silence* reads as if the author lived through the events that take place in the early days of the American Colonies, rather than so brilliantly imagining them. In fact, we do live through them, in the guise of Julia Park Tracey's bewitching, wise, and delightful narrator, who must navigate a narrow, superstitious world, and who in the process learns that being punished by temporal silence can unexpectedly open a wide and loving universe."

—SANDS HALL, CODIRECTOR, MEMOIR & NONFICTION PROGRAM, COMMUNITY OF WRITERS, AUTHOR OF *Reclaiming My Decade Lost in Scientology*

* * *

"Julia Park Tracey is a master of historical detail. Her deft eye brings alive the story of Silence Marsh, a woman whose unintentional acts bring persecution for the sin of female weakness so intense, it seems unbelievable yet true to the religious practices of early 18th-century America. The loss of her mother, husband, and child, her precipitous fall and subsequent rise with a man from the Age of Reason, cleaved me to her story and ultimately brought me to tears. I didn't want *Silence* to end!"

—JULIA CHIBBARO, AUTHOR OF *Redemption*

* * *

"With disarmingly restrained yet empathic prose, Julia Park Tracey introduces us to Silence Marsh as she wades through immeasurable loss and grief in pre-Revolutionary Massachusetts. However, it is her journey towards redemption that makes Silence a timeless heroine in the wake of the Puritanical strictures of Hingham village. What an achievement. I love this character and I love this book."

—MIAH JEFFREY, AUTHOR OF *American Gothic*

"Tracey's writing is sumptuous and absorbing, transporting the reader to a provincial, eighteenth-century Puritan village while weaving together a deeply felt story that packs a considerable punch."

—GREG HOULE, AUTHOR OF *The Putnams of Salem: A Novel of Power and Betrayal During the Salem Witch Trials*

* * *

"To grieve is a crime in Julia Park Tracey's lyrical novel *Silence*, unflinching in its depiction of the tyranny of religion and patriarchy and yet strikingly tender. Tracey deftly explores how one woman's unfair punishment of silence soon becomes her power. In a world that silences women all too often, Tracey has given lush voice to a story that is historical and yet timeless."

—JORDAN ROSENFELD, AUTHOR OF *Fallout* AND *Forged in Grace*

* * *

"In *Silence*, Julia Park Tracey shows how a woman who has lost everything, including her voice, finds her way out of grief by leaning into the silence of the world around her. Meticulously researched and beautifully written, Tracey contrasts the harshness of Separatist life in the colonies against the budding industrial port of Boston Harbor."

—HOLLY DAY, AUTHOR/POET, *A Perfect Day for Semaphore* (Finishing Line Press)

* * *

"The author brings the reader into the tale in a measured way in this convincing and compulsively readable book. The engaging characters unspool the story so that it slowly settles into the reader's heart and mind, building in power and tension until barreling forward like a locomotive, rushing to the powerful climax and satisfying ending. A stealthy, stunning gem of a book."

—SUZANNE PARRY, AUTHOR OF *Lost Souls of Leningrad*

SILENCE

A Novel

JULIA PARK TRACEY

Sibylline
PRESS
AN IMPRINT OF ALL THINGS BOOK

Published in the United States by Sibylline Press,
an imprint of All Things Book LLC, California.
Sibylline Press is dedicated to publishing the brilliant work
of women authors ages 50 and older.
www.sibyllinepress.com

Distributed to the trade by Publishers Group West
Sibylline Press Paperback
ISBN: 9781736795491
Library of Congress Control Number: 2024934176

Book and Cover Design: Alicia Feltman

"The Cucking of a Scold" is a traditional English song,
dating from about 1615.
"Adam in the Orchard" is an original lyric by Julia Park Tracey.
Authorized King James version of The Holy Bible,
1604; World Bible Publishers, Canada, 2005.

SILENCE

A Novel

JULIA PARK TRACEY

Silence isn't empty. It's full of answers.

—AUTHOR UNKNOWN

To the woman deprived of a story

In a strange bed

MY BODY IS SORE; my breast hurts when I draw deep breath, but I am not drowned, and I was not hung in the gallows for a common witch. Silence Marsh has landed on her feet like a cat, and like a cat, I lie quietly with eyes slit, watching motes of dust in morning sunlight. Where am I? In whose abode? It matters not, does it? Nothing matters. I have finished whatever toil has been set me, I'm certain. I fear naught, as there is nothing that could wound me more than the events of the past two years.

I had not known that I could be so damp and cold. The cosseted youngest child in my father's nest, then cherished wife of the town constable, I had always been safe and cozy, as warm as a bright hearth and a woolen garment can make one. But my week in the cell at the gaol was bone-chilling, the earth floor mucky where others had pissed and shat, the straw filthy, the corners occupied by spiders and the wooden beams overhead a highway for rats. I had crouched against the cold wall all night, my gown and petticoat stained with the mud, manure and green slime of rotting foodstuffs. Sharp stones bruised me to the bone at my brow, shin, knuckles, and I can still feel the sharpness of a tooth that caught a direct hit, chipped at the corner.

My hour in the pillory was not wasted in contemplation; the townspeople—my congregation and neighbors—vented their pent-up rages upon me, the next unfortunate fool caught in a misdeed. A sinner in the stocks, jeered at, pelted with mud and filth—what an entertainment on a Saturday! Many's the time I've paused to watch the fun on Hingham Green of an afternoon. 'Tis not so pleasant to be upon the other end of the rod, is it?

I am nor adulteress, thief, nor murderer. I am no witch, unless all we women are. I am fallen from grace with my open mouth, bewailing my inmost sorrow, at the loss of those most dear to me, one upon the other. Folk said I lost my reason, but I know only that my heart is shattered, and in crying it aloud, I paid the cost. The pillory, the gaol cell, the lash, the other degradations—and the silence. The silence was the capstone, meant to instruct me on my path toward righteousness, and I bear it still.

From my groanings, my rage, my unheard cries, I am grown hoarse and ragged. I couldn't carry a tune if an angel asked me for it. Nay, my voice is broken from weeping. A fitting manner to end this hellish year. I could speak upon it—but for the rule, and the law, and the eyes that are always watching, and the ears always pitched to hear dissent.

Let us go back, instead, to where it began, when I was but a Separatist bride, firm in my faith, and knew nothing but that for my freedom.

Part the First

ANTE SILENTIUM

To make one flesh

David Marsh and I were contracted as husband and wife on a summer day in 1721, in the village of Hingham in the Colony of Massachusetts Bay, under the reign of King George I of England. The morning began with a fresh breeze off the waters but grew sultry by the nooning. Arrayed in our best Sabbath black, white collars stiff with potato starch, we stood before the district's old magistrate, Sir Charles Naughton, in his summer regalia. My mother and father and David's mother stood to witness and approve at the whitewashed brick government office, an hour past midday; then we walked as man and wife to our little house, newbuilt of Hingham stone and timber by David and his brothers for our beginning.

That night, we became one flesh (our duty and our marital delight) in a bed couched with new sheets of English muslin, and a red and white woolen coverlet woven by my own father as his gift to us. The bed, its posts graven with leaves and vines, was the gift of my elder brother Jazaniah; he cut a red maple in the forest, dried, shaped, smoothed, and joined it with stout pegs. It would last our lifetime and longer. Over our heads, a swag of English-made muslin summer-curtain hung across the top and down each side, a sweet bower for husband and wife.

I, a maid of twenty, and David, constable of Hingham and planter of maize and tobacco, age thirty-one, thus began our life together. David wore eyeglasses withindoors, although they hurt his temples after long. He was a book-lover and reader of law, though we must have the Indian corn and the tobacco to sell, so he was planter as well, despite his inclination for study and thought.

My father, the weaver Israel Nichols, teased David.

"If you are so blessed, your wife will be as silent as her name, and not chew off your ear early and late with her nagging."

Betwixt us two, despite my given name, David was the quieter. Separatist families often name children for traits they find desirable, deeming English names like that of King George too worldly. My sisters Thankfull, Ruth, Charity, and Experience, and I myself are exemplars of this naming habit. But my father had two wives and many children, and over the years, ended with a Nathaniel, Solomon, Roger, and Thomas in my father's quiver. Mayhap he wanted such names only for his daughters, to lead us into righteousness.

Nonetheless, though baptized *Silence*, I am neither silent nor staid. The youngest survivor of fifteen children born, I have had much to observe, from the deaths of my siblings and cousins to the wonder and terror of the natural world we live in—and I have much to say about it. Too much, perhaps.

The first morning of our wedded lives I lay in my husband's arms, looking up at the swaths of muslin like a canopy of billowed cloud overhead, morning seeping its golden light through the closed shutters of our bower, knowing myself now surfeited of the knowledge of Man's carnal act, hitherto unfathomed, and I prayed myself full with childseed. *Let my first act as wife be to become mother.* I had eaten of the knowledge of the act of Creation and found it very good. Husband David's unshaven face prickled with whiskers, and I smelled clean sweat on his skin. I had never known that a man's skin could be so delicious in texture and savor, or that my own skin would thrum like a viol when touched by a husband.

The morning rose, and, my nightgown rucked against my side, my husband's flesh greeted me with eagerness. I welcomed him as Eve, as any willing handmaid: feeling righteous in duty, in the literal embrace of our roles as two made one, cleaving onto and into each other, hand in glove, his need enfleshed in mine. *Make me a mother, make me your wife, keep me in your arms, husband,* while we count our heartbeats and ride the sun across the sky. My very core shivered with his spasm, my legs wrapped around his; I climbed him as a tree, letting him tear me ope, my loud cries melting with his. Our love was made in this bed, for each other, as glory to God, as a gift, as a taste of eternal life to come.

Although I believe we are all born in sin, I had not been a sinful child. But this glory and this earthy married pleasure, perhaps, is where my downfall began.

* * *

Father and his brothers had grown to manhood in the young colony village of Scituate, down the coast a day's walk away, and they were glad to take new land up Hingham way when the opportunity presented itself from the Crown. Father built his first house on the spit of Hull, at a sea-facing place called Green Hill, which was indeed a green hill amongst the empty sand dunes—the only green thing there, I imagine. The rest of the rolling dunes are dull shades of tan and dun and brown and umber. There is no true color there but the sea, the marvelously moving waters of the Great Ocean. Next to the blue, the green, the purple and the gray of its waters, the earth is a leaden shade.

Father, a young man then with his first wife, Mary Wise, and my eldest brother Nathaniel but an infant, built this house with four log walls and a lean-to. They bore the brunt of the seawind for a handful of years, but Mary Wise did not care for the never-ending draught sweeping beneath her door and the dash of foam against her very shutters. She appealed to her husband and Father conceded. When bitter winter froze the water in Straits Pond, Father and his brothers pushed the little house over across the ice, and dragged it, with the aid of four strong oxen, to the crook of what we now call the Jerusalem Road. Mary Wise so named the horse-path because Father, Israel by name, needed his road to Jerusalem, she said, or at least to Hingham Village, where he could grind his corn and fetch his post new-arrived from London and Boston Town. And she bade them build a little seawall made of flat stones they dug from the garden, with a stile in it so she could climb over and walk on the sand when she wished.

I played on that very stile as a child.

The crook in the road, the turn away from the ocean to face inland, changed their outlook and their fortune. Now Mary Wise looked across the pond toward Turkey Hill, Planters' Hill, and the sharp slope we still call Weary-All. With a different prospect and a floor that was no more scattered with errant sand, Mary Wise and Father built more rooms to the house, adding plank floors, a weaving parlor and storeroom, a raised cooking hearth with a bake-oven in the kitchen, and a larger keeping room at the front with its own rock hearth. Father built a dining chamber with a fine, varnished table and chairs from England. The loft above became bedchambers with plastered walls, and year by year, the house became somewhat of an eminence amongst humbler neighbors, in the shape of our wooden saltbox, and so the style of house was called.

By the time I took my first breath, Mary Wise had long gone to her rest, along with two of my infant brothers (Israel the first, and Israel the second); my mother, Mary Sumner, had finished her own brood of nine. As the last child in the nest, I grew to womanhood with an empty bedchamber, sometimes bundled with a cousin or a houseguest, but, for the most part, it was my own little queendom. My shell collection, pretty feathers from my bird friends, colorful rocks, and a diamond-glassed window that faced the Great Ocean and the rising sun, were some of the treasures that spoiled me. I had no younger sister or brother to baby and protect. My wooden doll with a painted face and silk petticoats, and a London-made ribbon loom, my child-sized attempt to mimic my father at his work, kept pride of place upon the deep windowsill. Featherbed and linen sheets were my bower. Dried bunches of lavender, woven by Mother into wands, kept the rooms scented sweet through the winter.

This Silence, as a child, was nor silent nor still. My mother often brought me to heel, my good father corrected me, and the kitchen wenches swatted my netherside. I wanted to know the why and how of every living thing and imagined vivid tales that charmed my father and drove my mother to despair. My brothers gave me leave to follow in their chores, then buried me in hayflowers in the field or flicked seaweed at me when we mudlarked for clams.

If you were wise, you had brought sheep from England when you set forth for the New World, and if you were lucky, they survived. My grandsire Nathaniel Nichols had done, and was lucky; here we are today, three sons who run flocks of ewes on their land, four daughters (late of mothers) who card and spin. My father, webster of Hingham, weaves fine coverlets and table-carpets from our Hog Island longstaple sheep, a mixed rabble that call to mind the Lincoln from England, with wild Merinos that have inbred. We keep a single tup per pasture, moving them between flocks each year to keep the breed strong. The tups service the ewes; wethers and ewes provide wool, mostly white but sometimes black or gray, and meat for table. Father also weaves rough seed-bags, floor matting and the like with local hemp, and with whatever the villagers bring him, of their own flock or spinning wheel, when they've need of his loom, and we trade for our needs with his loomings.

Our success is no mistake; by the grace of His Majesty, my father holds much land, both at the neck called Hull, and a small nameless island in Hingham Bay where our sheep graze free of predators. Foxes, wolves, and other beasts had once preyed on our lambs, but our grandsire cleared the beasts from these sanctuary spaces and our ewes grow unmolested. Other planters' flocks did not fare so well, but they had chosen their land to be arable, and so over the years we swapped meat for Indian corn or wheat, lent our tups, and grew for ourselves a name for good breeding and wool. Father betimes takes apprentices to learn his tradecraft, and there is wool aplenty from his herds. In the spring, little spotted lambs with their pert black ears gambol in the green pastures, a sight that has always brought me joy.

In February, the lambing season begins, at times in midst of snowstorms, often in icy rain. Jazaniah, Roger, and Nathaniel must need be cautious in their work when young lambs are about. I remember a spring when they had been building a lean-to on the island, hoping for some shelter from that incessant wind, when they must stay the night with the flock. The postholes were ready-dug when it rained for several days. Nathaniel was to set the posts with rock and sand and some lime, but the holes, topped with rainwater, were not empty. I arrived by rowboat with Jazaniah just moments before, with a basket of warm meat pies for their nooning.

Nathaniel reached into the hole to see what were amiss and, as I watched in horror from a few feet distant, he pulled up one, then another drowned lamb, their speckled baby bodies stiff and waterlogged, one after another in each posthole. The boys wouldn't make such an error again, but the sight of those drowned wooly bodies is burned into my mind, a memory that returned to taunt me, especially after I had a babe of my own.

Year by year, we gathered the lambs in the shed, the traveling shearers stripped them naked in spring, and then we wives and daughters carded and spun, dyed and knitted. Father wove the red, gray, blue and black hanks of spun wool into coverlets and carpets to adorn bed and table. By winter, my hands were cozy in wool mitts as I sat in the meeting-house and breathed out puffs of air in the chill, and my feet were warm enough in woolen stockings, every inch of stuff from our own flocks, combs, vats, and needles. I could not be but thankful for our industry in our cold winters, when the summer work of our hands kept fingers and toes from freezing off.

I wore the red cloak to meeting, and my prim sister, Experience, wore the blue. She threatened I would be sold like Joseph to the Natives if I did not cower before the Lord and sit still in the meeting-house. But she died in her fourteenth year, no more to tease nor chide. Then I put aside my childish ways and turned to study the Good Book, in memory of her. The printed word enticed me, and once I was learned to read and put to the pen, I made a pretty hand. The lesser-known tales in the pages of the Testaments took me afar in my own study, to the story of Jephthah's daughter in Judges, and in that selfsame book, I read of the Levite and his poor concubine, whatsoever that was. I was fond of mother- and daughter-at-law, Naomi and Ruth, who stayed together and helped each other; I knew my own sisters would do the same for me, if ever I had a need.

We had come from afar to these lands to seek freedom to worship in our own Pure way. Yet such Bible stories made me wonder about the making of rash vows—we Separatists do not vow for any reason but marriage. Who would keep a vow so foolhardy? We Separatists keep the Commandments: Obey our parents, observe the Sabbath. We do not kill, steal, lie, covet, idolize, swear, adulter nor cuckold. These Commandments are a gift of God the Father, and the blessing of this Law is our shield and our sword. Thus, the stories instructed me in the ways of the Puritan faith.

Who was I to question it?

My David's family, the Marshes, were the first come to New Hingham Town. They picked up part and parcel from Old Hingham in England, whence half the town sailed aboard the *Diligence* to Massachusetts Bay Colony in the year of 1638. Carpenters, coopers, millers, farmers, scholars, and a handful of gentry made the journey, all Separatist worshippers, pure of mind, stout of heart. They were prepared to face wilderness, the unknown folk of the forests, savage weather, and a lack of anything they had not carried across the ocean themselves. If your shoe-sole broke in the New World, you shaped one of wood or seamed yourself a moccasin from a skin, like the Native folk, until a cordwainer arrived to settle amongst us.

The Marshes took the land the King had promised them as freemen, and felled trees, built the town's palisado and a house of their own; they broke soil for tobacco, Indian corn, beans and the pompion. When there was village and bad behavior enough to admonish, David's grandsire was elected constable, and it became the Marsh family's civic duty to keep the peace and read of the Law. They were swift and stern, for the Law must be obeyed—actions speak louder than words, so actions must be controlled. The Marsh men held the position of constable for three generations in the New World, and David was not one to shirk his duty. In truth, his upright zeal was attractive to me, and I longed to be Mistress Marsh instead of Miss Nichols, knowing I would be a help-meet for him. I wanted to marry a Master, not a Goodman, aiming for a position in our small society that would have the townspeople calling me Mistress and not Goodie.

When David and I joined as husband and wife, I learned that, although he was a loving mate, he was also strict and particular, and his actions in the community were to the letter of the Law. His father before him had also been a strict enforcer, and so, among those who were less admiring of the rule and the love of order, resentment of the Marshes grew and simmered. It is always thus: No one likes to be told what to do, but what God asks of us, one must accede to. It is our Separatist duty. It is *our* Law here in the King's colony.

David taught me that, even if committed by your dearest friend or your own family, to break the Law is to seek, nay, to ask for punishment. All these things I knew as true.

The grinning wolf

When I first knew David, he was still a farm lad with a faceful of carbuncles and no beard, sitting in an overlarge dark suit on the meeting-house bench with his father and family. I have always known him, in our small village, our insular congregation, though that was when he first caught my attention. David's mother came to the house to call upon my mother and to order coverlets from Father's loom, and betimes David or his sister Elizabeth came along. His elder brothers Stephen and Ephraim were already in the tobacco fields. His father Ephraim the Elder was a man learned in the Law, who also kept his lands farmed and prosperous. When David grew to manhood, his brothers had the plantation well in hand, which left David free to learn constabulary from his father.

David learned his letters and numbers at the grammar school for boys in the village alongside my brothers, and their first years of Latin with a shared tutor; he read the rudiments of Law from the books his father kept. David was sickly when young, and never as sturdy as his brothers, but he grew hardier over the years. He was strong enough to lift me in his arms upon our bed when we married, and I never knew him weak in physic nor in spirit. Ephraim the Elder died in winter of 1720; David was elected constable soon after, the year we married, and held the position with principle and dignity.

As constables, father and son had been required to patrol the village by night to watch for fire, housebreak, and disorder. They kept an eye on the Natives, servants black and white, the enslaved, and the local taverners. Drunkenness and brawling, fisticuffs and gambling, reckless shooting of guns, and misbehavior of many sorts filled their watch. The strictness of our Pure Law meant that debauched Christmastide or New Year's celebrations were not tolerated, although there were always ruffians who preferred the bottom of a tankard to the Lord's Grace. David and his father secured the pin on the public stocks many a time over these rowdies' necks.

Constables also ordered the traffic of wains and horses in the village on market days and made arrests if a warrant were issued. My father-in-law had a reputation for keeping the peace, with a stout stick, if necessary, and he had browbeaten many miscreants into behaving. Truth be told, my late father-in-law was perhaps too hard on the rough-and-tumbledowns. Those poor folk could not help being ignorant of the Word, and perhaps were unaware they were going to end in Hell. But to spare the rod is to spoil a child, or an ignoramus, so the old ones said.

David, though he had learned at his father's heel, preferred serving warrants, testifying in the court, and other less physical aspects of his duty. He was fascinated by the workings of the government and planned to present me as his wife to the newly appointed royal magistrate and justice of the peace, Sir George Fellows, at a council meeting, upon our marriage.

Once married, we did not attend many public evenings, preferring our own cozy company, but betimes a visiting minister or magistrate required all elected officials to present themselves, and David liked me to accompany him. The meeting-house was brightly lit by lanthorns on every post, and the doors were open to allow the night air to cool the warm room. The moon was bright and as many villagers were outside as in, enjoying the moonlight. At the dooryard, David bowed to the magistrate, declaring me his bonded help-meet. I was not yet with child then, but enjoying my newlywedded title of *Mistress*.

"Mistress Marsh, a delight to meet you in this new estate," Fellows addressed me, bowing correctly. I bowed in return, holding fast to David's arm. I was awed by the tight curls of the gentleman's white periwig, his precise posture, and the keen gaze of a politician in a position of power.

David was called away that moment by a planter concerned over missing calves, so I stood, moonstruck, a nervous bride unsure how to fill the silence. I folded my hands as if in prayer.

"Are you enjoying married life, young Mistress Marsh?" The magistrate smiled down at me, but somehow, I did not feel comfortable under his gaze. The moonlight and my early years of helping my brothers with the sheep flicked one word through my mind: *Wolf*.

"Yes, your Worship." I glanced about for David or one of my brothers, also in attendance. I hesitated to speak more than in answer.

"What do you like most about cohabitation with a husband, Mistress? Are you feathering your nest for young?" He stroked his stiff white collar in an almost sensual manner. His eyes seemed hooded in the moonlight.

"Of course, we wish for whatever children the Lord sends to us," I replied. The man was indeed wolfish, I avow, leaning ever closer to me. I instinctively crossed my arms as if cold; I wanted to step away from him. But I was younger then, and afraid to cast a poor light upon David, so I stood there like a mouse under a glass.

"Do you enjoy the act of marriage?" Fellows leaned in very close to my ear, as if pushed from behind, but no one had bumped him. He was asking if my husband and I had the congress of Adam and Eve. The suggestion was impertinent, but he was a magistrate, and I a new mistress, just twenty, with not much knowledge of how great men spoke with ladies.

Perhaps I misunderstood his Lordship's intention, but suddenly I flashed my ire. "I enjoy being married to my husband," I said clearly, my voice louder than he expected. "I shall tell him what you've been asking." Nearby, heads turned to see which lady spoke up loudly.

Fellows straightened and brushed at his suit as if he had been sullied or snowed upon with dandruff. "Pray, remember me," said he, all politeness, and bowed away.

Whatever that was, I did not care to experience it again. But every few months David asked me to join him at council meetings, and as his wife, I had no reason to say him nay. I met his lordship Fellows on other occasions, and though I greeted him in the correct manner, I made no attempt to stand nearby him. My first introduction had been enough for a lifetime.

I encountered the magistrate some months later at Election Day, whereupon David had been reelected to constable. In my best indigo shortgown and petticoat, and a new white coif freshly starched, I stood proudly to the side, hearing the huzzahs of the village folk acclaim the new sheriff and the reelected constable, and we hailed them with spiced pompion-cakes and new cider.

Sir Fellows laughed and cheered, as did my brothers Jazaniah and Nathaniel and their wives, David's brothers, and all our neighbors. It was a pleasure to see all the folk, and know we had made a good election, and could celebrate, which meant a great deal to a community with no other holidays. We had no Popish nor pagan days and celebrated but so few days through the year. Fellows made the rounds, bowing and stroking his starched collars like a child pets a cat. Later, when I saw him in his formal winter robes and saw the miniver at his collar, I understood the habit. His long wig bobbed as he bowed. Idly I followed him with my eyes, wondering how soon David and I could leave the assembly; we were still newlywed, and I treasured our evenings alone.

I saw Fellows bow to Prudence, a young woman new to the village who had but recently married the son of our apothecary, Mr. Henry. And I witnessed it again: The leaning in, the impertinent question, the puzzled, then shocked look on the girl's face. The wolf was leering again at an ewe. I left my place on the wall and strode with purpose across the room.

"Goodwife Henry, how do you fare?" I spoke aloud, interrupting whatever he was saying, causing heads to turn to see who had cut off the magistrate. I took her arm familiarly, although we were but scantly acquainted.

Flustered, Prudence Henry turned to me. "Oh, very well, Mistress Marsh, I thank you."

Fellows turned his wolf-eye upon me. "Mistress Marsh." He bowed. "Many congratulations on your husband's re-election."

"My husband the constable has so many friends," I replied, returning the bow, seeming to accept his plaudit. "He is grateful for the chance to protect the people of this town. As am I." I kept his gaze and squeezed Prudence's arm. "I do wish all the folk to feel as safe in their homes as in the meeting-house."

"He is blessed to have such a *forthright* wife." Fellows gave a false smile, more a baring of his teeth. "Have care that he does not curb your tongue for speaking on his behalf. Some husbands would find it grating, if not offensive."

"My husband speaks for himself. I take my instruction from his actions alone. Pray you pardon us." I jutted my chin at him, then bowed and turned Prudence away with me. "Now, Goodwife Henry, as to the receipt for your apple-wine, I should love to hear it." I started walking, towing Prudence alongside.

She came stumbling, flustered, next to me. "Did you *cut* him?"

"I did not. I was correct enough in my attentions. But he is not. I pray you stay away from him if you can. He is a wolf in magistrate's clothing, that one."

"Mayhap you are right." Prudence squeezed my arm back. "Want you the receipt for my apple-wine? Or was that pretense? I should not like to tell an untruth."

"My dear, tell me now and we shall neither of us have pretended. And our consciences will be as new." We continued our stroll about the meeting room while the festivities ran on. I knew I had a devoted friend in Prudence from that moment.

As we walked home in the dark from the Old Ship meeting-house to our home on Water Street, David, chatting over the evening's success, queried, "What said you to Fellows? He called you a scold, though in a lighthearted manner. Were you sharp with him?'

The tin lanthorn's piercings lit our way like a cluster of nightflies lighting us along.

"He was bitter that I stole his prey from under his nose," I laughed. "He says wolfish things to young ladies and enjoys their shock. I saved a lamb from his jaws this night and he cannot forgive me it."

"Why, Goodwife Marsh. You are become a regular politician these days. I shall have to bridle your tongue, as his worship said, and ride you 'til you drop from exhaustion." He spanked me playfully and when I squealed, he grabbed me, pulling me to him, and bridled my tongue with his own.

I forgot about Sir Fellows, but he did not forget me.

Marked by suffering

efore my lifetime, there were raids and battles here betwixt the Natives and the Colonists. Betimes the Colonists won, with the aid of British soldiers in their lobster-red coats and the mandatory service of each man in the new towns. Alas for the Natives, the smallpox took many sagamores and their families, as it has done with us here and in England at times. Who among us hasn't a pock-mark upon cheek and chin? The Natives' loss was to the gain of His Majesty's subjects—land was opened and bestowed upon Colonists, and the Natives were pressed to move on.

But those feathered sachems and braves were no dupes of His Majesty's Army. Clever in the ways of this unknown wilderness, they have had the advantage over every citizen of England, with the benefit of Native alliances and, sometimes, the Papist French. The farther west the Colonists push, the more we tangle and upset with those already living on the land, who then seek their revenge.

One tactic has chilled the marrow of every man, woman, and child in the colony: Some Natives have been known to take English families captive, a fate from which few have returned. The White men rot where they are slain; their women and children are driven afoot long marches to the Native or

French villages up north to Canada to be ransomed or sold; betimes the captives are marched westward toward the dread mountains, gone forever.

Boston Town is the home of a number of redeemed women and children who were captured and released, ransomed or rescued. The Rev. Cotton Mather penned a history or two, writing the facts of these redemptions, so my father read in *The Boston Newsletter,* our colony's royally approved press. In that publication, he sometimes finds reports from other colonies or outlands where hostages are taken, where men are slain but the women let to live. It seemed a distant danger to our settled village until recent times.

Such a redeemed woman lives now in our little town—the Widow Mary Reeves. She does not speak of her time with the Natives, and she has not remarried, choosing to remain faithful to her dead husband, and to raise her ransomed children alone. The Reeves family are the like of us, but strange, too— as if their time in the Native village has materially changed them, made them something other than Nonconformist, a goodwife and her stainless kin. There is a cloud upon them despite their redemption. We know not what to make of them, living as resurrected, thought dead but returned, and her children half-wild. They speak a tongue not known to my ears; I hear the children rattling Native words to each other and whistling like the birds. The Reeves boys have an unnerving habit of walking without sound in the woods, appearing suddenly. Then they melt from sight into the trees, soundless as a puff of pipe-smoke.

From beneath my eyelids, lowered as they should be to prayer and to read the Gospel, I observe the Widow Reeves on the women's side of the meeting-house. She bears an inked blue line, the color of indigo dye, from lip to chin that the Natives forced upon her, but they were interrupted in their disfigurement and did not complete their design. To me, it looks as if the woman has been chewing on her quill tip and spilled a line of ink down her face. I saw such on my brother Roger's chin when he was a lad, thinking deeply about his letters before blackening a page with his careful blots.

She seems alone in her station as redeemed; one of us and yet not. She should be glad and grateful, and at peace among her brethren, yet she seems not at ease. I would speak with her, but I have not been alone or near enough to converse. I nod my greeting as I do toward the other Pilgrim fowl—the black-attired women of the congregation who cluck and fuss amongst each other like scratching hens. (One is never safe from their beaks and claws, no matter how deeply one prays or studies, no matter how starched or stiff one's garment.)

In truth I am not quite brave enough to approach the Widow Reeves in friendship. She frights me a little, with her ken of the wilderness and her blue-line chin. She *knows* things, has been intimate with the uncharted land outside our village boundaries. Her acquaintance with the world beyond the village and the woods seems sinful, whether her fault or no. And all of us secretly wonder—was she also intimate with the Native men?

A person who has sinned often has the physical demarcation on his or her person. Our parsons tell us this: that one can see whom God has favored and disfavored. Has your child a lazy eye, or crooked legs? What did you to make it so? The Elect are so few, and no one knows until the end who will be favored, but we Separatists look upon anyone strange or different with suspicion, with narrowed eyes and pursed lips. (And yet, what if *we* are incorrect, and the Lord has tricked us? Sometimes our Lord is fickle, pronouncing one edict but enforcing another. Why were the second-born sons favored? Why did the innkeeper offer his daughter to the strangers? Why did

Lot's own daughters lie with him? My mother hastened the book from me when I, a maiden still, asked her of this.)

So what of this widow? Is she marked by her misfortune, or by the Lord? Is she redeemed in the way the preachers tell us? Is she to be embraced or shunned? And why mayn't I stop staring upon her?

* * *

THIS FEBRUARY DAY, my mother was ill, and had not been well for many months. She had some wasting disease, an ailment of the breast, and within first the left, then the right, hard lumps formed, and spread until her body was riddled with small lumps. Mr. Henry the apothecary bled her again and again, then said she would not live long regardless. I told him he was mistaken, by God's grace. I could not yet be without my mother.

We had wondered if I was barren when no child filled my womb immediately, but our mighty God took pity on me, perhaps, and granted us a bud to fill our flower-urn. I broke the news to my mother—that I was with child, my firstling, after a year of marriage. I spent as much time at Mother's bedside as I could, to cheer her, pray with her, love her along her path, we hoped, toward healing, or Judgment Day, to be judged one of the Elect, and to wait for us in her heavenly abode. Such are the stories I told myself in the wasting days, and she, in her turn, told me how to bear and raise up a child.

"You must not lift your arms above your head, lest the baby be choked on its own cord." Mother held my hand and admonished me from her bed. I had never heard such lore until now, but I had been a virgin, and then a childless woman, so childbearing tales and strictures were not for my untried ears. But now, the truth was revealed to me. I did not know of what cord she spake.

"The cord that binds mother and child is forever. The midwife cuts the navel string when you birth, but the tie is eternal," Mother half-explained, her blue eyes sad, remembering her lost children mouldering in the burial ground on the hill.

I asked the expected question. "Does it hurt so very much, the birthing?" Every Eve must labor and travail, saith the Lord. That much I knew.

"The firstling takes the longest, for the womb has not yet learned its duty. Firstling babies are blessing and curse. They open your heart with more love than you can imagine, daughter, but the pain of bearing and delivery, suckling the child, the healing of the womb afterward, and the fear of your new babe's precious life—those are the curse of Eve upon us all. This is the way of all women." My mother, loving and fecund, had birthed ten children to my father and also raised up four young ones by the late Mary Wise.

"Pour out my tea, daughter, I pray you."

I steeped my mother's herbal brew of strawberry leaf and lemon balm, plucked and dried by her own hand in her herbal garden, sweetened not with maple sap that most settlers used, no, but honey from her own hives. In cold February, the honey crystalized and turned opaque in the crock, but it melted like butter when stirred with a spoon into hot water.

The silver sipping-cup was too hot for her to hold, but I had knitted a cozy to slip around it, and she warmed her cold, thin hands on the soft little shawl wrapped around the hot flagon.

"You warm me twice," she said; to the tea or to myself, I wondered. "I am so very cold these winter days."

"The fire is bright enough; do you not feel it?"

In faith, it was almost too warm in the small chamber, but a sickroom has its odors, and when a window mayn't be opened, the fug grows thick, a miasma of night-water, bleeding basins and flux. I set the flagon aside and pulled the cover higher up her shoulders.

Mother quietly pressed her lumps, caressing them as a meditation. "'I can count all my bones,'" she quoted the Psalmist suddenly. "Daughter—the parson, I beg you call upon Parson Hobart and send him hither; let me hear him read to me the Gospel. I feel I won't tarry here long."

"Mother, don't say such things. The Devil is waiting around the corner to take you up on such an offer! Take your rest, and I'll bring your lavender salve. It will help— you'll feel aright soon."

I massaged her hands and temples with the springtime sweetness of her beeswax and lavender balm, then kissed her weary head and left her settled in woolen blankets. I donned my warm red cloak, then set forth toward Parson Hobart's home near the church meeting-house, on my way back to my own home. It were a long walk but I was strong and heedless in those days. I tramped over puddles rimed with ice, a cold ocean wind at my back, pushing me back toward the village of Hingham. My hands were warm inside the wooly blue mitts, at least for a brisk mile from the Jerusalem Road to the high street on a frosty February forenoon. It were still early days in my motherhood when a walk could not hurt me, before the quickening, and I was not yet confined to home.

I rapped at the Hobarts' door, looking at the ground, at last feeling the cold in my leathern shoes, until the door opened to me. Parson Hobart's wife, Aphra, one of the sourest of the Pilgrim fowl, held the heavy door just a handsbreadth open. She did not invite me in from the cold.

"Aye?" This single word from her thin lips felt like a burr caught in my stocking.

"My mother bids the parson to tend her soul, if he is within." I blew out a breath of icy air, like smoke from a sachem's pipe. "May I see him?"

"Your mother is poorly. She will not last the winter."

If my ears could lie flat like a cat's, they would have. Such a sharp tongue in this holy man's wife. Goodwife Hobart eyed me through the narrow opening.

"He is at study. I shall tell him when he finish."

"*Goodwife* Hobart," I said to indicate our social difference. "Mistress Nichols expects his comfort anon. Pray that he attend her shortly. My father the weaver would be displeased at any delay in attending his beloved wife."

Aphra Hobart looked as if she were smelling piss and closed the door. Overly chilled from standing in the wind at the doorstep, I was glad that my house was not far. I walked over a slushy path through the township. But on a moment's thought, rather than toward my Water Street home, I went down the North Street to the harbor, where a dozen ships were creaking on their ropes, as idle as a Sabbath day. A gray seal was yelping its prayers at the wheeling gulls from the rocky mud of low-tide shore. Screeching gulls trotted on webbed feet, stopping to snap up tiny crabs or clams foolish enough to open their shells. The rotted seaweed smell at the wharf was as familiar to me as the oily scent of lamb's wool and the yeasty smell of small beer.

Thinking on clams, I asked Neriah Ware, one of the mudlarks at the harbor wall, to bring a pot's worth of clams to my house, for stewing with milk and crumbled biscuit. My David loved his codfish or clam *chaudiere*, or as we called it plain in Hingham, chowder. Sister Charity made a peppery soup and thin, crisp hardtack to crush into the broth, and it was so warming on a winter's day. I had learned her receipt and made it almost as well as she. My palate was not bold enough for the African flavor of the kitchen pepper that some servants brought to the board in other houses. As I had only David and myself to please, I did not pepper it so well. Perhaps when I grew great with child, I would not pepper it at all.

I took myself home, and tended my rising dough and my soaking beans, awaiting the delivery of clams. When Neriah came, I paid tuppence for the shellfish and gave him a farthing besides from David's coin purse. Quietly, in my little house, I stirred the fatty pork in the kettle, added the clams and chopped potatoes, the dried herbs from my mother's garden, then the pat of butter and the pint of milk that made the chowder so rich. I pounded black Malabar peppercorns and left the mortar on the table to season our broth to taste. My own crisp hardtack filled a small plate, and I laid two shining silver spoons, a wedding gift, on the table. David's tankard of cider, foaming gently, sat next to my smaller flagon. I added another thick chunk of oak from the log-well next to the hearth to keep the fire blazing and waited for David to return after his monthly Court Day.

In a chair by the fire, I carded batts of wool and rocked gently, holding my newly rounded innards where I knew my womb, and my unnamed child, blossomed. What should we name it? The sun had long since gone down and a stormy night arisen when David arrived at last.

"Fair evening to you, Goodwife." He shook his head and droplets of melted snow rained from his hair.

"Fair evening, Goodman." We teased each other with this form of address, although outsiders might find this drollery a bit coarse. We were higher in station than the goodmen and goodies of the town, and always received the Master and Mistress address; however, there was something loving about the word *good* in the lower address, and we both counted it an endearment to address each other so in private. David was, to me, so very good.

He hung his hat and great cloak on the peg near the hearth where they would steam dry. He washed his hands and face at the wash-basin; I handed him a clean cloth to towel dry. He smoothed his hair back into the queue at his nape and turned to take my hands.

"How did your mother this day? Does she rally?"

"I hold hope of her return to health, but today was not the day for rising from her sickbed. I sat with her a while and told her of our good news."

"My son." David was determined to know this mystery before time.

"Your *daughter*!" It was another such playtime between us, wondering which sex would the new child be.

"Every man desires a son first—the eldest brother should protect his younger sisters and brothers, like your brother Nathaniel. And a man needs his worker in the field." He put his hands on his hips, playful in his argument.

"A mother needs her little maiden in the kitchen and garden." I placed my hands on my belly. "Mayhap there are twins, one each, to please us both."

"Bless me, if you were to bear twins. You'll need the entire bed for yourself at term, my good lady. Twice the womb for two infants! And then two cradles?"

"And two bonnets, and two blankets, and two trenchers."

"And two pair of shoes, and twice the taxes! A blessing on this house." He laughed.

"Such a blessing! But we will always have room for more children. A houseful. Two houses full, if the Lord calls for it!" I stirred up the chowder and ladled it into a crockery basin for our supper, shared between us. After soup, I scoured the board and tidied the hearth for morning. There was yet wood aplenty in the log-well for the night and the morrow.

"Wife, I should like to name the newborn for my mother, Elizabeth, if it be a girl."

I liked my mother-in-law well enough; it was her cow that gave us the milk and butter. She was a kindly woman and had welcomed me as a daughter, not as a thief of her son. But I had a request of my own.

"Aye. And if it be a boy-child, might we call him Israel? Father gave two sons his own name, and both died in cradle. He has longed for an Israel these many years."

"Agreed. Let us take ourselves, and wee Elizabeth or Israel, to bed and give it the rest it needs to grow strong and hale. I long to hold him—or her. Will this house not be a castle meet for a young Marsh?"

"T'will."

I filled the warming pan with red embers to heat our frigid bedlinen and slipped on its woolen cover. I leaned on his arm a little as we passed through to the bedchamber. With the candle blown out, and the light from the banked fire barely lighting the kitchen, our chamber was very dark, very cold, but we soon reclined into comfort with the warming pan at our feet, the woolen bedcurtains pulled, and each other, curled together like a barn cat and its long tail. Into such dreams of warmth, love, and security, I could sink forever.

It was my intent to visit my mother next day, after the noon hour, as I had every day, David accommodating my request to be away from the home so much. I worried for my mother in her illness, and he knew I honored my parents in this way. But as I lifted a bucket of water outside at the well, I felt a strong pain in my nether area, and soon after, a trickle of blood marked my stockings and garters. I found my monthly rags and bound myself, wondering what to do. I could not leave the house to see my mother nor ask anyone for help, and David had gone by horse to his mother's land at Stoddar's Neck at Weymouth Back River, to see how the cattle did in the cold. There had been trouble with the split-rail fences over the new year, and kine wandering away from the Neck.

I didn't know what to do but sit in my rocking chair and worry if it were normal to bleed. Childbearing was still a mystery to me. My gut stopped its cramp, and there was no further flux, but I yearned to consult with my sisters or my mother. I waited for hours for someone to come past my home, someone I could send in errand. Perhaps it had been only the effort of lifting the heavy bucket that had bothered my middling or staying too long in the cold of yester. I could not know, without a woman to tell me.

Long since, the door sounded; my father's neighbor Master Catlin the warehouseman came by. Mother and Father must have missed my visit greatly to have sent the merchant to find me. Mayhap he was on his way to the wharf anyway.

"Oh, Master Catlin, I am so grateful to see you. I—" But I stopped when I saw his face, so sober was his mien. "What is it, sir?"

"Mistress, your mother took a turn late in the night. The good lady has gone to her rest. She passed this morning." He bowed his head. "May the Good Lord bless her name."

I felt the pain come to my womb again, and I slumped to the floor, unable to stand. I couldn't believe my ears. "My mother is gone." I curled over my sharp pain and wept. She didn't know how much I needed her that day. How much I still need her every day.

Master Catlin helped me to the chair.

"Sir, my husband—and the mid-nurse, I pray you."

He left me swooning in my rocking chair with pangs in my womb and a sharp pain in my chest. I could barely breathe. My mother gone, not my beautiful mother.

David came through the door sometime after, followed by the town's midwife, a plump, black-skinned woman called

Huldah who served in one of the planters' houses. She wore rough brown linen and tied up her hair in the brightest yellow kerchief I had ever seen. She shushed me and sent David to stir up the fire and fetch water. Between them both, they managed supper, and she brewed oat straw and raspberry leaf tea for me. She said the raspberry would tighten my womb like a draw-string and hold the child in place. The oat straw would soothe my temper.

But she were wrong; nothing could soothe my heart. I wept and wept, my mother gone forever. If only I had one more day with her, to tell her how good she was. To tell her I wished I could be like her, as strong and as capable. I felt limp as a hank of wet string.

Huldah comforted me with her low voice. She spoke nearly all the time, under her breath, in prayer and in narrating her work. "Huldah gonna feed you some more sup and get your strength back. Your husband, your father need you now, Mistress. No nettles yet, wait for the spring. Your baby gonna be strong come summer, gonna tear you open but make your heart big. Your baby gonna make a woman out of you, yes, Mistress. Yes, Mistress. Huldah got your tea; Huldah got your baby in her hands."

Next day I was well in my body, no pain, no bleeding, but David disallowed me to ride in the wain to my father's house.

"I must see my mother laid out; I must pray with my grieving father." I could not stop the tears that overflowed and fell down my face like a child's unguarded emotion.

"You can do that here, until you are hale enough for the visit." David used his master voice—it meant he was not playing, and he intended me to obey. I could not say against him, so I missed my mother in her winding sheet, and I missed her burial. No matter that I read the sorrowing Psalms, it was never the same as being present at her enshrouding, a daughter's duty that Thankfull and Charity took up. Another week went by before David allowed me to attend meeting and hear the sermon. After Sabbath service, I returned with my father to his home, and when I walked into my childhood's house, it felt tilted, broken as a cracked plate without my mother's calm presence, her sweet humming to the bees, her cheerful face under her stiff white coif and her bright white apron pinned on.

Perversely, God turned the weather bright and sunny after my mother died. It seemed more appropriate to me for the sky to storm and the clouds to hide the sun, but the weather turned suddenly springlike, and snow melted away, fooling the fruit trees into budding, causing the dark earth to suddenly glow green with a scant tinge of new grass.

It had been just two weeks since my mother's death, and I realized that no one had yet told the bees. Mayhap to Christian folk, who think the bees are dumb beasts, it was a silly thing, but it was long-held tradition back to England's mists to tell the bees of the beekeeper's death. My mother had told her hives thus many times, when she lost a child or a neighbor passed from this Earth. But the death of the beekeeper was the most important telling of all, if the bees were not to swarm away without her.

I asked my father and he said he had not thought of it. "Will you do it for her, then?"

I knew then I would be the keeper of these wily creatures. I was wearing a gray striped shortgown that day, loose at the waist for my blooming figure. But I went up the stairs to find Mother's yellow bee-gown and changed into it. I asked Father for some black linen-cloth and brass pins, and he gave me all this from his storeroom.

The air was terribly still, not a breath of winter or spring breeze, so rare for this shoreward home. No wind, from near or afar. I approached Mother's bee skeps, humming Psalm the sixth,

> *I am weary with my moaning;*
> *every night I flood my bed with tears;*
> *I drench my couch with my weeping.*
> *My eye wastes away because of grief—*

I tore the cloth into strips, singing the words through my tears. Ready at last, I knocked on the board next to the first skep. I wore no veil, just the yellow gown my mother had always worn. I wore no gloves. The bees did not bother me. Were they listening?

"Hear me, my sisters. My mother is dead. She has gone to her Judgment. Pray for her salvation." I pinned a strip of the black cloth to the top of the skep, where it fluttered a bit, settling down the side. I knocked again, next to the second skep.

"Hear me, brothers. My mother is dead. She has gone to her Judgment. Pray for her salvation." I pinned another strip of cloth, and repeated this again, at the third skep. "Hear me, queen. My mother is dead."

I repeated this for the fourth and fifth skeps, pinning strips of black like sad flags. The breeze returned, catching the light cloth and tossing it. I might as well have been a leaf on the wind, for the lack of attention from the bees. But they knew now. They would not flee. It were only superstition, of an old, old tradition from before time. But God made the bees to serve us. We need follow the customs to keep them as happy as we, when eating of their honey.

Strangely, my tears stopped flowing. Neither did my middling pain me. Was it the light breeze or was it the ritual of mourning with the bees?

"God be with you, bees," I said, backing away.

I turned back to the house and caught a flash of color, standing out from the dun of the sandhills and dead scrub on the shoreline. Parson Hobart's wife in a blue shortgown, sitting in her husband's wain, watched me from the roadway. I waved a hand to her but she perhaps was not really looking at me. She turned her head away, looking inland, as if not at all interested in my movements. In the second seat of the wain sat their daughter Zuriel, the child of Parson's first wife. I guessed her age about twelve just then, on the cusp of womanhood. Goodwife Aphra Hobart had borne no children of her own. There was something amiss there, I understood now, with my thick middling.

And I had not seen proof of it, but I sensed there was no love between stepmother and stepdaughter.

Zuriel waved her hand at me and I returned the wave. Goodwife Hobart kept her face turned away, perhaps annoyed that the child had greeted me. The parson's wife had no reason to shun me, and every reason to offer me her condolences. It was the only polite thing to do, and yet she did not. I walked back to my father's house in wonder at her rudeness.

Parson Hobart stood at the front door, speaking again with my father. They shook hands as I entered the room.

"Mistress Marsh, pray accept my pity," he addressed me.

"Pray that I may be as strong as she," I returned. "I would that she be called the Elect. But we cannot know."

"You will know it in your heart, if you are to be Elect," he admonished, lest I slacken. "Our God separates the sheep from the goats, and it is written upon their souls. I will pray for your family to be found worthy."

"Your goodwife sits outside in the wain. Will she not come in?" I looked toward my father to confirm the invitation—it was not my house for issuing the welcome.

He nodded back and offered, "Pray, Parson, your wife?"

Parson Hobart coughed into his fist and made excuse. "She wanted a bit of sunlight today, after so many months of indoors. My girl is in the wain as well. We turn back to town anon. I'll join her, no more to trouble you. God be wi'thee."

"We thank you, Parson, for your prayers and condolences. Fare thee well." Father bowed him to the door. When Father turned back to me, he frowned.

"What vexes you, daughter?"

"Why would not Goodwife Hobart come to the house? Does she fear the wasting disease? One does not catch it from another person like the pox." I could not hide the scorn in my voice.

"Respect for the dead, I'll call it." His eyes drooped with sorrow and lack of sleep, but he did not weep. "Time you got back to your own house, daughter. Be with your husband, he'll comfort you." He kissed the top of my head, my starched coif, in a rare show of affection. "I will drive you there, worry not."

The smallest savage

After Mother passed in February, I had no more cramp nor bleeding. My sister Thankfull, six years my senior and with three of her own, said I was fit enough to return to my usual tasks. Since Mother's passing, I saw my father often, bringing him soups or maple sugar to tempt his appetite, doing the little things Mother used to do for him. I rubbed his shoulders after a long stint at the loom, and I sought out the largest egg, the earliest onions in the patch, for his sup. It comforted me to be in my mother's place, standing in the sunshine at her bread trough, or sweeping her dooryard of sand and grasses, though he had a kitchen wench to feed him. I could not step into Mother's shoes, but I felt closer to her in the shadows of where she used to live.

Standing in a kitchen, combing the fine wool, awaiting my husband at home, carrying my unborn babe, made me feel a paragon of womanly grace. I did my duty, and I was Elect, I felt in my inmost heart.

The third week of March completed the first month since Mother passed. I could not believe it had been so long already, so swiftly passed, and that life had continued, sunset following sunrise. David and I went by wain to sit with Father so the men could discuss the tups and ewes. Jazaniah and Roger came ahorse. But they did not bring their wives, so I had nought but time on my hands. I had even forgot my workbag, and I had wool aplenty to card at home.

Father laughed at me, saying, "*A man works from sun to sun, but a woman's work is never done.* Go you out and tend your mother's bees, girl. Leave us to our business."

My brothers laughed with him, and though David smiled, he saved his laughter for our private teasing.

Bees were actively embracing the first blooms—dandelion, wild plum blossom, even the herbs and grasses roadside. I would check to be certain the hives had no ants, mice, nor other pest worrying them. I put on Mother's yellow beekeeping gown, her gloves and muslin veil and, imagining myself as Mother, walked from the house, through the still-dead garden, the light muslin wrapped around my shoulders.

When I got to the bee-yard I spoke to the bees.

"Creatures, it is Mary Nichols no longer; it's Silence Marsh this time. Pay me no mind. I am looking only to learn, not to steal your wares today. Teach me how to keep you safe and thriving." I hummed a familiar psalm that we sang often on Sabbath, a tune Mother had hummed to her bees many times. I pulled the featherweight muslin across my face, my world dimmed of its brightness. I leant above the rough log bench to look, through the veil, more closely at each hive's opening. The bees buzzed around my head, butting my arms and face through the veil with their hard little heads.

I was not afraid. I have never feared the hives. They must needs warn me; it was *their* duty.

I stepped around to the back of the bench, so that my form did not block the light, and felt from the outside of each skep, pressing gently on the bulrush as Mother had done. Three of the hives felt full already. Full hives meant honey. I should ask Father to order new skeps from the basket-weaving Natives down Scituate way. A handful of Natives lived in the woods hard by, working for trade when they felt like it, swingling flax, chopping wood, weaving baskets and chair-bottoms, and, if asked, bee skeps made of dried rushes. Father would trade a warm coverlet for skeps, a fair exchange.

I would move the bees into new skeps if I could, the way I'd seen Mother do it. Working among the hives felt indescribably right to me—as if my God had made me for just such a purpose. It felt dutiful, wholesome, useful, and I felt at peace with the usually cruel natural world. What better symbol of industry than the toil of bees, the parson has preached? What better example of the *promise* of toil and duty than the expectation of sweet honey, like salvation for the Elect. I needed this feeling, bereft of my mother and the misfortune when I could not say my farewell to her.

"Goodwife!" I heard David call for me from the top of the rise. I hadn't expected company and with the veil wound over my face, it were difficult to see well. I turned quickly toward him, out of instinct, not common sense, and tripped over my own clumsy feet. It happened so quickly but it seemed as if I were falling slowly, as in a dream. My left hand went down to shield my quickening womb, and I tried to catch myself with the right arm. I knocked the far skep off the bench with my elbow and it tipped back. My hand caught on the bench and I felt a scrape up my arm, then my knee hit the ground, jarring me through and through, and my hand reached for grassy ground. I scrabbled at my veil.

"Silence," David shouted, running, and at my elbow already. I saw him at my side dimly through the veil. He helped me to my feet.

"The baby! Are you hurt? Let us away from the bees. They are fiercely angry now." He pulled me along.

I was tripping over my feet, clawing at my veil. "I can't see."

"Leave it."

I could feel the ground roughly underneath us as we re-climbed the little rise. I managed to get the veil off, my coif coming undone with the veil, my hair caught up in the cloth.

"Are you hurt?"

"I'm fine, no injury to myself or the babe." I hoped this was so. I felt no pain in my womb, only the raw scrape on my elbow.

"How can you even know that? You ought not be down there, taking such chance."

I shook out my veil, hoping to find my starched coif with-in. In snapping the cloth, several bees flitted free.

"Get you home," I told them. "I must go back, husband, tip the skep upright again."

"Get off, vermin." David brushed a dead bee off his fore-arm and looked at his skin closely, the linen of his sleeve drawn back.

"Not vermin, Goodman. They're more like livestock than pests." I jested in our playful tone, but David did not jest in return. "Did it bite you?"

"It did, but no matter." Yet he did not look aright. "Let us go back to the house."

My husband turned and we walked toward my father's house, David not speaking, but walking rather faster than I could in my condition. I plucked off my gloves, thinking what a fuss he made over a simple bee's sting. I had been stung be-fore and, aside from the initial fire, it faded quickly. Was my husband mayhap one of those who weakened in the knees at the sight of blood? I had never seen this side of him. And there was no blood anyway, not even a tiny bead.

By the time we got to the kitchen dooryard, David was perspiring and pale in his mien, so much that in fact his arm was damp and sweat dripped down his face. The sting was a hard white lump on his arm. He looked as if to faint.

"Father," I hallooed the house. Then I called again and again, until his hoary head peered out the door.

"He's bee-stung, just on the arm there. But he's fainting."

"Vinegar and flour for bee sting," said Father sharply, and withdrew indoors.

"Bring wine, ale—he needs drink," I shouted after, as David weighed every heavier on my shoulder, slumping to the ground.

Then Roger, hearing our raised voices, jogged in from the far field. We half-carried David inside and I untied his stock and opened his blouse. His lips and eyelids were swelling before our eyes; he looked like a man beaten in a brawl, a monstrous fish. He coughed, seeming to struggle for breath.

Jolly, the kitchen wench, brought a cup of cider and Father tried to give it. David choked on the liquid and began to quake, his lips blue.

"He's cold! But—he's burning up!" I knew not what to do.

"Fetch a blanket!" Father sent Jolly upstairs.

"Lord save him!" I could not choke out the words to any prayer. What kind of fit was this?

Roger was at David's side with the vinegar, splashing it directly on the bee-sting. I took the offered blanket and a cool cloth for my husband's swollen forehead. I kept calling his name, more desperate each time.

"What is happening?" I sobbed. "Do something, Father! Roger—Oh, David! David!"

But at the end of half an hour, my beautiful David was a misshapen, ugly monster who died gasping for breath, gurgling in his throat, and there was not a blessed thing any of us could do. He had been felled by a tiny beast no bigger than a toenail, himself the slain Goliath. I could not move from where I sat on the floor, David's head in my lap, as the night dropped upon us and Roger lit the candles. Jolly stirred up a potage of lentils and offered them to me and to my father, but we could not eat.

I stayed on the floor, David's head against my rising midriff, the closest he would ever be to our baby.

At last we covered him with a linen bedsheet, and my brothers carried the body to the downstairs bedchamber, where David was laid out for his Judgment. His swollen face did not look at peace, and I knew he'd had no chance to repent aloud before his sudden death. Had he said a silent prayer? Had he somehow begged for Salvation with his blue lips and fish-like gasp? Was he down below us in Hellfire even now? I could not believe it, not my good David.

Was it my fault the bee had stung him, or was it God's plan? Was it God's plan to take my husband so soon after my mother? Was it God's plan to leave me a widow with a quickening womb? Was it my fault I had tripped, that I could not see where I was going—an accident, or God's plan? *So clumsy!* David had surprised me, startled me—but I did not blame *him*. How could I know he would come to find me? Why did I trip and fall? Was God's plan to punish me, with two sudden deaths? What had I done to merit such censure when I had been so faithful?

I recalled Psalm the 118th:

> *They surrounded me like bees;*
> *They were extinguished as a fire of thorns—*

And I remembered our bed-loving, our little jokes and our laughter, and knew that my sin lay there. I had laughed aloud during the marriage act, I had spoken my thought, and I had wanted carnal knowledge of my husband. It must be sin.

I had killed my husband.

Would God also take my child, with cramps, or such falls, or such a grief? But my child must live now, and be another

David, rather than Israel, a new David Marsh. This was my only aim now: to bear this child and hold him up, a staff and a shield against the world. Numbly I sat near the hearth in the keeping room, sipping at the warmed wine brought by the wench, as the sun went down. My brothers bade me farewell and went home to their houses. Father knew not what to say.

At long last I made up a bed and lay in my old childhood bedchamber, and when I blew out the candle, I clutched my pillowbere and wept into it, sobbing my anguish in the dark. *My husband is dead. He is gone, like a puff of wind, and I am holding onto this precious babe inside me to keep me going. It is the only thing I have to stand me strong against the terror that the world is become. My unborn child, never to know his father. What a tragedy this life is.* Was David being judged, this very moment, and found wanting? My good, sweet husband, unshriven, in Hell. I could not stomach it, not knowing.

There was no point in going home to our little cottage. My brother-in-law Ephraim Marsh took it and moved in, giving me my widow's third in silver. I went only for my robes and my wools and workbag, and our marriage coverlet under which we had coupled, then returned to my father's house ever after that, both of us bereft of our mates.

We drifted like ghosts in fog, silent, moaning inwardly, passing each other without words in the empty chambers, Jolly tending us with her calloused hands.

March left us, poor lambs, like a lion that year.

A knife at hand

E arly in the morning in late summer, dark as midnight, I felt the stirrings of my womb. Huldah the midwife had checked on me when she passed through the village, and she had foretold the babe would come on a Wednesday. I knew it was not a false pain; this was deeper, and I felt the babe lower in my middling than it had been before. I arose, with some difficulty, all but a tortoise stuck on its back, and went for the chamber pot, set in a stool for my ease. As soon as I settled to release my water, a gush flowed out and I felt a deeper still pang through my gut. I waited until it eased, then crossed back to my bed, looking for a toweling cloth for the waters. I had no candle and thought I would bide a bit and see what became. My nightdress was damp.

A footstep on the creaking stair, in the passage, and Jolly tapped and put her head in, candle in hand. "Mistress? I heard you moving around. Is it time?"

I held my hand under the tight dome of my womb. "Seems like it. It is a tight pain that lasts a long count."

"I'll tell your father to fetch the midwife," said she, and left me a long time.

I felt the tightness grow and fall away like the waves upon the pebbles of the shore, growing in feeling and length, as the time passed and the candle melted away. At last I heard a bustle in the kitchen and boots on the stairs.

"Daughter, are you well?" Father stood near the door, not looking within for modesty. I could see his shadow by candlelight. I could not answer, at that moment, feeling another spasm. He poked his head around and saw me in the chair, rocking back and forth through the pain.

"Huldah is here. This, too, shall pass," and he edged away. I saw him no more until my strife was over.

Midwife Huldah came in with Jolly and a fresh candle, her hair wrapped in a brown and white printed cloth tied tight. "We get you ready to be a mama. Untie that gown! You choking that baby."

Jolly plucked at the string at my neck keeping the gown closed while she bustled about with sheets and cloths and a basin of water. I sat in my rocking chair by the window and leaned over my great belly, another pain making itself felt. Another pain, and another, no closer, no slower, just one after the other, as waves on the shore that I heard from my window every night. My baby boy was coming. My son, to be named David, my tiny soldier against the great world—another pain, and I felt every moment of that spasm.

"I will greatly multiply your pain in childbirth; In pain you shall bring forth children," saith the Lord, my mother had told me. I breathed deeply when the spasm had passed.

I was aware of more bustle and steps on the stairway, and Huldah shuffled in again. She had brought her groaning stool and her sharp knife, set aside for now, and made me walk with her across the room and back, the length of the chamber, and about again.

"As long as you can walk through it, the faster t'will come, child. Baby must slide down, and if you're lying abed, he take his time." Jolly brought up a trencher with the groaning cake and a mug of ale, and it gave me strength. Whenever a woman belabored a child, Huldah baked the groaning cake: good molasses and cornmeal, dried whortle-berries and apple, with ginger and black pepper for warming. With a pull at my ale every few pangs, I felt warm and heartened. I was grateful to have the victuals at my elbow, and the women at my side.

Later, Jolly brought up raspberry leaf and dried rose hips steeped well together, not too hot. And so, through my window, around the curtain, we saw the sky lighten and the sun creep across the waters of the sea. The sun came up and passed over the house, the heat of day mitigated by an ocean breeze outside, but we had no open window and no fresh air, which might catch the child, or myself, and whisk us away.

As my agonies increased, Huldah placed the knife under the bed, "to cut the pain," she said. She sang a low song in a crooning voice, with words I didn't recognize but thought to be from her African home.

I heard a hurly-burly belowstairs, and voices, and when Goodwife Hobart put her scraggy face into the room, I knew the parson had come by to sit with Father in prayer. I didn't want that woman in the room with me; her suspicious eye, her untoward sneer upset me. Her nose sniffed at everything she disapproved of, and I am certainly one of those people.

"What is that knife on the floor?" Her voice cut through the room.

"Nothing, mistress. Just set it there out of the way," Huldah rubbed my back as I leaned over the bed, paused between walking the chamber. "To cut the string, mistress."

"Woman shall toil and travail in birth. It is our curse," Goodwife Hobart said, her voice like a spray of piss in the air. She had no spawn of her own; how would she know? "It is God's gift to us to suffer."

"I pray you, get out!" I waved her away. In the moment, with another pang bearing down on me, I did not trust myself not to shriek at her.

"The open door bring a draft, Mistress. I closing it now." Jolly closed it firmly.

With a harrumph that lingers in my ears to this day, the parson's wife withdrew and left me to my labors. Huldah and Jolly exchanged glances but did not speak ill of the parson's wife. I soon forgot the annoyance, with my girth tightening again, always a little stronger than the one before, and a little longer in duration. As the day progressed, my sisters came to help spell Huldah, brought me ale to drink, more tea, helped me to make water in the pot, where squatting felt so good. Jolly wiped my sweating face, rubbed my temples, my back with my mother's lavender and beeswax ointment, my swollen womb with the oil of benne seed and rosewater. These women cared for me, body and soul, when I was naked and suffering, and though I could hardly rub two thoughts together in extremis, I never forgot their kinship and sisterhood in those dark moments.

The long afternoon and evening crept past; the night came again, and stretched onward. Huldah kept me walking until I almost collapsed, only letting me rest occasionally. The pains were faster and closer together, and I finally started to feel pressure below. I had moaned and sighed before, but at this point the pressure was great, and I had no thought of words or speaking, only the animal pressure to bear down and cry out with the effort. The women helped me to the groaning stool and suddenly, in that crouched position, I felt all my muscles working at one thing, and bore down on the pressure, pushed with my whole body and soul, on the one thing I had to live for: My baby, my child, its head crowning into life and breath.

Jolly held me up from behind and Huldah worked from below, and at once, in a gush of liquid and blood, I felt the body slip from my core, a great loosening. Almost at once the pressure ceased, just a light cramp now and again as the afterbirth followed its master out of the womb. I heaved and sobbed, exhausted. My boy was born, my little David.

Jolly held me, laughing, "Good lass, you made a baby!"

Huldah held up the damp bundle of red arms and legs and greasy dark hair and looked at me, smiling. "She a li'l girl baby, Mistress."

"Oh, my sweet child," I whispered, tears on my face. I held out my arms, but Huldah said, "Soon, Mistress—let's wipe her down, change you gown." Huldah washed my face and sponged me and helped me don a fresh nightdress and my soft monthly rags. I sat in my rocker for a moment, as they sheeted the bed anew in sun-dried linen. Jolly put me to bed and handed the baby to me at last.

"You're no David." I gazed into the tiny, wrinkled face. This precious child. She must be named for my mother-in-law, as David had asked of me. I could do that for him, if nothing else. The late David Marsh was the father of a daughter, Elizabeth. And Father said, by the clock on the keeping room's shelf, it was past midnight, so it were the Wednesday, as Huldah had predicted. Tuesday's child is full of grace, and Wednesday's child is full of woe, so say they, but I would not let anything happen to this precious gift.

"Elizabeth means *My God is Bountiful*, or *God is My Oath*," the Rev. Hobart said at her christening at the end of the month, when I was allowed back into the meeting-house to worship. At the time I thought it the most beautiful name I had ever heard. Now I think it the most exquisite curse— what kind of God takes a child? What kind of monster-god would do that? And what fools would believe such drivel?

As *God is my oath*, Elizabeth Marsh lived two months, until the first of October, when an infant fever stole my child, my last hope, from my arms. A weakening from flux, emesis, inability to suckle, and a cruel god—that is what killed her. No plea or supplication would have been enough.

And with her passing, I became as one living in death.

Whence it came

The trees had all turned to vivid flames of color when we laid my child in her cold grave. She had been baptized, she was a child of God, she was one of the faithful, if a newborn as weak as water can be said to have faith. Was she one of the Elect? I had not worried over my mother, who had lived such a saintly life, dutiful, kindly, wise, pious, that I did not fear her election to Salvation. My David was a good, upright man; he surely must be one of the Elect—but for his sudden end, when he had no time to beg for his soul. I suffered tortures at night for David's soul, if he had not been Chosen after all, because of his bitter, untimely end.

I was numb to this in the days after Elizabeth's death, only bringing it back to mind as I felt the full force of my anguish. I was grateful to be in my father's house. He paid for the winding sheets, the pine coffin, and gloves for the parson and my brothers the bier bearers. Father carried the tiny pall. The bells rang and we walked from the church up to the burial ground, where Jazaniah and Nathaniel, the only bearers needed, set her tiny casket into the wee grave, so small that it was no burden to dig it even in cold soil. Father had ordered a stone for her head, but it was not yet graved.

Beloved daughter
Elizabeth Marsh. 2 months 1722.

And that was all anyone would ever know of the wisp of heaven that grew in my womb, kept me alive whilst I mourned her father and grandmother, and died in my arms. And though I walked as one somnambulant to her burial, awake in death, rode home on the wain in shock, sat in my chair and did not eat, lay in my bed and did not sleep, I held myself together as a member of the congregation until the next Sabbath, the following week.

Father walked me to the wain and helped me in, tucking the rug over my knees and the flapping ends of my red cloak in around me. I sat as a stiff wooden doll on the seat, and at the Old Ship Church, walked toward our bench like a poppet on strings, joining my sisters Charity, Thankfull, and Roger's wife, Bethia. I was present but not hearing, standing for the Psalm but not singing.

Parson Hobart noticed me, and I had come to expect pity in people's faces over the past few weeks, while my baby slipped away, or lay on her tiny bier. But his pity I saw not. Rather, Parson seemed to be speaking directly to me in his sermon, a phenomenon I had never experienced. And in his holy words, his sing-song voice, I heard everything I had ever feared.

"In Paul's Epistle to the Romans, chapter 7, verse 18, the Testament says, 'In me, that is, in my flesh, dwells *no good thing.*' We are filth, the dregs of all the privies and muck-piles of our village—and we carry this vice of obstinacy and selfishness in all that we do. We must resist the temptations of the world and stay true to our faith, no matter what challenges we may face. For if we were *true* to the Lord, then evil would not come to us."

Had I been *true*? I began to take account in my mind as he preached.

"For far too long, we have allowed sin to permeate our lives and corrupt our souls. We have turned away from God's teachings and embraced the ways of the world. We laugh when we should pray, we play when we should work, we jest when we should preach the Word. We have become complacent in our faith. But I tell you now, sin is a *disease*, a distemper that eats away at our souls, destroying everything that is good and pure within us. It leads us down a path of lust, pride, and frivolity."

I felt his words like the cut of a pillory's whip. I had felt pride in my comely husband the constable, and in my estate as married woman, as *Mistress*. I had hungered for his loving touch, his heated kisses, all in our marriage bed. Was that blasphemy? Was it sinful? Was I sinning even now, to question the sermon, and the Parson's words? I had laughed, played with, and teased my David. It was joyous, it had overflowed my days with happiness, and it were gone now. What was the sin? Playfulness? Joy?

"We are surrounded by jocularity and the inconsequential, by frivolity and shameless acts. People are more concerned with their own selfish desires than with living a life of virtue and morality! The Evangelist Matthew tells us, 'on the day of judgment people will give account for every careless word they speak.' It is a plague that has infested our society and corrupted our souls. Sin is the reason we suffer. We have become so accustomed to sin that we have forgotten what it truly means. It is not a mere error or a slip; it is a deliberate act of rebellion against God. Every time we sin, we turn away from the path of righteousness and embrace darkness."

The rafters of the old building seemed to shake with his rumbling voice, as if God Himself were rattling the timbers.

"And what does this darkness bring? Pain, suffering, and eternal damnation. We must turn from sin, follow His Commandments, and pray, pray for salvation, lest it be refused you at Heaven's gate!" The Reverend Hobart slammed his palm down in emphasis, his rostrum resounding like a drum, so that we all jumped in our seats.

Was my playful love with my wedded husband a sin? Should I have stayed dour and silent instead? Had I killed him twice over? I blamed myself for the bee-sting, which might have been an Act of God—something I could not have foreseen. But I'd stumbled, and he rushed to save me—my hero, brought low by a single insect bite. And all of our love-play, our saucy bedroom games, our pillow-talk—was that a measure of sin? Had I killed him with my lust, and did he suffer outside Heaven's gate?

Yea, my heart was breaking—and I had lost our child as well. I had failed David thrice, then: by failing to keep our infant alive, the very least thing I should have done as a mother.

I wept silently at first, as the Parson preached to me, *at me*, then my tears poured out like a burst weir. A howl of grief was building inside me and I rocked on my bench, moaned into my handkerchief, pressed to my mouth to cover my sobs. My sister Thankfull put her hand over my other hand, shushing me. Bethia nudged me with her shoulder for silence. The watcher came along the aisle with his shushing stick and tapped my back, once, twice, then knocked harder, against the back of my head to silence me. Other heads turned and frowned, I heard women shushing from nearby benches, then men from across the aisle.

But the parson continued in his screed, louder, over my sobs. "His authority over us knows no bounds. His authority is utter and complete. He owns us as we own chattel and kine. We are His to dispose of in whatever way He chooseth. The Lord giveth bounty and the Lord taketh it away. He giveth life and he taketh it away. His works are not ours to question! If you do not sin, have no fear—but if you sin, the Lord will smite thee down. He taketh all away—and smite those who doubt and question his Righteousness!"

"What kind—of god—smites down a babe?" I found myself on my feet, screaming. "What god refuses salvation to a little child? To a brave husband? How could our love be sinful? Why were they taken from me?" Rage and horror and grief were a hurricane in my chest. I could not stop, I remained half-crouching, my hands like claws.

My sisters pulled at my dress, my sleeves, to sit me down. I flung them off.

"What kind of god takes away *everything*? What kind of god? I rebuke this god! I curse him, I spit his name from my mouth—"

"Take her out," Parson Hobart shouted. Father, tears on his own cheeks, half-dragged me down the center aisle, shushing me.

"She has defiled our sanctuary and our Lord's holy name!" I heard the parson's thundering voice and other murmurings swirl over me.

"There is no god," I sobbed, heaving, howling. "Just this cursed Hell!"

Somehow Father bustled me through the door and out of the church, where I fell to the ground, my hands clawing at the dirt.

"There is no mercy; this is a horror—" I would have cursed and sworn had I known any curses at the time. I would have said anything to ease the pain in my heart. I wanted to die. I was walking as a dead woman bereft of hope and faith. There was nothing left in the world for me. I could not go on. I was already dead.

Mr. Henry the apothecary bustled to Father's side to see if he could help in my madness, slapping my cheeks hard, repeatedly. I sobbed and screamed. Fists and cudgels could not touch my pain. Together the two men half-carried me to the wain and lifted me to the seat. I covered my face with my hands, pulled my bonnet down over my face like a sack. I heard Father thank Mr. Henry and untie Ginger, climb up and shake the reins. The wain started down the hill toward home. I tipped and almost fell out of the seat, but Father grabbed me and pulled me upright.

"Hold on, girl—I pray you!" His hands were busy guiding Ginger down the slope.

"I want to die."

"Shush. Hush now. You're not yourself. You're ill from grief. Let me get you home, put you to bed. We should not have come today. That's all right, girl, hush now." He trotted Ginger once we hit the flat, and kept saying, "Hush now, hush," all the long way home.

Father sent me indoors while he put the equipage and horse away. I poured myself a half-gill of sack from the kitchen shelf, and swallowed it fast, leaving the wooden cup on the chopping block. My filthy hands shook. Jolly watched me, her eyes wide with shock, and tried to attend me, but I pulled away. I climbed up to my chamber, where the empty cradle stared at me like an accusation, a torture—*my babe is dead*. I couldn't keep her safe. I failed David. I had killed my husband and his only progeny. He couldn't keep any of us safe because I had brought the bees upon him. I had failed my mother in caring for her bees. I failed everyone and everything, and there was no one left to save me. I was living in hell.

And God help me, I could not quite remember what I had just done in meeting but I knew I was doomed. I had burnt my boats and had nowhere left to go. Who would stand for me now?

I doffed my shoes, shortgown, stays and petticoats, down to my shift. I closed the shutters and slid under the coverlet, pulling it over my head. I stayed there for some days, until I lost count.

* * *

Jolly and my sisters tried to feed me, get me to rise, drink some tea or ale, but I didn't even need the chamber pot. I was a dried-up sinew. I wanted to die. Mr. Henry came and Father asked him bleed me to cool my blood. They hid the cradle and swaddling clothes from sight, stowed in the attic eaves or in the stable, perhaps. Thankfull bathed my face with a warm cloth, my arms, my now-slack breasts, and soft, empty belly; my hands which were curled into fists she opened and bathed, scraped my filthy nails. Bethia and Charity sat with me, but when Charity read me from the Bible, I screamed at her to leave.

Father brought Mr. Henry again and he dry-cupped all over my back and breech to pull poison from my corpus. He left me lying bruised and humiliated in my shift, and I pulled the cover back over my head.

Father tapped at the door some time later, bringing a lanthorn.

"Parson is here, and his wife. He wants to speak to you, but Goodwife Hobart will see you first. Get you a comb and your bedgown, daughter."

Jolly came in and helped me pull the blanket to cover my shift. She handed me a flagon of ale to swill my mouth and swallow. I gagged but got it down. She helped me set my coif. Heaven forbid I be seen in my nightdress with my hair uncovered while ill, by the visiting minister. I could not hope for a charitable visit. I knew it would be anything but. The hypocrisy sickened me.

A knock at the door and a brusque opening revealed Goodwife Hobart, in her blackest of gowns and petticoats, her severest bonnet. Her cheeks burned a high red color, as did the tip of her sharp nose, whether from chilly wind or zeal, I could not say.

"Sit you up, Widow Marsh. Cover yourself, your head." I had already done so. She merely wanted to scold me for it.

"My husband Parson Hobart is waiting to speak to you." She looked down at me.

I hated the sight of her, judging, sneering; I had felt this way since knowing her and had always held my tongue. In my madness, I wanted to tell her to go fornicate a cur or some other such abomination but I couldn't form words. The Pilgrim fowls of the town must have food to eat, and it was with tales like the one she was then gathering of me, taking in every detail to regale her cronies. I wouldn't waste the spit in my mouth upon her.

She stood aside, bowing her head as her husband entered the room.

"Widow Marsh." The minister was dressed as for service, in his dark suit and white starched collars against his chest. His hat was pulled over his beetle-brow and his prominent nose stuck out like a beak.

"You have disgraced yourself and defiled the meeting hall with blasphemy and obscenity. Your lack of faith is a shame upon your family and this house. You shame all of us in the congregation. You will come before the magistrate and elders on Tuesday next, the 31st of October, for censure. Do you hear me, Widow? Do not shame yourself by dissembling any further. May God have mercy upon you."

He turned and left the chamber. Goodwife Hobart lingered a moment longer, her head shaking like a nanny goat pulling hay from a rick. She fixated for a moment on my daughter's ragdoll in the bed with me, the only memento I had left in the physical sense, then swished from the bedchamber in umbrage.

I didn't care. I didn't fear her or him or whatever god they represented. I lay myself down again and stared at the wall, fuming. They came to stare and sneer, and now they would judge. What did it matter? I willed myself to die. If only I had the power to just close my eyes and disappear. I would join my husband and daughter somewhere in the great beyond, the Happy Hunting Ground of the Natives, or somewhere beyond the edges of the sea. Or in Hell. It mattered not to me. I was already dead inside.

On the next Sabbath I stayed away from meeting. I couldn't face the congregation, and I wouldn't drag myself from bed. I waited until Father was gone out the door to the village, and Jolly to her own church down the road. I went down to the kitchen in my bedgown and made some tea and ate from the pan of potatoes and bacon of last night's meal, back of the hearth. What I wanted was water, deep enough to cover me, over my head. I wanted to wash away the fog and try to think clearly for once. The task of filling the washtub for a bath seemed insurmountable. So many buckets, and I doubted I could focus long enough for the job of work.

I could wash myself in the surf, mayhap. I wandered out the kitchen door and headed to the stable. Ginger's half barrel of water was full and clear, mossy on the staves and the bottom, with a few drifting leaves atop. I picked out the leaves. The water was cold, and so was the wind. I didn't care. I shed my bedgown and pulled my shift over my head. Sky-clad, I stepped into the water barrel. It was sleet-cold. I crouched into it, gasping at the chill. I made to bathe myself using my hand as invisible soap, splashing myself, wetting my face, my chest. I stood and stepped out into the dirt, then sat arsy-varsy, my entire body sunk down to the mossy base, my head and hair hanging out the side. I untied my braid and let my lank hair blow in the cold wind.

It was raw weather, much colder than I imagined. I scooted to one side and tried to bring my head under, but the barrel was too small. I was not a child, sharing the tub with my sisters, aye, long ago. I struggled to sit, to get up again. I must wash the stink off my body, the loathing, the judgment, the sin. I turned around and went to my knees in the grass, the mud, and plunged my upper body, my entire head and hair down into the dark water. My head pounded and throbbed with the cold headache. I swished my head back and forth to wet all the length of it. My wet hair was pulling me, holding me under. I needed to take breath. What if I held it until I let go, lost consciousness? What if I stayed here, until the silver bubbles of my breath blew out and away, like the drowned lambs my brothers had found in the postholes?

I heard a shout and felt myself seized from behind, my damp gown thrown over me to hide my nakedness.

"Miss Silence, what you done?"

Philadelphia, the African slave of our neighbor, pulled me from the depths. He grasped my face in his hand, met my eyes, saw that I was alive still.

"Mistress, don' do that! Please, mistress, don' do that!" His wrinkled face held such concern that I was swept with shame.

"I still live. I'm sorry, Philly. I'm sorry." Taking his arm, I stood and wrapped my bedgown around me, my muddy knees and feet slipping on the dirt path. I felt the cold wind in my wet hair and was suddenly quaking from the cold.

"Wait, Miss Silence. Wait a minute." He shook out a horse blanket and wrapped it further around me. "Come let's git to the fire, git you warm." Guiding me as if I were an elder too frail to walk alone, he walked me back to the kitchen and through the door. I stood on Jolly's scoured floor and looked at the kitchen, knowing I was ridiculous, I was disgusting, I was lost, with my wet hair and horse blanket and muddy feet. Philly pushed me to the wooden chair. I sat.

I had rarely met Philly in the village or on the road, and much less withindoors, but he clearly knew his way around the hearth. He blew the flames up and found a knob of ginger, with his folding knife shaving a piece into a basin. He sought out the honey and some red kitchen pepper, and with the former made a ginger posset in hot milk for me to drink. He added the pepper to a larger basin of hot water for my feet.

"Jolly gon kill me if she see all this, Miss." He shook his head at me. "I'm get a better blanket for you, a cloth for your hair. She'll be here soon, comb out your curls."

I sat, sodden and stupid, tears rolling down my face, in a horse blanket in the kitchen until Philly brought me a clean sheet and a woolen blanket.

"I'll go outside a minute, miss, so you can wrap up?" He placed the sheet and blanket on the bench and stepped outside the door and closed it.

Was I losing my senses? I was sorry for what I had put upon Philly, ashamed to make his life any harder. I dropped the horse blanket and wrapped the sheet around my body, then pulled the blanket around my shoulders. I was still dirty and cold, as browbeaten as a naughty child. I was a fool.

Philly tapped and cracked the door. "Are you covered, miss? I'm coming in."

I sat in the chair and looked at him in despair. My mother, my husband, my daughter, my whole life, as ruined as a tobacco crop in a late rainstorm.

"Let's git your feet into that hot water and drink that posset. You'll catch your death!" He fussed like an old tabby and I couldn't fault him. He was too kind.

I should have drowned myself when I had the chance.

Both the saved and lost will be judged

On the last day of October in the year of 1722, I dressed in my somber Sabbath blacks, my freshly starched coif and linen collars, my sable-colored bonnet over my coif, my hair pinned properly underneath; I felt the heft of my prayerbook inside my pocket, a linen handkerchief in my hand. I wore my warm red cloak over all. Father nodded when he saw me, approving, but he did not make comment until we were almost at the meeting-house. The Magistrate Sir Fellows and the church elders, under the leadership of Parson Hobart, were come to censure me there.

Father also wore his Sabbath blacks, his black hat as sober as a parson's over his curly white mop. His red face was barely lined but his frosted pate showed his great age—three score and and seventeen, by the church record. His back was straight still, despite his many years at the loom.

"I'm sorry it has come to this, daughter." Father finally spake as our wain rumbled past the harbormaster's warehouse on the Hingham waterfront. "I don't know why you fell to pieces in the meeting-house, of all the places, but you'll have to pay the piper. It won't be pretty."

"I was afflicted, my mind addled." But this was, to my true self, a lie. I knew a righteous anger in my breast, but I kept it inside. Because no one wanted to hear me question faith, question God, question the bedrock of the Separatists' world, no matter how much pain I carried. No one wanted to hear what I had to say of anything.

"I know you were wroth, taking on so after such sadness. Your dear mother," he choked, his voice watery. "Your husband, your daughter—it wounds the spirit, so much at once. I remember—we lost your brothers, the first little Israel, then the second, both just nurslings, and Thomas, just a wee lad. Little Solomon lived a scant year, and Experience, that sweet girl—just fourteen when she left us. It breaks the heart, I know. But you *must* trust in God, daughter. You mayn't give up. You must pay the piper for your sins."

In my own misery, I had forgotten how many child-deaths my father had seen, and two wives as well. I was sore ashamed, hearing him beseech me. I had been so weak where he was strong.

"I'm sorry, Father. Pray you forgive me?"

He took my hand and held it for a moment, then let it go as we made the turn up the hillock to the meeting-house sheds and wain yard.

I hadn't expected so many people in the meeting-house of a Tuesday, but the benches were filled, as all the goodwives and goodmen of the town came to witness my shaming. My villager neighbors were not the sort to fill their hours with books or news from afar; the business of their near neighbors was much more agreeable. One wants to know if one's neighbor is a sinner, lest that person be a danger to one's own salvation. And one wants a full basket of dirty laundry to share across the washing green on a Monday, if one can get it.

A hum and buzz in the air when we came in the door reminded me of Mother's hives. I wanted to sit upon the family's usual bench on the women's side with my sisters, but Father urged me forward, his hand on my elbow. We passed to the front row where an elder directed us, and sat in silence until eleven of the clock. Then Sir Fellows and the elders came up the center aisle and seated themselves at the long board table facing the congregation. Parson Hobart came in behind them all, taking his chair at the table up front. I saw the hatchet face of his wife, Goodwife Hobart, off to the side, where she usually sat to hear her husband preach. That bench supplied her with an excellent view for the day's censures. Her basket would be quite full by end of day.

Parson Hobart stepped forward and began the proceedings with a prayer, and he made it a long one. He asked for forgiveness of my sins, and for a blessing upon the proceedings, to show me the error of my ways, and to heal the community for the damage I had done. He noted my weakness as a woman and my infirm heart and mind, then implored our Lord to punish me harshly, for to spare the rod is, as we all know, to spoil the child.

At last, he said, "Amen." My neck ached from hanging down so long. I longed to rub it to ease the strain, but I dare not, no more to add to my list of freakish behaviors.

Sir Fellows, resplendent in his winter robes of black silk with miniver collar, his long wig curled and gleaming like silver, called my name, his rich voice rolling through the meetinghouse. "Widow Marsh, born Silence Nichols, come you forward." He remained in his chair, his narrow hands resting on the smooth board before him, his brow furrowed and his nose pointing at me like a finger.

I slid my red cloak and bonnet onto the bench and went to stand in the space before the table, clad in my prayerful black, prayerbook now in my hand and handkerchief inside of my pocket, my long twist of brown hair respectfully pinned up and covered by my starched coif. I hated to stand before the man who held my future in his hands, with my back to the dozens of eyes of the congregation that blamed and shamed me. I recalled how Fellows had spoken to me when my husband was not listening, the uncouth suggestions from his lowered voice. The way his eyes had slid along my figure, as if I were a haunch of fresh venison, and he a starved man. How he had made free to insinuate and suggest with his tone and his eyes, if not in specific words, and how I had defied him. Sir Fellows, a gentleman and royally appointed lord of our town and region, held absolute power over me now, and I stood alone, my soul naked before him.

He had not forgotten.

"I see you have brought your prayerbook. Pray you make better use of it in the future." He looked upon me as a man inspects his maize for worm. "You are the daughter of our congregant, Israel Winslow Nichols, are you not?" As if we were new to the town, and he had never seen my face nor made my acquaintance before.

"I am, sir."

"And you live with him since being widowed over the spring?"

"Yes, sir."

"That was proper. A woman need be ruled over, and clearly you were unable to guide your own steps after the death of your husband. It is fitting that you should have returned to your father's house. And in your father's house, do you pray and study the Word of God?"

"I do." Once upon a time I had done. But not of late. The first lie.

"But surely not enough. Israel Winslow Nichols, come you forward."

I was mortified that Father must stand with me in my shaming.

"Israel, you have failed in your duty to your daughter. She profaned the name of the Lord, blasphemed in meeting, spoke out of turn, and caused mayhem while questioning her faith. I call this the fault of a weak and ineffectual parent, and we hereby censure you for your failing."

Father bowed his head, so humbled. I could not stop my tears from flowing.

I spake, "Your Worship, 'tis not fair—"

"*Silence!*" Fellows exploded, his face red as my mother's quince jelly. "You will speak no more unless spoken to. *Bridle* your tongue. Let it utter not a single word more."

The meeting-room was still as the grave. No one dared break the hush. I stood, quaking, weeping without sound. I had not the strength to stand up to such bullying this day. The volume of his shouting hurt me as much as the words, like whips, reminding me of my husband's absence, of all I had lost.

"Israel Winslow Nichols, you shall be fined *fifty* pounds in gold or silver for failing to bring up your daughter to meek and silent womanhood. I pray you will correct her ways, seeing she has no husband to correct her. A further outburst from this woman will result in a fine of an hundred pounds, and if there is a third offense, and she betray your parenting again?—shall get you a week in the gaol. Pay the exchequer of the town by Saturday or the fine shall increase. You are dismissed."

My father nodded in acquiescence.

"And pray get you another wife." Sir Fellows looked down at his scrolls, dismissing my beloved father without a flick of his eyes.

Father had not the money in coin or gold. He had woven products that he made, aye, and materials—wool and lin-en, and all the rugs and coverlets and hempen bags he could make for trade goods. But he had not a storehouse of wealth. My sin would clean from Father his savings against his elder years and any storm that might burst upon him. Not me, not *my* storm. His own. I felt sick at the thought of his punishment and knew mine would be worse yet.

Father bowed his hoary head and said, "I thank thee, your Worship." He stepped back to the pew without brushing my hand or meeting my eyes. More than anything, I felt Father's mortification over my own. The shame ached like a black tooth.

"Widow Marsh, born Silence Nichols, you will now hear the charges against you and answer them, and the consequences. Then you will be chastised." The look was in Fellows' eyes again. I knew he should enjoy my downfall, and I knew it should be hard.

"You interrupted sacrosanct proceedings in a place of worship, and questioned the Lord, the Faith, and your place in this community. For that you must bear consequences in some or all of the following." Fellows shuffled parchments before him and pulled at a certain piece, blackened with writing, holding it at arm-length to see it clearly. He did not care, it seemed, for the look of spectacles upon his long nose. He read the chart aloud.

"Firstly, if any interrupt or oppose a preacher in season of worship, they shall be reproved by the Magistrate, and shall pay five pounds or stand two hours in the pillory, with the inscription on paper pinned to him, *A Wanton Gospeler.*"

"Secondly, if any person *swear*, rail or revile in the church or in the bounds of the town, they shall stand with their tongue in a cleft stick for an hour on the Village Green, at the place of the pillory."

"Thirdly, if any person shall blaspheme the Name of the Lord, they shall be set in the pillory one hour, with a paper on their breast with the word *Blasphemy* wrote in Capitals thereon, to suffer one month's imprisonment or to be bound to their good behavior for one year and to pay costs."

"Fourthly, if any person deny the Lord thy God in a place of worship, a charge of *Atheism* is made upon them, and they shall wear the white gown and sit in the center of the church for a month of Sabbaths so that justice may rain upon them in the place of worship."

"Fifthly, if any person has entertained familiarity with *Satan*, the great Tempter and grand enemy of God and mankind—and by his help has acted without faith for which, according to the law of God and the established law of this commonwealth, they deserve punishment and censure." He let the parchment fall to the table and leaned upon his elbows.

"Widow Marsh, do you understand these charges?" His eyes drilled into me, like to pierce my soul. His voice rolled across the congregation as richly as any minister of God.

Shaken, I was afraid to answer in the affirmative, but I understood not the fifth charge.

"I have not entertained familiarity with Satan, your Worship."

"Must we read the witness statements?" Fellows, irritated, looked across the board table at Parson Hobart, who shuffled through his parish book.

"I have it here," Parson said.

"Then let us hear it, Hobart, no delay! The accused has asked for *proof*."

The parson cleared his throat. "'On the day of her daughter's birth, in August of this very year, Widow Marsh did knowingly use a magic charm to ease the pain of her childbirth, breaking the commandment of our Lord that women are to labor in pain, from the Holy Writ of Genesis; with the spell of a knife beneath her bed to reduce the travails of her labor.'"

I recalled that Parson Hobart had served on the panel of judges for the witch trials before my birth. The recollection chilled me as he continued his recitation. A shudder went through me, as I fully grasped what was happening. They thought me a witch! They called my simple life a bond with Satan! Then I could not still my trembling. I clasped my hands tightly together and clenched my jaw.

"Secondly, on that and other occasions, Widow Marsh did prefer the company of African servants to the companionship of her English friends and neighbors, which association is against the rule of mixing with a different class and grade of companion, according to the Holy Writs of Leviticus and Deuteronomy; yea, in many of the Holy books, as we hear of a Sabbath Day.

"And thirdly, Widow Marsh does knowingly keep a poppet of her dead daughter in her bed chamber, as a magical charm and tool of the Tempter.

"These three charges are sworn by my Goodwife Aphra Hobart, who witnessed these herself, and is, of course," he coughed. "Of unimpeachable character."

Goodwife Hobart eyed me from the side-bench, her pinched nose held high and righteously. She all but preened herself in importance.

"Do you deny these statements, Widow Marsh?" Fellows, who did not suffer fools, of which Goodwife Hobart was surely such a one, nonetheless knew the law well. He had me plucked as a grouse on the kitchen block.

Still, I refused to acquiesce. "I did not use magic nor consort—"

He cut me off, sharp as a blade. "Confess and be punished as fitting, or be silent and lie to yourself instead. Was there a knife under your bed, yea or nay?"

"Aye, but—"

"Do you keep the poppet of your dead child? Yea or nay?"

"Nay—well, but it was her—my babe's—" A wave of grief washed over me, checking the words in my throat. My empty arms. Elizabeth, cold in her grave. I covered my mouth with my hand to stop the wail from rising.

The Magistrate did not hold nor hesitate on my account. "Do you prefer the company of *African* servants over the company of an English neighbor and Christian such as Goodwife Hobart? Yea or nay?"

That woman. The accusation pushed back my sorrow, knocked clean off my mind with a wave of rage. I looked across at Goodwife Hobart. I did not hide my revulsion. "Aye. That, I do."

She screamed then, "Her eyes! Don't let her curse me!" and other women and children in the hall set to shrilling, "Witch, witchcraft—Satan's handmaid! Lawbreaker!"

"Order, order! This is not a witch trial; we will have order! Silence the chamber!" Sir Fellows had had enough of them, fools, and of me, obstinate. "Widow Marsh, you admit to the witness's statement, and you admit to the charges as stated. We will proceed to the sentencing forthwith."

He shuffled his pages, the writ already prepared, disregarding my defense.

"We require that the town of Hingham and Cohasset village observe a Day of Humiliation to atone for the sins of Widow Marsh, on Friday of this week, November the third, with no meat, fish nor fowl, and no strong ale for any citizen or resident of this township, in consequence of Widow Marsh's faults. And you all shall pray for her redemption."

There were murmurings behind me as this settled among the pews. They had come for my punishment, not theirs. So not merely my father and myself, not merely my family, but the entire town would share my punishment, which, I knew, would cause them to resent me. I heard hisses behind me. Such degradation. I knew aright what they would pray for—not my salvation. I closed my eyes. But the Magistrate had not finished.

"At the Superior Court held at Hingham Town on the 31st day of October, in the year of our Lord seventeen hundred and twenty-four, Widow Marsh, born Silence Nichols, wife of the late David Marsh of said Hingham, is convicted of being disruptive of the parson at church; is sentenced to two hours in the pillory, with the inscription on paper pinned to her, *A Wanton Gospeler*. For swearing, railing, and reviling in the church or within the bounds of the town, she shall stand with her tongue in a cleft stick for an hour on the Village Green, at the place of the pillory. For denying the Lord in a place of worship, a conviction of *Atheism* is made upon the said Silence Nichols Marsh, and she shall wear the white gown and sit in the center of the church for a month of Sabbaths.

"For having attempted to thwart her woman's place and entertained familiarity with the Great Tempter, rather than according to the laws of God and the established law of this Commonwealth, the said Widow Marsh, born Silence Nichols, deserves correction, which will be ten stripes of the lash at the pillory and a fine of ten pounds in gold or silver. Her hair will be shorn at the time of that correction.

"Furthermore, Widow Marsh, born Silence Nichols, is hereby indicted for blaspheming the Name of the Lord. She shall be set in the pillory one hour, with a paper on her breast with the word *Blasphemy* wrote in Capitals thereon."

He paused, weighing the moment, his mouth pursed, his head cocked. He had me right where he wanted this time. His mouth moved as he savored the moment. I prepared for him to announce the one-month prison sentence, although I feared so much to hear, my body shook. The prison, with filth, lice, maggoty bread and dirty water, shackles and irons, the ravages of guards, the violence of maddened prisoners—I was sick with dread.

The moment stretched, weighted.

He finally spake.

"A week in the goal to think on your sins," said he, with a kind of malicious delight. "And lastly, Widow Marsh, born Silence Nichols—let your name, that Christian virtue given you by your loving parents, be your penalty. You shall be bound to silence for a twelvemonth, and you will pay the court's costs of 40 shillings." He looked at me with scorn, perhaps even satisfaction.

"You shall sit the pillory on Saturdays in the month of November, and in the church aisle on the Sabbath days of December. You will provide the white gown. Your silence begins January the first. Your fines are due by November the last. May God have mercy upon you. This court is dismissed. Take her to the gaol."

Part the Second

SILENTIUM

The silence begins

I have been silenced for a year. My crime was in voicing my broken heart, my distraught spirit; and they called my boldness a sin in questioning God's will. I was a fool to have spoken so publicly. I was so broken I did not know my place anymore. I did not know myself. I spoke aloud, out of turn, in church and expressed myself so fiercely that the Magistrate and the elders convened to sentence me—to a year of silence, to suit my name: Silence Nichols Marsh, daughter of the weaver, widow of the constable, mother of none, now that my child has also gone to the grave. My heart is a sieve, and no love is left for myself or this world. And yet, I live and walk each day. I am yet alive in death and dead in life. The silence fills my ears like the roaring of the sea.

I have nothing to say at first. I have naught but my reeling thoughts, my heart like an anchor, my head wooly as a handful of sheep's roving. My stripes have scabbed over. My back will always bear the welts of shame, but they have closed after two months. So has the lump and great bruise in my tongue after an hour with the iron cleft stick forced into my mouth. My chipped tooth remains sharp as sin. Now I have the year to endure. If I live.

I had often played with my long hair, made a dark ringlet around my finger as I waited for Meeting to end; the Sabbath-master swatted me when he caught me fidgeting. It was a habit, a soothing little pastime, to play thusly with my tresses. As a young girl I had dreamed of a proper goodman come to ask my hand in marriage and, looking at the dark band of hair around my narrow third finger, my cheeks pinked as I pretended to reluctantly agree.

Now, shorn of my locks and of husbands real or imagined, there is nothing to play with, no comfort to be had from my witless diversion. My ears are naked. My neck is bared. I feel the cold bitterly this January, and my linen coif does nothing to warm me. It is light as a bit of sugar on a cake. I wrap my head and neck with a knitted woolen shawl, to muffle the sharp draughts in my father's house, or in the meeting-house when I must attend on a Sabbath. I am thus able to hide my bare scalp, and fight the cold of a New World winter without my crown of hair.

Father owns but a single looking-glass by the kitchen door, as he does not hold with prinking for company, and so goes about cockhatted or with his brows grown like tree-moss. I had been known to pinch my pale cheeks or lips, and to wash my face with milk in the spring and summer when I was receiving David's court, or imagining myself a shepherd-ess in a fairy-story. To pretty up my face, smooth my wind-blown hair before the glass, when I come in from a walk. Nothing to prink at now, if I were even so inclined. I see my pink head carved like a dinner fowl at a tavern, uneven drifts of short hair all that remain of the hacking and the blade of Mr. Henry, who was pressed into doing the deed at the pillory. My dark tresses, once grown past my waist, were stamped into the mud, then plucked at by the wharf-urchins and made sport of, as I limped away toward Father's home.

I stay with my father, as there is no place elsewhither I might go. He has dismissed his servant Jolly for his sudden poverty and we are alone as two can be.

My sister Thankfull brings from her household the loan of a writing tablet, four sheets of ivory an inch wide and three inches long; they are fastened with a brass rivet at one end so the tablet might fan out. With a lead pencil, I can write my thought and show it; if my companion could read my simple letters, he would thereby understand my desire or expression. I could make use of the tool, I could. But it seems to me that the ivory tablet is against the spirit of the sanction, that silence means *absolute and utter silence*, of thoughts, of psalm, of prayer, of song or humming, of exclamation and ejaculation, of any expression of feeling or sentiment, most of which are meaningless to the Lord anyway.

And my father has already paid dearly. I dare not risk causing further harm. I nod my thanks to her and wave her away, the ivory fan tucked into a box where it shall be ignored; if it were mine I should sell it, to repay my debt to Father.

I lay my clipped head on the smooth linen of my pillowbere. I look up now at the plastered ceiling of my father's house, the sleeping chamber I had used as a child coming up in the ways of the Lord and of the household. The winter wind howls at the eaves. My shoes make noise upon the wooden floor. The house rattles with the regular thump of my father's loom: *thwack* and *slam*, *clack* and *thrum*, some three thousand times a day, while the design grows under his hands, his own canny skill. The weather, my earthbound feet, my father's loom do speak, but I may not. It seems another of the world's cruel jests at my expense.

My mother had not lived to see last spring's new lavender, and I, heavy with child and grief, had not the heart to gather it in high summer. What remains in each bedchamber now are fragile twigs that catch the dust and shake seeds and dried blossom to the floor if disturbed. Her scent is gone from my life as surely as the joy, the heart, and now, the speech.

I miss my mother fiercely. The house is empty without her presence, despite my father's noisy production of table-carpet and coverlet. Both of us sit at board in silence; we eat our silent sup and wash it down with our new cider, and go alone to our sad beds. His house is not perhaps the best place for me, but Jazaniah has seven at his table, Roger with nine, Nathaniel in a small house with his four sons and his new wife expectant. I might have gone with my married sisters, but Father needs me to keep his house now without Mother or Jolly, and—I must confess it—I had thought I'd be petted and adored as of old. He grieves our mutual losses—but he is deeply humbled by my punishment, my silence and my shorn head. We each need the other forbye, and despise our circumstances.

How do two sorrowful people pass the time? Father sits at his loom and works all the day, and into the night if he cannot sleep. Weaving sends him into a kind of transfixed state, where he can travel the world in daydream or prayer without leaving his bench. I believe he walks with my mother on shores and in meadows full of flowers, and recalls their courting days. His work keeps him from having to see me in my shame all day, only at table, where we of course do not speak. I fill my days with carding, punching down the risen dough, sweeping out the cold stone kitchen, boiling up the Great Wash on Mondays, and all the little things that make a man's household run smoothly.

I have no joy in life, nor life in my body. I have nothing, not even a voice to profess my penitence. Only a still, small voice that tells me I have been brutally wronged.

I can sew a seam, stir the porridge, knit a cap, or darn a hole, but I have no special craft to speak of—nor a soft hand with flour and lard like sister Charity, nor a memory-keep-er like Roger, who can recite scrolls of Scripture and knows Psalm upon Psalm by number, every word. Thankfull has a lilting singing voice just right for singing the old songs of Eng-land, but which she has tamed for singing the Psalms. My sister Ruth has healing hands—she can soothe any squalling child, unstick an eggbound hen, save frostbitten toes, pull out the tiniest splinter, and unknot a stiff neck with a twist of her hands. I can do all of those things well enough, but I am nor adept nor scholar. I wish to leap over the stile and feel the ocean wind at my face, hear the crash of waves, collect shells and stones and wonder at the wildflowers, like a child. And none of those will fill the larder.

My days are long, the nights longer. I feel sin and pun-ishment sucking me down as a sodden wool cape, heavy as a dank fog. I do not know myself.

Without trying, however, I seem to befriend the wild and tame creatures, or they come to me uncalled. They scorn me not, and I have no intent to harm them. I snap my fingers, and call them not. I scatter dry breadcrumbs and cobs of In-dian corn for the hens, and black seeds from the sunflowers Mother had planted along the edges of the dooryard. I pet the little black hen that likes to be held in my arms. I whisper her name, Blackie, when no one is about, and am pleased that she seeks me out for crumbs. She doesn't understand my sin.

Father's horse, Ginger, lips my hand when I feed her a carrot top. She nuzzles and rests her head across my shoul-der like an overgrown babe. The creatures do not judge me, my shameful cropped head and my silence. If this affinity for mute beasts is my gift, so be it. Mayhap I will speak at Christmastide like the animals do, as the old stories tell of the stable creatures. A year hence, perhaps it will happen. *But Christmas is Papist sin, forbidden to us, and here I am again, dwelling in places I ought not to consider.* Shame, remorse, desolation lick at my heels like flame.

What I ought to have learned was how to ape or mum, so I can communicate my needs to my household—to Father, to my sisters when they call by. Father acts as if I am also deaf or blind, speaking loudly as if I cannot see and hear him standing before me. He shapes his words for a simpleton—does he think I have also lost my reason? Sister-in-law Bethia, if she is nigh, seems to read my heart, what I need or want, almost before I can gesture toward it. I make dumb-show when I must, but silence means not speaking. What the Lord hath put into the mind of a magistrate, I must own.

When it is too much to take, I slip away from the house and crouch on the winter shore, no one to see me, and there I sob aloud. I scream into my cupped hands my loss, my loneliness, my despair. My elbow over my face, or my face buried in my hands, I weep as hard as I am able, until almost spewing my bile, but I don't speak. Because why be bothered to form useless words? Who in my world cares to hear me speak, or even make the smallest groan? And what is there to say? What is left to speak aloud except emptiness?

Soon enough, I find myself using the same gestures over again, and they become my language. I mimic sipping a tankard or a tea-bowl, taking food, cutting bread or meat, indicate pain or a specific item by pointing, although I have been taught from birth how rude it is to point the finger. *Sleep* or *wash* are easy gestures, and so are the emotions of sorrow, gladness, anger; it is the simplest of all to show agreement or disagreement, or that hobgoblin, *I don't know.* The shoulder shrug means *I don't care, it matters not.* And this brusque gesture I make too often in my earliest days of silence. Because I do not care, and it matters not a whit.

I invent a sign for Father by stroking my "beard," and a sign for my brothers, using fingers to indicate which one of four I intend. My sisters are signed with four fingers as well. I have no hand-sign for David nor my baby. I have no words in my body to express their loss, or even to name them. They are words only in my heart. Difficulty arises if I want explanation, to ask why or how. I use my face to express myself, but I will not mouth words, which seems a breach of the ordinance. They said I mayn't speak. So I mustn't. I respond when spoken to with a hand sign if it suits, and with nothing if it means a longer conversation. I am mostly, as one would expect, silent.

I have not become angry yet, in these early winter days. I am still bereft, melancholic, stunned, thus, silence is not so hard to keep. But the melancholy worries my father. He scarcely speaks to me, and I know he is deeply wounded by the fine and my shame. But I hear him speaking with my brother Nathaniel in the workroom.

"She'll waste to nothing if she cannot brighten up. Melancholia will take her."

"Is she sleeping by night?"

They discuss me as if they talk of kine and crop. It matters not if I sleep or no. I have nothing to rise for, no reason to leap from my bed in the icy mornings beyond household chores, to make the beds or sweep. But they are all for directing my disposition and the arrangement of my face.

Still, Father does not stint, in reporting to my brother. "Master Henry said that the melancholic's habit of *phantasmata*, thinking terrible thoughts, subjects the sufferer to the most harrowing tribulations of inner life. Melancholia is a kind of madness, caused by the humour of black bile."

The men discuss my black bile and my *phantasmata*, and soon enough they have made their minds. If melancholia were a part of my constitution, there might be no cure. I hold not a glimmer of hope of feeling better, ever. Perpetual silence, in that manner, suits me.

My father dresses warmly and rides Ginger to town to call upon Mr. Henry. He returns with a bitter powder meant to be drunk in a draught at candlelighting, to help me sleep. I mix it as told, a scant teaspoon in a mug of small beer. I gag and cough and wish I could refuse to swallow it, but I sleep the night through, whatever was in it. Yet it is too successful: My dreams are terrifying, and I can scarce open my eyes in the morning, coming up from under the dreamscape like a person caught in the deadly undertow. I open my eyes and suck in a breath to scream but catch myself in time.

That is the end to bitter sleeping draughts. I wag my head and hold a hand over my mouth to show him I mean it. To Father's good grace, rather than fight me, he allows me to refuse, and returns to his loom. But over time, he returns to the cause.

After a three-day snowstorm, Mr. Henry arrives by sledge with his bleeding kit. I undress to my shift. I lie upon my bed, covered with Father's warm woolen blankets in my cold chamber, where breath hangs in the air. The apothecary, his stock tied high around his thick red neck, straps my arm to a board with a leather thong and chooses a silver fleam from his pocket case. He gives me the wooden case, a carven small box for his instrument, to hold tightly in the extended hand. He knocks the end of the fleam with his well-notched mallet; the sharp blade slips through my white skin, and from the crook of my arm a dark trickle flows. I have thought of blood as bright red, but this is dark as wine, thick as honey. My blood must be the curse that afflicts me: too much, too hot, too molten.

"Purging the wet, warm humour ventilates the blood and cools the spirit, allowing her to heal the breach with the Lord, and return a more righteous and penitent woman," Mr. Henry explains to Father. "Take away half the blankets and let her feel the cooling airs."

I feel my blood heaving within me, pulsing in my ears. Liquid velvet spots the sheet. In a moment he has done, and pulls the fleam, stabbing the wound closed with a brass pin. He makes a figure of eight with a bit of linen thread and the closure holds. The wound stings, but what is pain? My losses, my sins, they throb. I turn my face away. They leave me, and I wonder if this wobbly feeling is a sign of health returning or of life leaving my body.

Bethia brings up a glass of water she says is made from melted snow, so cold it makes my teeth ache and brings forth a sharp pain in my pate; it washes cool in my mouth, down my dry throat, and I feel it splash into my empty stomach. My humours must be cooling. I feel slow and stupid. I must become accustomed to feeling this way. There's no other alternative. She leaves me in my chamber to redress, with no words of comfort, only a sideways judgment, and I stay in the chamber until I shiver blue with cold.

The next morning I rise and dress without help, despite the stitch on my arm, knowing that whatever I do not do will remain undone, my mother cold in her grave, my father waiting for me at table. I am sick at heart, but I am not selfish. It is all my work, now.

I care for Father's house as if it were my own, only borrowed—keeping it neat and warm as any goodwife, holding a place for Father's next wife, whosoever she may be. When that happens, I will be moved back yet another square, to a lesser position, and then a lesser: a widowed woman with no sons, no children at all, no property, and a public shaming to haunt the family for years to come. We shall see no visitors. We shall receive no courtesy. And it is my sin, my own, that has done it.

I keep to my chamber, rather than sit in the keeping room near Father, as I would have liked better. I arise, aye, and dress myself, drink my tea, but after breaking our fast and Father leading the prayer, I drift up to my chamber like sea smoke, my heart an anchor dragging below, my eyes glassy, unseeing. I pick up my carding combs and sit in my cold chamber, my hands no longer idle, my mind asea.

I am a drowned corpus, washed ashore, eaten upon by crabs. I am silent, voiceless, adrift, alone. The winter days drag on.

In wrath they hate me

February is ever the longest month—it is the shortest of the calendar, but its gray weather and chilblained fingers and toes, the end of harvest bounty all too near. Folk have sung their songs and told their stories a dozen times by now, and the lingering cold is a tedium to endure with patience and prayer. The tree branches are yet bare, not a hint of the green and blossom to appear in March and April. The English say, *Half the wood and half the hay by Christmas Day*, but we are well past that pagan debauch, and the woodpile wanes.

The potatoes and turnips in the cellar have grown beards. Father's braided onions begin to powder black with mold. Ginger's haystacks are farther from her stable now, as the winter ekes on. The last pompion has grown soft, and we are counting the weeks until new life appears in the field and we might have new milk, fresh eggs—soon, please, soon!

As the short month passes, I become more at home in my skin, as it were; I am used to the silence now, and no need to pinch myself to keep from speaking aloud. I am not at all well, however. My punitive wounds have healed, but my heart has not. I feel the absence of my mother in the cold indoor days, by the hearth, where we would have chatted amiably and knitted stockings for our husbands, or a swaddling blanket for my coming babe. I still have so many questions I would have asked her, about love, and loss, about caring for babies beyond the birthing, about a babe's sleepless nights and refusal to latch onto the teat, or when the naval string should fall off. I would love to have seen my mother's face as she beheld her grandchild, although she had plenty others. As the youngest of Mother's brood, I am the last to bear young, and that made my firstling infant precious to us both. She missed it all, and I have not recovered from the sorrow. Shall I ever?

I feel as formless as a shawl dropped on the floor some days. On other days, when work is over, I rock in my chair and read the Psalms. I long for something else to stretch my mind, take me out of my head, and I find comfort in only some of the Psalmist's words.

> *I mourn in my complaint, and make a noise;*
> *Because of the voice of the enemy,*
> *because of the oppression of the wicked:*
> *for they cast iniquity upon me,*
> *and in wrath they hate me. My heart is sore*
> *pained within me:*
> *and the terrors of death are fallen upon me.*
> *Fearfulness and trembling are come upon me,*
> *and horror hath overwhelmed me.*

Psalm the 55th seems written directly for me; I know it in my bones. But the remainder do not comfort me, and that, I know, is a sin. I do not feel delight in the Lord, because—I must own it—I question my belief.

In Psalm the 15th, I read: *Who shall abide in his holy hill ... He that sweareth to his own hurt, and changeth not.* I swore to my own hurt and refuse to retract it. That caused me to be punished—in the house of God where I should have received comfort. I am abandoned now by my congregation, at a time when I need them most. As if they don't want me back. Or at all. And how am I to live this way—isolated, yet captive? My still, small voice badgers me: Do I belong or do I not? As the statement of a community, it hits me hard.

I venture away from the Psalms, into the Old Testament stories, of the Angel of Destruction that wiped out Sodom and Gomorrah, and I wonder about the infants who had not learned to sin yet, and how an angry God allowed them to be obliterated. About Lot's wife, who wanted but a single glance back over her shoulder at the life she had loved and was losing. I brood over that story and wonder if my lesson was not to look back, but only to look forward in obedience, and if my repining had turned me to a pillar of salt. Such a fierce God, such a cold-hearted Lord. What kind of father treats his children so?

I have always ignored the spark of doubt in Parson's sermons, in a Heavenly King—who can know who is saved, whom God chooses? They say there is no clue to our future unless we are confident in our goodness. But if we are confident, are we not sinning through pride? If we are confident, then we must have overlooked some sin. Being certain of salvation by its very nature feels like temptation, saying one knows the will of God or God's eternal plan. No one knows God but God himself. One can never be certain. One must always wonder, at least for themselves. I am in knots from chasing this string.

One may not doubt. To doubt one's redemption is not to trust, and to rely on one's redemption is to err in pride, so one must linger in a place of uncertainty. One's works and one's faith are not enough. Wars have been fought, souls have perished, in the argument of this dilemma. One must "fear God alway," as King Alfred had preached. Indeed, one of my grandmothers had been christened Fear as a reminder to be in awe of the Lord every day. I have wandered onto the thinnest of ice, a breath away from the expellable, cardinal sin of Atheism. It is lucky I might not speak aloud, for what I hold between tight lips is a shriek of anguish that I am more than thrice punished.

The one rock in my life has always been my Separatist faith, and when I try to turn to it, the bosom of my congregation shuns and censures me. Why belong to a church that possesses you only conditionally? It seems the sheerest of muslins to me, a tissue of untruths between piety and disbelief.

I sit erect in a wooden chair by the hearth, carding wool, keeping my hands ever busy; I have never known my hands to be still until the melancholia sat upon me after Elizabeth's death. A goodwife keeps her fingers always in motion, a psalm ever on her lips: knit at stockings and caps, darn at holes in those selfsame stockings, and when the household work is finished, fill the time with prayer or corner-cleaning, or stab upon a sampler to practice stitches and adorn the walls with pious sayings. A woman mayn't have time for her thoughts, for her thoughts make her rebellious, and her yoke is eternal. Why, in my twenty-two years before, did I see it as a grace instead of a punishment? And how am I to return to that state of blind bliss? The small voice of my inmost heart tells me I am not wrong. I ply the two cards against each other, the greasy smell of lanolin and ewe-scat clinging to my hands, as the batt combs smooth.

I may be silenced, but I cannot stifle my thoughts.

My entire family, including my late husband's kin, every friend I have ever known, my village, the Colony of Massachusetts, the Kingdom of England, and the world in which I have grown to adulthood—they all depend on that sheer muslin of faith. It is terrifying, if all of that is falsehood. What if it is all a lie? What if we fall through it, and find ourselves faithless?

I know not what to believe any longer.

A measure of potherbs

Snow no longer falls, but it is still quite cold as the rains come; rainstorms wash out the snowbanks, from even the shady lees of the hills, and leave in its place green grass of a hue so vibrant it almost hurts my eyes to see it. The early grass is as tender and soft as silken threads, and the little white lambs, their long tails jerking, gambol across the meadows and back to their dams in comical bursts. Each returns to its mother and butts her bag, taking a teat in mouth, forming a picture fit for Bible times, a lamb lying in the green grass—a symbol of peace? Or of danger to tender newborns?

The weather more forgiving, we return to meeting on the Sabbath, though the road be all in mud. We cover our laps with the mudguard, a coarse blanket, when riding in the wain, to arrive in the village unbesmirched. But a mudguard cannot shield my face, my bare ears and neck, from the probing eyes and the whispers of the townspeople. I want to scratch at myself like a loused wharf-child, so powerful are the stares of my brethren in the meeting-house.

When the week begins anew, Father takes his inventory for spring, what rugs and coverlets he had made yet to sell, and what materials he lacks. He sets out toward Boston Town on Ginger, keeping to the roadside where wains have not churned the way into mud. I should not doubt my father's love; he has forborne to bring Mr. Henry back to the house to torture me with his heavy-handed cures. Rather, he seeks out an apothecary in Boston, and returns to tell me the most curious news he's ever heard.

"Daughter, you will not stomach it—it seems like a grand jest! But 'tis truth!" says he. A Mistress Greenleaf, wived to the Rev. Daniel Greenleaf who preached so strongly in Newbury town and Boston, keeps an apothecary shop in Court Street—a *woman* practicing apothecary *alone* and raising her twelve children by herself like a sea captain's wife, whilst her husband orders his congregation in Yarmouth.

"I never thought I should tell such a tale—a woman to keep a shop!" He slaps his own thigh in astonishment. Proud of his own curiosity, he has crossed the threshold of the business without prejudice; he finds it a wonder of sweetmeats and elixirs to tempt the palate, as well as tinctures, teas, powders and potions for the infirm. Perhaps the sweetmeats turned his opinion of the woman. He is always led by his gizzard. Father brought with him a pokeful of goody made with benne seed and burnt sugar rolled in the finest pounded sugar. The Greenleaf woman is an alchemist, it seems, turning common sugar into gold.

"She is a force, daughter. She knew answers to my inquiries, when I asked her of this or that malady or cure, and she knew it *as well as a man*! I was heartily confused, I tell you, that she be as learned as a man! She reminds me, in a way, of your dear mother." His voice catching, he pauses.

La! A married woman in the busy town of Boston keeps a shop on a prominent street, where she is, one presumes, permitted to wait upon men and women alike with her knowledge. It seems there are places one might go and not be told what one might say or feel—it has never occurred to me in this way that my punishment is that measure of unfair, or, mayhap, overblown for the crime.

I turn my back to him and cover my mouth to hold in the retort. I am being punished, daughter of Eve, for the sin of women's weakness—can it be that I am not altogether in the wrong? Or am I in the wrong place? My rage rises. Yet Father is only trying to help me. And mayhap he has—might this apothecaress (Mistress *Greenleaf*—her very name sounds like a promising herbal) cure my bleak outlook?

"Don't take it amiss, daughter, but Mistress Greenleaf suggested me a treatment for you that is far different than Mr. Henry's advice." He tugs at his linen cap, which keeps his head warm when withindoors. "Remember, girl, *'The Lord created medicines from the earth, and a sensible man will not despise them.'*"

I am not a man, but of course I do not say this. I touch the scabbed-over mark in my forearm from Mr. Henry's fleam. I do despise them. But I wonder about Boston and the wonders therein.

Two days hence, his impatience for my improvement showing, Father takes me thither by boat.

It has been some years since I visited Boston Town, just the one visit when I were still a maiden. Since then, ten years or more, the town has grown considerable, and I am astonished to see, from the chilly gunwales of the small vessel, that the Long Wharf has even more warehouses than before, and that houses of brick and timber crowd the streets. Last year the town was swept with the smallpox again, which cut through the population like a scythe, but there still live more than *ten thousand* souls in this town, nay, we might call it a *city*. The sheer number of beings is difficult to comprehend after my humble village of three hundred heads.

Boston Harbor is a busy center of commerce and travel, ships creaking at their ropes, porters and dock-wallopers unloading crates and barrels. More wharves and landings than I can count confuse me, but the hired captain knows where to land us, and brings us smoothly into a secondary pier near the Long Wharf. What would have taken a very long rattling day in the wain has taken a scant two hours by sea with the wind behind us, and I feel rushed and flustered at the speed of our travel, indeed, sea-wind-blown. My cheeks are cold and, if I reflect my father's countenance, pink. I have been glad of my red wool cloak and thick mitts amid the plash of seawater and salt-mist in the wind.

The streets are mud and puddle, but I have pattens for my feet and so I pluck alongside my father in his boots, holding up my petticoats as I can. I have heard countless sermons on the horror of city-dwelling, of the unfettered sin and tempting devices that lurk in corners and shadows. But, God's truth, we have those same temptations in the smallest village, in the smallest mind, and I am not inclined to fear much these days. Most threats leave me numb; what worse can happen now than has happened me thusly?

The journey has awakened me from my slumber, however, and I feel more fresh and alive than I have in some time.

From the harbor, we follow King Street up to the new-built Town House where the colony's governance takes place, and thence a little turn onto Cornhill Street to find the Old Church before us. In a wide, bricked building shouldered next door, two or three small operations are housed: a tailor, a silversmith, and the apothecary of Greenleaf & Greenleaf. The heavy door is Dutched and in fine weather should stand half-open, but the mud-season wind off the harbor is still sharp as a cleaver.

The door knocks a little bell on a wire and so we are announced by this bit of brass hanging overhead—a clever invention I wouldn't have thought of if I'd a month to ponder the problem. The clean bricked walls are lined with shelves laden with wooden boxes, glass jars, pottery vessels and casks of oils, wines, and vinegars. The room smells of lavender and mint and other scents I can put a name to: ginger, cinnamon, burnt sugar, and the earthy, dirt-smell of mushroom; and more still that I cannot name. A dish within the glass case is laden with dried amber circles that resemble flowers; a folded parchment before it is labeled "Pine-Apple, of Jamaica." A slate hanging on the wall, writ upon in chalk pencil, declares, "A wise man should consider that health is the greatest of human blessings," and beneath it, the word *Hippocrates*.

Good health, yes, but I should like my husband beside me and my infant in my arms. I turn to Father, who is perusing the etchings in a medical book on the polished wooden countertop.

What is Hippo-crates? I gesture the question to my father, mis-saying the unfamiliar word in my mind. But before he can explain, a voice cuts through the room.

"Hippocrates," says she, "the Greek doctor who was the father of modern medicine two thousand years ago." A motherly woman of some two score years, perhaps more, comes through a muslin curtain at the back of the counter and meets us here.

"Master Nichols, you have returned. Had you a pleasant journey in all this mud?"

"Good day, Mistress Greenleaf. Nay, thank you for asking; we've come by boat this very morning, and there was no mud until we arrived at the foot of King Street. May I present my widowed daughter, of whom I spake before: Silence Marsh."

We bow to one another. I note her waved dark hair threaded with silver, the dimple in her cheek, her clear gray eyes, her coif far fresher in appearance than mine after a windy morning asea. Her hands are no rougher than mine; her height is as tall as my father, and her figure is slim, not stout. When she opens her mouth, her teeth are strong like a bonny child's, nor pitted nor missing. I can trust a woman with my health who looks the very picture of it, as does she.

"Come you again for sweetmeats, sir?" she chides him, and Father does not deny it. "The gentlemen cannot eat enough benne brittle, and it will rot their teeth," the lady laughs to me. "Sit you down, sir, and I will bring you a potion to warm your gizzard whilst I speak with your good daughter."

With busy hands and efficient moves, she soon has Father in a seat by her hearth drinking a ginger tea and reading the latest *Boston News-Letter*. He has missed a woman shunting him about, telling him where and when to sit, and I know he must find himself a wife again soon.

"Now, then, Mistress," the lady draws back the curtain. "Come you into my offices here and we shall parley over a cup of my special tea." She gestures to an anteroom with a cabinet, more shelves, and two leather-padded chairs. "Please sit."

I sit, and she follows.

"Now," says she in a low voice. "I have heard of the—imposition of a punishment upon you." She looks into my face with frank curiosity. "I am not a Separatist; we are of the royal faith, the English church—and such penance is more than we impose on our most frequent sinners. Such a penalty—I—" She halts her speech.

I know where she is going with her opinion. I myself am torn between believing this is barbarity and believing I am hell-bound. Even as I reject the idea, I still believe I am damned. I cannot say. I shrug my shoulders without smiling.

"I shall not press you to make confession or break your oath," the woman assures me. "But I should like to assess your health thusly. May I?" She holds open her two hands and makes to touch my face.

I nod.

"Very well, then. Your eyes?" She holds my eyelids open and looks at my naked organs with interest, then releases them. She feels my face near my ears, then drops down to my throat. "And your neck?" She gently clasps my throat and feels along my jawline. "Ah, and then—" she feels my wishbone, and presses further along the breastbone. She holds her hand over my heart. "Breathe through the nose for me, my friend, a long breath?"

She nods. She pinches my cheek, then the back of my hand.

"Do you make enough water?" she asks. "More than thrice a day? It is good for the corpus to drink more liquid, so that you make water six times a day. Morning, noon and night are not enough, and you will know by the color. If it is golden in color, you are not drinking enough liquid. If it is clear, like pale wine, that is better. And your bowels? They move daily? Very well. Open the mouth, so I may see?"

Mr. Henry has never asked me such queries, and I should die of shame if he had. But I feel at ease with this wise woman, who exudes a robust health in all that she does. I wish I could ask her questions, hear her speaking, visit with her a long while, but I know we must return to the village by end of day—and I am silenced. I have no words to speak aloud.

She looks at my tongue and at my teeth, running her thumb against my chipped tooth. "How came this to happen?"

I pull back. Does she not know of my time in the pillory? Where mud and filth pelted me, and a pebble shied at my face left me with a broken mouth? I mime throwing a stone.

Mistress Greenleaf tuts and sniffs my breath, and then she rises with a rustle of petticoats and rinses her hands in a basin of water.

"Take a portion of these herbs to brew at home. I counsel you to take lavender and lemon balm in the evenings, to soothe the nerves and to help you sleep."

She holds the curtain open for me to follow, and at the counter, she makes a mixture from scoops of lavender, dried mint and dried lemon balm leaves, folding the little paper neat as any traveler's bindle. She takes my hand, folds out my first finger and places it on the folded packet. "Hold that, if you please."

I warm at this motherly exchange. I did the same to help my own mother.

She unspools a bit of hempen twine and snips it with her scissors, then ties the packet closed, nudging my finger aside. "Thank you, mistress. Take this home with you and make the tea nightly for a fortnight. A cup of this will change your life." She smiles, her bright eyes shining.

"And I shall send my son the doctor out to see you in Hingham. I believe he has some good sense from the university—aye, he attended Harvard and is a medical doctor with all the training, not a mere herb-wife like me. I believe he cut up the meat of a drowned man to learn about the *anatomy*, so he told me. I could have told him about the anatomy by carving a lamb or a hen, but what does a woman know? Her kitchen and a baby's hind-end, no more."

She laughs aloud, and her laughter and her statement both so startle me that I almost laugh aloud myself. For all the world, I did not expect such a statement from a woman! The bright tangy air within the shop is so rejuvenating that I feel medicated already. Dizzied by the messages I have gleaned from her, I rejoin my father.

"Mistress Greenleaf, you have given me new life," Father says gallantly. He folds the news-letter and leaves it on the chair, and pays her the few pence for her goods. "We thank you, lady, although my daughter cannot speak now. It is a perilous—ah, a difficult journey, and we must navigate it to its end."

Shamed again by his explanation, my cheeks burn like a washerwoman's, and I gaze at the wooden floor. I bow my farewell to the apothecaress, not meeting her eyes.

"Let us find bread and meat before we return to the wharf," Father suggests, and leads us toward a tavern on King Street. "This one has a mixed great room; you'll not be noticed there." I'm grateful for that, and indeed I am one of many ordinary women dining or visiting with husbands and friends in the Merchants House. I cannot bear to be singled out and noticed amid company anymore. In this great city, no one knows me or my shame.

Father asks for boiled beef and potatoes for us, and cider from the barrel. A scrawny boy brings the platter and knives, some napery, and mugs of cider before overlong.

"What think you, daughter, this brazen city? Do you recall our early visit here? Aye, you were a scant twelve or fourteen, I mind, and your cousins were over from England. Such doings, then, traveling from the home and mixing in great company." He took a long pull of his cider.

"Best to get back to our own front door, our little saltbox by the sea, soon as we're able. There be too many dangerous ideas afloat in Boston Town, and not enough brain betwixt us to hold them all at bay."

So back we go.

Tonic of a new sort

The spring lambs do come, and the new calves as well. There is milk again for the table, and I boil the ground corn mush for our morning and our evening meals, with molasses to sweeten it. But our bowels grumble, without leaf or stalk to stir us, nor cider in the barrel by this time. The land is waking, but we still live on last year's bounty, on what remains from the winter stores. I recall that the young doctor was intended to call but we have seen no sign of him, nor heard any rumor that he had come to the village. I expect him not, feeling my melancholic self as little draw for a city gentleman. What sort of fool would travel to the netherlands to see a silent widow?

Another week passes, spring still freshening the earth. I feel my blood sluggish after a long winter without green pot-herbs or fresh victual, and wrapping myself from the stiff, cool ocean breeze, I set outside with a trug on my arm to look out for greens for a tonic—nettles, dandelion, cress, lambs' quarter, burdock, or sassafras leaf would cure my disposition, I am certain of it. I start out along the wain-road of Jerusalem way toward Hingham town, seeking plants off the side where they hadn't been trodden into mud or fouled by horse dung. I have some success, pinching up bunches of dandelion and burdock along the roadside, looking for the little rill where cress grows, along with baby fiddlehead fern and new nettles.

I continue my meander, seeking any sort of herbs along the roadway, finally turning toward the woody stand near Straights Pond, where a single sassafras tree remains. If it had tender leaves, I would add them to my tonic-broth. I am too precipitate, however, and too soon in the season for any green leaves. I cannot fill my trug enough to cook for potherbs, but sufficient to make a first tonic for the two of us. I find I am tired already. The winter has been hard on me. I am weaker than I imagined, fatigued by my ramble. I don't know why I even attempted such a venture. I am a foolish woman, no sense at all.

I turn about, heading home, toward the outer edge of Father's land, passing where Mother's skeps still stand, since last year, a twelvemonth now, unmolested, uncared for. Since then, I have not spoken to the bees, if there are any left. I cannot forgive them.

I cannot forgive myself.

I am weary from my excursion for tonic-greens today, but I make no excuse. I've done nothing but sigh and stare over my chores for weeks. Idle hands are the Devil's workplace. I continue the road back to Father's house—to *our* house, where I live now, again, being a widow without the house I'd lived in, the parent of no one, the leftover nobody in this family.

I hear a horse trotting up the road somewhat behind me but cannot bother to turn to espy the trotter. What difference is it to me? With my half-filled basket of weed and sprout, my hair windblown, and my cloak wrapped around me, I look a veritable witch-woman on the wain-road toward Black Rock.

"Good afternoon, mistress. I seek the house of Israel Nichols. Is it hard by?"

I glance across my shoulder to see a splendid black mare with dainty white socks and a perfect blaze on her face. On her back, a finely tooled England-made saddle, a stranger in a blue short-cloak; a shining brass button holds it at the neck. The man's woolen breeches are gray, tucked into glossy knee-high black boots, and his shirt looks a fine linen, though I am impolite to assess him longer than an instant.

"Do you know the house?" he urges me. I will not look him in the face. I hesitate; the town knows me and knows my crimes. Mayhap this man does not, and I cannot explain it him.

I nod and gesture with my hand toward the house. It is the poorest of manner to point the finger, of course, but I cannot open my lips and tell him thing one.

"So near? I thank you, mistress, er, *miss?* My good lady."

His fumbling address makes me almost smile. My David had fumbled his words sometimes, and it would strike me as amusing if I could still quirk a real smile. But I, merely on my impulsive scavenger's amble, have crossed paths with a stranger and am unable to speak even the commonest of greetings. What a brute I must seem. Such a misshapen fool.

I glimpse up to his face and meet a cheerful expression, inquisitive gray eyes, a firm mouth, a noble nose, and a new-shaven chin, no periwig but his own light brown hair tied in a queue with a simple black ribbon under a black hat. He looks my age, no more than five and twenty, younger than David, at any rate. This might be the Harvard man we expected, or it might be a customer for carpet. I suspect it's my Greenleaf visitor, and, overcome with shyness, I nod and begin my walk again.

"You go that direction as well? I shall stay nigh so I do not lose my way."

I give him a slight glance to acknowledge him. It is the King's road, and I have no right to deter him from following it, whether near me or by himself. But it irks. *Leave me be,* I wish I could say. The horse clops alongside, her nose almost at my basket. I feel her gently bump with her nose, so shift the basket to my left arm. The mare's eye is almost at my level. I smile into her eye and pet her jowl and throatlatch. *Pretty girl,* I would say, but I can only stroke her in silence.

"Aye, smart to move your basket. Raven is her name, and she'll eat your straw hat if you don't mind her. This one will eat her head off, given the chance. She went down with the colic last autumn and I thought to lose her. She's lucky I'm a physician."

I know now he is the one come to examine me, and I feel exposed before I were prepared. His voice drifts above my head as we walk. Of course, I do not respond, just a quick nod to show I am listening.

"A physician of *persons,* but it happens that the insides of most beasts are generally the same. The principles often apply to all creatures. Foodstuff goes in and must come out. The science is the same if the beasts are not." He speaks of such indelicacies.

A pheasant bursts from the brush at roadside, drab colors that signify the female of the race, and the bird's cry startles the horse. The lady Raven shies, wheeling on her hind legs, and the loquacious doctor aboard wheedles, "There, my lady, ho-ah, hold there." Raven skitters on her heels like a waterbug, her eyes rolling back and the whites stark against her black face.

I set my basket down and approach the dancing horse, her master gripping with knee and fist, and I hold a bundle of dandelion green flat on my palm. I shush her, whispering not words, but a shush like the hiss of water on the shore. "Shhh-pshhhhh-pshhhh …"

And she stops her dance, stepping toward me as if I had offered maple sugar and an apple in the same hand. Raven lips the greens from my palm and munches, then sniffs at my face with her whiskered muzzle, looking for more.

"Mistress, you have a way with wild creatures, I see," says the gentleman ahorse. I glance up and he is, to his credit, trying not to look ashamed at Raven's antics. He had at least kept his seat. "What magic is in your basket?"

What cheek! Such a thing to speak of! Simple herbcraft that all women should know, if their family suffers from stifled bowels, or needs a tonic in spring. I quirk my brow at him, saying, for all the world, "What must you take me for?"

"Ah, I pray you pardon me." He chuckles, but I see his grip tighter on the rein as we further our journey onwhither. "Not a witch. Just a maiden."

Cheeky! I have half a mind to snap my fingers at him, but I merely quicken my pace, to outwalk them. Yet I'm curious to know how he saved the mare; colic in horse is usually fatal. They get into the grain like gluttons and eat until they die of it, barrel distended, thrashing in pain, as the Reverend says sinners will die. More than one horse has met its end with a musket ball to ease its suffering.

In a half moment the pair are even with me again, a cocky smile upon his face. I stroke the pretty mare's jowl again, murmuring a little sympathetic sigh before I can stop myself.

"Oh, so you do speak," the gentleman laughs. "I thought you a mute. Or too aloof to converse with me. My mistake, Goodwife—?"

I shoot him an irritated look—David's lovename for me is not a sweetmeat for his mouth—and I step livelier toward home. The doctor laughs again though does not urge his mare to catch me. Where the road turns south toward Scituate, I gesture at my father's blue-painted door and the post out front where he may tie his steed and walk myself around to the whitewashed kitchen door.

I set down the herb-basket before undoing my cloak and hanging it on the peg, my mitts and bonnet in the catch-all tray beneath. I straighten my coif in the looking glass and push my wayward windblown hair back inside the cap. My cheeks are pink from fresh breezes but I won't say I look well. A harsh winter and a broken heart have made me anything but pretty, and vanity is a sin. There is nothing to prink over. I have long since learned this.

I warm myself at the kitchen fireplace, stretching my chilly fingers in the heat. The kitchen smells of rosemary and onion. My supper broth is bubbling, a mutton bone bobbing on the oily surface as the pot sways gently over the embers. I pretend there will be no knock upon the door.

Father answers the front door when the gentleman raps. They speak loudly in their hale voices. The men carry on for some time speaking news and about Boston Town and the Harbor tax and other such, and I bide my time at the kitchen fire, picking at my nails and thinking bleak thoughts not worth sharing.

Father puts his head round the kitchen door. "The gentleman is here for *you*, Daughter. The expected Doctor Greenleaf."

I nod, my innards a little fluttery, the mortification of having to face the stranger, be further examined, now as I've walked a half mile at his side. I stand and smooth my gown, then pass through the door and the dining hall, to the great keeping room where the fire crackles. The horseman stands with my father, both turning toward me as I approach.

"Daughter, our visitor—his mother spoke of him last sennight. Dr. Daniel Greenleaf," Father makes introduction. The doctor removes his tricorne and bows his head politely, but a smile in his eyes makes his politeness almost impertinence.

I return the little bow as equal in station, my eyes lowered in frosty annoyance.

"My widowed daughter, Mistress Silence Marsh. Do you both sit here on the settle and speak to the ill health of my daughter, sir. I am to my offices." Father excuses himself and soon I hear him beating the weft in his workroom.

I follow Father to close the door, to dim the clatter, meeting his eyes with a little smile so Father knows I am not troubled unduly. I turn back to see Dr. Greenleaf still standing.

"I thought you were leaving me," says he.

A flirt, is he? He is no Nonconformist, I can see, the mere cock of his head, the jaunt of his neckcloth. He fears no vengeful God. An adherent to the Anglican faith, said his mother, worshiping under the proud, tall steeple in the gleaming new North Church atop the hill in Boston Town. The Rev. Hobart sneers at the Popishness of such an ostentatious church, and praised our simple Old Ship meeting-house as more fitting for worship, but what matter is it to me, lost sheep that I be?

What is there to pray for, anyway? I sin again with the thought.

Nevertheless, Popish physicians must sit when visiting, and I am hostess now, so I gesture to the settle.

"Yes, of course, but you must join me," he returns, less an invitation than a dictate. "I shall examine you and discuss a course of medicament, if you will allow it."

I sit at the far end of the furniture, uncertain of what to expect, as I have always been hale and not sickly, a sanguine, benevolent in attitude and quick-witted. Now Mr. Henry says I am suffering an excessiveness of black bile, and I gather he holds little hope for me. If I were a Papist, I would leave the bleak world and turn nun; though God may smite me again for thinking such a thought. Perhaps the half-Popish doctor has a middling solution for leaving the world with neither nunnery nor death. His mother's tea has done me no harm.

"My dear mother explained to me your position—your tragedies. I am sorry for your losses, Mistress." His eyes hold caring, but his voice turns. "And your church's censure—naturally that makes your condition all the worse, in this physician's humble opinion. One cannot punish an ailing person for being ill," says he.

His face hardens as he speaks, and I find that I would not like to cross him in a dispute where I was in the wrong.

"I beg your pardon, Mistress, but it seems utterly pig-headed to blame the sufferer for her condition."

I have held that exact idea in my inmost heart, and it startles me to think anyone else might feel the same. I am filled with sin and am slated for hellfire. *Or* (I hear the still, small voice) *is it all stuff and nonsense? Am I not correct while all others are wrong?* My confusion may show on my face.

The doctor turns to his business. "I have a twofold plan for your return to health, good lady. One is to meet the melancholy where it lives: If in the kidney it lies, one treats it with medicaments to cool the black bile." His tone is wry, and he grins, reaches into his haversack, rustles through by feel, as a blind man. "I bring from my good mother these dried crane-berries, although you may perhaps gather them freshly later in the year?"

I nod. He pulls up a small Osnaburg sack, perhaps a King's pint in measure, tied with a bit of coarse twine.

We have all grown to love the beautiful red crane-berry, sometimes called fen-berry, that grows in bogs and floats if the water is high. The Natives showed the *Mayflower* settlers these wonderful fruit a century ago, and we have not left off eating them since. They are sour to eat of fresh, without stewing, but the berry makes a colorful sauce for a roast, and adds sharpness when baked into oatcake or pudding.

I take the sack from him, feeling the weight of the berries, smelling their sour tanginess through the cloth. Just their bright scent improves my disposition. I almost smile.

"That is the *old* medicine, of which you may have had your fill."

There is something to his tone which suggests he is mocking me, or the very idea of black bile. I cannot tell. I am not a worldly creature and I know scant few Nonconformists. Are they skilled at mockery?

He produces next a small, thick piece of paper with the receipt written out in a pretty hand, no blotches:

> *Steep a half gill of dried crane-berries in hot*
> *water and drink twice a day ~ may be taken*
> *hot or cold. A spoonful of honey or sugar may*
> *be added to the taste. Cooked berries may also*
> *be consumed. It may produce much water.*

"I know it a simple remedy, but we have found it an excellent tonic for the kidney and spleen." He hands me the paper. "I doubt not that you will feel healthful after a fortnight of this treatment."

The young doctor claps his hands once and makes as if to shake off the dust of them. "Now that I have given you the *old* medicine, let me give you the *new* medicine."

I look at him quizzingly. Is there a new medicine?

"Oh, mistress," he laughs. "We have newer ways in the city than in the countryside, and yet newer ways in the capitals of Europe and beyond," says he.

The doctor leans toward me a little, not impertinent, and lowers his voice. "I don't like to broadcast this when I'm out in the provinces, but the small towns in the Colony might be considered *parochial*, that is to say, a bit primitive in the sciences of reason and medicine."

Does he deliver blasphemy or truth? If there is a new way of reasoning, I want to hear it. I cock my head, willing for him to tell me more.

"There are learned men in London who say that the best remedy for the evil of melancholy is to take exercise or labor," he says. "They say that rugged, rural living produces hearty, robust people, while city life saps their resilience and makes them vulnerable to depressed thoughts. I think them mistaken only in blaming *city life* for the evil. I believe it is small-mindedness, which we betimes find in the countryside, that produces half the evil in this world."

He keeps his voice low enough under the clack of Father's loom that he cannot be understood from afar. The doctor speaks plainly to me.

"I know your religion's great men call for treating the bodily humours and for obeying the will of God, but God has given us the great gift of free will to learn and grow. That is how we achieve wisdom. Great men in Europe have opened up an Age of Reason, and we are all learning new and exacting ways of looking at the earth and the heavens—with learned eyes, open minds, not with superstition and fear. Will you stay in your darkness of shadow and shame? Or will you let me treat your illness—for I believe it is an illness, *not a sin*—through this new method?"

These words are overmuch to absorb, and to be honest, I do not understand everything to which he alludes. I nod, as I am not permitted speech to ask all the many questions bubbling up within me. Is there a hope that I might feel better, to put an end to my melancholia that does not end in me swinging by the neck on a hempen rope somewhere? I expect leeches, bleeding, and noxious and painful medicaments from Mr. Henry. If it is some other form of treatment, I would, selfishly *(oh, the sin!)*, like that better.

Have I even a choice? I can flounce from the room if I wish, and were I a younger girl, I might do. But in this moment, I have not the fortitude to flounce. I'm as artless as a bit of seaweed out on the shore. Whatever Father, the master of this house and of my whole life now that I am widowed, says I should, I will do.

They say silence is golden, but it is gray as mist and smoke.

I make a gesture with my hand—*do what you will, sir*—and he cocks his brown head.

"Very well, then, Mistress Marsh." He claps his hands once again, and the sound of it echoes in the room like a blunderbuss, startling me. Dr. Daniel Greenleaf leans on his hands on his thighs and looks me in the face. I lower my eyes, but he gazes a moment longer.

"Will you trust me, my lady?"

Who am I to fight? I must do as I'm told. Yet I flick my eyes up to meet his.

He winks at me.

The desire to laugh erupts from somewhere deep within me and I clap a hand across my mouth, strangling the sound before it emits. Such a doctor! I will not meet his eyes now for fear of laughing. *The sin, the silence!*

He continues his speech: "You have taken your exercise for this day. Very good, my lady, exactly so. Thus, your treatment begins tomorrow—with exercises to improve your mind and body, to chase away this black funk and give you a fresh face and a lighter spirit. That is the endpoint of this prescription, and though it may conflict with your friend Henry's treatment, I ask you to trust that I have your *whole* welfare in mind. My mother will prepare mixtures for you as needed, and I will deliver them every fortnight or so. I expect your return to *whole health* ere the summer is ended, or sooner, perhaps."

I have never heard of such balderdash as his before—the only proper healing, I have ever learned, is through repentance, punishment, and prayer. Boston Town ways might be downright dangerous to my soul. *If I even have a soul.* In the moment, I have no belief in anything, so what matter if I go along with the attempt of doctoring? So long as it does not involve branding me for blasphemy or worse. And I can live quite cheerily, speaking or silent, without ever a leech or bleeding bowl come my way again.

He seems convinced. He speaks with such good humor in his voice, his countenance, that I wonder, does he laugh at me? I have had no cause to laugh for ages. I have forgotten how, and it is all but forbidden me—certainly would send me to a further depth of punishment if I were found to be *laughing*. Nonetheless, I am cursed aready, and glad to avoid the rope and the brand, the Separatists' treatment of sins.

"Will you trust in me?"

I nod.

"Good girl, then." He gives a sharp nod. He clears his throat. "I prescribe," he says in a voice of authority and perhaps a little edge of humor, "—that you take another such walk as you made this afternoon for your green herbs, but each day, in the morning, when the day is new.

"If it rain or snow, you might stay withindoors, but do, every *sunny* day, take yourself out and walk the shore or the path, for a quarter of an hour by the clock or the sundial, in each direction. Count your steps to 500 or say a poem—a Psalm? Very well, a Psalm, then—recite to yourself three times each way, howsoever you like to keep the time. Find the distant point at which you may turn about and return.

"But it is *imperative*, my lady, that in sunshine, in fresh air, you must move the blood and the body. This is the primary medicament I prescribe. Do you take my meaning?"

I do, with a nod.

"I leave the berries with you and trust you shall procure more when you need them, from the mercantile or from your own stores, or send word if I might bring more hither." He looks for my agreement. "Drink cider or tisanes, aye, but keep away from milk. Butter and cheese aright, but no liquid from the dairy. It clogs the passages of the nose and throat. And *see to* that walking for sun and air," he cocked his head at me. "I will guarantee an improvement in health before the spring is done and gone."

He stands and makes to leave.

I arise and rap at Father's door, opening it. The clatter flows back into the keeping room, an ocean wave of sound. Father waves from his loom.

"Send me your bill, sir, and I will pay it," he calls, pressing treadles and shifting the shuttle again, without breaking rhythm.

"I will bid you good day, then." Dr. Greenleaf dons his black hat. He turns back to me, his voice low again. "Mistress Marsh, O Tacit One. I shall find a means to soothe your spirit—if you'll let me."

If I were a forward lass, or a spinster I might go to his horse and wave him fair journey from the footpath. But I am only a tired, broken widow, and the world has taken too much of me. I close the door, lean against it, and listen as the hooves trot away back to Boston Town. After a moment, I take the stairs up and into my father's bedchamber, the better to see the shrinking horse and rider trotting away, leaving me to think on many new ideas.

I trail back to the kitchen and look into the glass. My cheek-apples are pink, my nose as well. My blood is stirring.

I shall make the crane-berry decoction tonight.

Mistress of bees

I will confess that my corpus feels better when exposed to the sunlight and exercise as prescribed by the Doctor, and that I feel lighter in my person after a two week's course with the tonic of crane-berry. If I had been any other woman, I might write to the Doctor's mother with my thanks for her attention, but I should not communicate from my silence—I would not have anyone say I have not taken my sentence wholly, with good grace. It seems churlish not to own this censure, wrap myself in it like a mustard plaster that blisters and sears, but shall cure me in the end. An opportunity for growth, one might call it—a stretch of my spirit, a lesson in the byways of the Lord.

Dr. Greenleaf comes again ahorse, and this time he brings a fold of paper holding mayweed, that which makes Father sneeze so in the summer; the doctor calls it a French word, *chamomile*, to steep as tea, to aid my spirit and my gut, and a sachet from his mother's herb garden, of lavender, for sleep. He knows not that I keep lavender wands in every room, in the linen chest and in every pillowbere, but his mother's handiwork is a soft linen, finely sewn, sheer enough to see the grains of dried flower but not so sheer as to shed its powder. I wonder if she has woven it herself, though when might she have had the time? I feel my mother's absence deeply, and I treasure this kind, motherly gift from a near-stranger, more than I expected.

The doctor vexes me with his teasing, prying eyes, seeking to meet mine, but I like his advisement and will take of it. An herbal drink, a sunshine walk, air afresh each day—there is nothing to dislike about his medicine, not when compared to Mr. Henry's methods. But to my Separatist soul, it feels like a cheat and a con—if the treatment doesn't hurt, can it be good for me? And am I breaking rules or making sin by easing my path and growing back to health?

I stretch my spirit to accept the chastening fire. I say this to myself many a time, until it comes to me, one restless Saturday even, that I'm no longer holding this chastening like a penance I must endure. My silence has kindled from weeks of sorrow and isolation to anger, nay, *rage.* I have absorbed it as a white rag soaks up blood.

Next day, I ride in the wain with Father to our Sabbath meeting, and my anger simmers like a bone in a pot. *Look upon me, test me,* I dare the congregation with my sealed lips, with my presence, with my name. *You'll hear nothing from me, not a squeak, nary a sigh. Fie upon you for punishing me.* I'll not speak again, until the moment of my own choosing, if ever.

In the Sabbath sermon, I do not love what I hear. The voice of the parson is as the tuneless buzzing of so many bees to me: noise I must sit through as the remittance for belonging in this town, in this congregation. I know there are other worlds, other towns, communities, congregations—but they are distant as the moon to me, beyond this one church, the Old Ship on the rise above the village. This congregation is the length and breadth of my entire world, and I endure every service, noticing, not drawing attention if I can help it. I am silent and still, as they want me, as they want all us women to be. I am their model now, molded as they desire. I am the cup that is clean on the outside but filthy inside.

Within, I burn.

I cannot do otherwise than sit in silence. I attend this congregation week by month by year, because this is all I know. In my world, my town, my family—there is nothing but this path.

As we file from the meeting house after the Sabbath sermon, Parson Hobart, his starched white collars lying crisp and stiff against his black robe, greets Father with a bow. He shoots a curt glance to indicate he sees me but need not speak to me, a disgraced woman. Goodwife Hobart stands with the other women, their eyes darting to me, my shorn head under my bonnet. They do not cup their hands over their mouths to whisper. It is easy enough for me to read their bodies and their expressions. They are aghast that I still come to services and would be equally horrified if I had missed. In their black clothes and white coifs and cuffs, meet for the Sabbath, they are Pilgrim fowl scratching for grit. They cluck as I pass them walking sedately toward the wain.

Young Zuriel, Parson's daughter, stands off to one side by herself, her indigo shortgown and petticoat a sharp contrast with her starched white collar, her coif. She is an indifferent-looking girl, neither pretty nor ugly, with an attitude of unhappiness drawn on her face. If she does not take care, she will end up with a pinched, pursed look, like her step-mother Hobart.

Father lingers to talk with some of the men, so I continue around the back of the church to where the wains await, horses under the spring shadow of the ash trees, still patient after two hours of sermon. I set my prayerbook on the seat of our wain and am about to step up when I hear someone behind me. I turn to see that Zuriel has followed. I meet her eyes and give her a little nod of greeting. As my inferior, as a child still, she drops a courtesy and bobs her head. In that instant, she shows more spirit than I have yet seen.

"Good morrow, Mistress." She looks at me full in the face, unabashed. "Is it true what my father says, that you do not speak?" She had not attended my trial, which were unmeet for children.

I hesitate. This is one of those open queries too complicated to answer easily without words. She reads my hesitation for answer.

"I mean, *might* you speak?" Her curiosity is inquisitive, as a child, rather than rude.

I nod.

"But you are not permitted to? You were *cursed*." Her eyes widen, and her cheeks pink. Excitement does her well.

I wag my head and sigh a little. *Is this what people say of me?*

"I would find that too much to bear. I hate being told what I can and cannot do. I should speak if I wanted to."

I am forced to hide a smile, for what creature enjoys being ordered about? We are nor oxen nor curs.

Catching my hidden mirth, Zuriel breaks into a charming smile that lights her face and brightens her eyes. "I suppose you cannot do anything about it."

I share my agreement known with a single raised brow.

"I hate the Sabbath," says she with a hiss of a whisper, shocked at her own vehemence. "'Tis the beastliest day of the week. Pray, don't tell my father I said so." Then she covers her hand with her mouth, her eyes wide, shocked at her own temerity, because of course I mayn't *tell* on her. Speaking ill of the Sabbath, using slang, dishonoring her parent—and her own boldness—startles both of us. I hadn't expected it of the daughter of the parson or her prune-faced step-mother, but I see it now. The little rebellion is coming from *inside* the palisado. I bite my lips together not to laugh, just as Father comes around the corner of the barn with other congregation men.

I glance at Zuriel and quirk my eyebrow, just enough to let her know that I agree with her. But we mayn't laugh on the Sabbath, not in the churchyard. Not anywhere. My father has suffered enough by my misdeeds, and it isn't safe for Zuriel, either. People are punished for such words with the lash and the stocks, and she is almost of an age.

"Good Sabbath to you," says she properly to me and to Father, as he unties Ginger.

I bow my head as Father returns her farewell and helps me into the wain. I know Zuriel watches as we leave the wainyard. We edge down the slope and through the village up to the wharf, where gulls screech as if they didn't know it was the Sabbath. We roll through the town, past boats rocking at harbor, resting over the Hallowed Day. Canvas sails snap in the harbor breeze, and the splash and creak of water and rope, the fishy smell in the air. A white gull upon the post of the pier opens its yap and shrieks, demanding attention, crowing its story.

A senseless rage sweeps through me. The gull asks no one for permission, heeds no Sabbath rule. The God who tells it to call out is the same God that silences me. I am less than a common gull to the God we worship. I am on the verge of shrieking aloud in like manner, cawing back to it like a crow myself—my mouth opes and I draw in air—

"There, girl. I know it pains you." Father breaks in, his voice gentle. He reaches one hand for my clenched fist, opens it with his thumb. I clench his callused thumb as I did when a wee child and we were walking. "It is hard upon you. It is a hard, hard thing. Nigh four months you've toed the line, held your tongue, and there's yet long seasons ahead. You can do it. You take your medicine, my girl. Take your medicine."

Tears spill down my face, though I stifle my sobs. His voice wraps me in love and sorrow and shame and duty, my steadfast father, my loving father, and I hold his thumb in my hand and blot my tears with a folded linen kerchief, white as mayweed petals, white as the feathers of a gull.

* * *

A scant few days later, I accompany my father to the wharfinger and warehouse to collect the dyed goods he has ordered, and to purchase fresh cod and other victuals. I am a hindrance to Father, unable to visit the market without a list, which I won't write out myself, and I mayn't answer questions at the market. We must together go, and it takes him from his job of work. I am a drag and a nuisance and a shame to him. I carry the basket, and point at salt and tea, green coffee beans, dried black peppercorns and curls of cinnamon bark, whilst Father banters with the warehouseman and pays his coin. My bonnet hides my face, but I know I am watched askance. I am like the beetle on a pin in the glassed case in Master Henry's apothecary's shop: something to ogle and fear and hesitate to touch, despite being one of God's own creatures.

At the edge of the village, just past the wharves, I tap at Father's sleeve, to let me get out and walk. My fingers walk across my palm and toward home.

"It's a bit of a way. Are your shoes up to it?"

I show him that I've worn strong leathern shoes, not my light kid slippers.

"Very well, then. Get an appetite for dinner. You've promised me fried ham and spoon bread, and I'm groaning for my sup." He holds my hand as I back over the wheel and alight at the roadside. He looks up at the sun. "Don't keep me waiting for table!"

I blow a kiss to him and he smiles at me. I am grateful, as always, for his understanding, even under difficulties. He is a good father, and he deserves more than me, the shame, the expense, as a millstone about his neck. With a chirrup, he sets forth, trotting Ginger toward home, the wain still rattling the remainder of the way. I wait until his dust swirls past me before walking on.

My habit now is to walk the hard-packed shore, or to follow the horse-path down toward Scituate, but today, the worn wain-road back to Father's house at Black Rock is pleasant enough for my exercise. The path takes a gentle grade upward for a way, until at the crest of the hill I can see out to the horizon beyond Father's house. A blue line of ocean meets the sky, with fishing craft and a sprinkling of schooners and the like, rocking at anchor near and far. I pass the cutoff toward the sheep pastureland where my brothers stead at the Estuary.

A horse and wagon head toward me, and I step to the edge of the path. I am warm enough in my woolen gown, the sharpness of the April breeze just cooling so that I needn't perspire from my amble. As they close in, I see it is a planter, Young Goodman Henry, the apothecary's son, and his wife, Prudence, who had been my friend before. I have already hidden my face in shame once in town this morning; I'll not do it again out here in the fresh air. I keep my chin up and meet their eyes with a nod. I know my station, and I know theirs. She meets my eyes with a sympathetic glance, but mindful of her husband, does not speak. Young Henry chirrups his horse to hurry past.

It stings, to be cut this way. But I walk on forthwith because I have no other option.

Soon I reach the little bridge at the Weir River crossing. The river, more of a wide creek, still runs swiftly after spring thaw and rains, and I see fingerling fish glinting in sunlight below me. The river broadens and gurgles out into marshlands, heading to the bay beyond. The sound is pleasant to my ears. Then I hear another sound, familiar but almost forgotten, so I follow my ear a little way off the horse-path. The buzzing grows louder, and there, clinging to the low branch of a blooming serviceberry bush, about six feet over the ground, is a swarm of striped honeybees, the very like of my mother's own.

Swarm in May, worth a load of hay. But it is just April.

I foreswore the bees when David died. It wasn't their fault, but I simply could not have stood amongst the bees after that. I had not tended them, and neither had Father, nor and one night a bear or some other such creature ravaged the skeps, and there were no bees left at all. It was another such way I had destroyed my mother's legacy: her bees gone because of my carelessness and melancholia.

I hold in mind my dead mother and my David and my dead daughter and myself, and consider my silent place in this sad world. What I want right now is to save a life, make something grow, bring life back to the world. I want to work with the bees again, to prove that I can do something and not poison it with a touch, with a word, with my voice. I may work amongst the bees in silence, and they would thank me for it. I might sing to them or declare a Psalm, someday, and they wouldn't mind that, either. The bees will judge me not.

Swarm in June, worth a silver spoon. There is no rhyme for April.

I look about for a branch or a stone for a marker, some way to flag the site so I won't forget. I would return with the wain and a skep, I could get Roger to help me, mayhap. But the swarm might not stay to await my return. The ball of bees might fly again. I must take them now or not at all. If only I were wearing my apron, but I had dressed for the warehouse and the village market, not for labor. I have my best blue gown on—the bodice and petticoat, lighter woolens for spring's finer weather.

I have no one to help me; I must do this alone.

I find a fallen branch, about the breadth of my arms and as thick as my wrist, and gather up my blue petticoat, revealing the white chemise underneath, the lowest hem grimed in road-mud. Holding the blue petticoat like a basket before me, with my other hand I reach with the stick, and in one swift move, knock the buzzing ball of bees off the branch. They fall together with a heaviness into my skirt, and I need both hands to hold up my petticoat before me.

Bees on the swarm will not sting; they hardly have the thought of it, so anxious are they for their queen and a new home. I will give them a home now. Some hundred bees or more fly up around me like a puff of dust. But the mass of bees stays as one, squirming together in my petticoat before me, a monstrous insect-baby, heavy as a ripe watermelon, humming to each other in consternation.

I hurry back to the horse-path, knowing another mile lies ahead of me, and that the weight of the creatures will wear on me soon enough. The road is flat, the sun is high, but soon enough the marshes on the shores of the bay send a breeze to fan my face beneath my straw bonnet. The tavern at Turkey Hill lies off the road ahead. I see a few horses tied at the Cart and Wheel, recognize the fine bay, the dusty brown, and that pretty gray one; a few men talk in the sideyard, smoking, or coming from the privy.

I do not want to meet up with any folk but it is the King's road and I have to steel myself to pass without turning my head. I ought to be used to it by now. I know they see me because there had been conversation, and it stops as I walk past, my petticoat in my hands, and some hundreds of bees buzzing around me like a small storm cloud. A Massad-Chueset Indian sits against the outer wall in the sun, his arms folded over his chest, and watches me, his face unsurprised whether

I had grown wings and flown or stood next to him in silence. But no one molests me, and I continue toward home, my load before me like a gravid belly. I can't think about what people might say: *Bee-witch, swarm-herd*. They already say things I cannot control.

Swarm in July, not worth a fly. But it's April, and I've caught a swarm, and a reason to live on.

My back aches, and so do my curled fingers, my bent nails. I can't release my grip on the fabric of my petticoats, my arms tired and trembling and, by now, I perspire muchly. Nantasket rises afore me and I hear the geese and ducks making a clamor on Straits Pond, when hoofbeats come from behind me, meeting the road from the countryside, a light lope, or a light horse. I wonder when I will see Dr. Greenleaf again, but it isn't he.

To my surprise, a little white pony pulls to, carrying Zuriel; a light halter and a child's saddle dress the beast. Zuriel wears a faded rose-pink linen shortgown with a flowered petticoat, and she rides astride the pony like a lad. Her coif is flown down her back on its ribbons. She looks as startled to see me as I she.

"Are those—bumblebees?" She hunches her shoulder as if to ward them off, but my bees are not about to bother her or her steed. "Won't they bite you?"

No, and I am not afraid either, she can see.

"You haven't far to go now. You're taking them home? I can see your father's house. Your mother kept the bees, did she not? I heard my father speak of her. T'was a shame when she died, he said, best honey in the town." She prattles freely now, a guileless child.

I look at her over my burden, at the pony, at her limbs peeking from under her skirt, and back at the town, then back at her face, my eyebrow raised. She understands me.

"Father is in his study until sup, and *she* is resting—with The Curse." Zuriel impugns her step-mother with a sneer. "No one misses me. This is my pony, Angel. I might ride him so long as I don't come home dirty or late."

I envy her the companion; I used to wander the shores as a girl and always wished for a pony to ride through the sandy dunes. I would pat the beast but my hands are full. I smile at Angel unreservedly, then catch myself. Zuriel walks the pony alongside, seemingly content to accompany me home, chattering like the blue jays that swoop and dive in the dooryard. At last I am able to veer off the path toward the vegetable patch and the lean-to where the bee skeps are stored. The bench is empty but needs a sweep to clear pine needles and dried leaves and dust before I can release my burden.

Zuriel slides off Angel and ties him to the post at the stable, then returns to me, standing well back of the buzzing ball in my skirts.

"May I help? What should I do?"

Gathering my petticoat in one hand for just a moment, I gestured at the bench and made a whisking motion, shaking my hand to relieve its cramp.

"Sweep it? With what?"

I gesture at a fallen pine twig that will do as a whisk-broom for now, and she obliges by sweeping the brown pine needles and dead leaves off the bench.

"And now?"

I point my toe at the stack of skeps, untouched for the past year.

"You need one of those. Shall I—?" She tries to lift but one but they are stuck together, no doubt with propolis and old wax. "Let me try this—." She pulls hard between two skeps and the top one comes loose. Zuriel shakes it free and looks inside it. "Should I brush out the cobwebs?"

I nod. She gives a quick pat, shake, and whisk with her twig, and sets the skep on the bench.

No, I gesture at her. *On the ground.* She sets the open skep before me and I jerk my head at her to stand back. The bees likely won't hurt her, but I don't want her to panic and alarm them, and I can't bear another accident such as David's. Wisely Zuriel steps back a few paces to watch. At last, I am able to unburden my petticoat of its seething insect ball, a strange birth as I roll my skirts over the open skep and shake them over the basket. The bees land with a light *chock* in the skep's hold, always cushioning their queen in the center. A cloud of bees flies up around me, and some warn me, head-butting like tiny goats defending their space.

I take a deep breath and in one swift motion, I pick up the skep and turn it over onto the bench top, with the finger-wide bee-bore, their front door, a few inches above the flat bench-level. The whirling bees continue to fly about or land on the skep, no doubt seeking their queen. I shake my skirts again and back out of the bee-yard. With a sigh, I search my blue petticoat for bee-stains and see yellow pollen spots, a few broken wings from servants who had died in the service of their queen. It will come out on Wash Day next.

I ease my back and shoulders, spreading out my hands and fingers, bees swirling about the yard, and then I turn to my assistant. I put my hand to my heart and nod at her, my thanks-gesture.

"That was heavy work for you," she responds. "You must be tired."

I mime being thirsty and invite her to follow me. She looks at the sun. "For a short while, but we sup early." She doesn't want to get caught out, I know. We make sure Angel can drink at the water barrel and give him a few handfuls of hay so he won't crib at the post, then take the path past the kitchen garden to the back door. I wash my hands in the bucket by the door and shake off droplets of water. Zuriel follows me into the kitchen, where my beans have baked for hours and scent the air with smoke and molasses.

I owe my father his supper of fried ham, but I gesture at the chair and then take myself down the cellar steps and pull a jug of cider. When I come up the stair, I see Zuriel looking around the kitchen with a half-smile on her face. It is a cozy hearth, thanks be to my mother and Mary Wise before her. I have been blessed with women who knew how to make a chamber feel warm and homely.

I pour a wooden cup of cider for the girl and one for myself, then catch a glance in the looking glass at myself: a tatterdemalion if ever there was one. My coif is crushed, my gown and petticoat spattered with pollen-spots, and my short hair as mussed as a wee child's. I ruffle my hair with my fingers and try to straighten my coif. No use. It is ready for the Great Washday like my skirts.

I slice the ham from its bone and stir up a corn batter for spoon bread, pushing it into the cob-oven's front when I pull out the beans in their sealed pot. Father will be wondering where his supper is gone if I delay any longer. As I take the plates and the silver spoons and knives from their place in the cup-board, I show Zuriel that I have taken three of each.

"Oh, ma'am, I cannot. I would like it, but my father expects me at table for sup before midafternoon. We make an early table," she makes excuse. "But I might come another time?"

I nod and smile at her. I like the girl.

"I would like to see the bumblebees again. Will they make honey?"

They will, if God allows it. If I have not failed the bees, my mother, and the rest of the world again. Of course. Zuriel curtseys at me and closes the door behind her like a lady, then dashes to her pony. Through the window glass, I see her run, a blur through the diamond panes. Soon I hear Angel's light hoofbeats as they return to town.

The ham wants frying, the spoonbread shall soon be baked through, and the beans are mellow and tangy from their long bake. I'm worn out from my burden-bearing. What possessed me to rescue, or steal, a swarm of bees from a bush and carry them home in my petticoat? A demon or an Angel? It is a question for the ages.

* * *

DR. GREENLEAF SENDS A LETTER within a packet of herbs. Neriah the wharf boy, on a pot-bellied Spanish pony, brings the packet from Hingham town and Father gives him a farthing for his trouble. I open the package, a linen bundle with a folded letter inside, tied with hempen twine, my name writ prettily upon a tied-on label. Within, cleverly folded to hold the dried herb, is a paper packet of flowerheads with a grassy scent, fit for horses or sheep—or for me, it would seem.

> To Mrs. Marsh:
>
> There is much spring fever in Boston so I am unable to call upon your house this sennight. I send you this in my stead: St. John's Wort.
>
> My mother Mrs. Greenleaf bids you take a tisane of this mornings or evenings with or without honey and more often if you feel it comfort you. St. J's Wort soothes the nerves and improves sleep. She asks you to increase your meals with a gill or more of green pot-herbs at least thrice per sennight. Pray sow some green herbs in your kitchen garden for summer harvest ~

your parsleys, spinaches, cabbages, and whatever herb is native to the soil here.

Do you increase your walking to a half of the hour by the clock each way, or twice what you have walked in the past. I expect you shall be much improved when I appear next.

Yr obdt svt~

Dan Greenleaf

I see the enormous flourish he has given under his own name. Such a man, no shame at all.

The spinster and her nephew

Mr. Henry calls upon my father out of the blue—he rarely comes from the village, from the shop where he stocks his tools in trade: his decoctions, elixirs, and tinctures, most mixed with spirits and cane sugar. Sometimes they work, sometimes not, and if effective, Mr. Henry takes all the credit. If his attempts fail, it is surely the fault of the sufferer for misusing the medicament, or applying for Henry's help too tardily, or the ever-present Hand of God.

I am in the kitchen boiling a scrap of rennet for cheese-making, now that the cows are in milch again. I hear a guest arrive and Father's voice greet him. I do not go into the great room because why should I so display my mortification? The weekly trial of Sabbath services is more than enough for me. But presently, Father opens the kitchen door and calls me in.

"Mr. Henry has come by with his recommendation for you," he says, bringing me into the great room. I greet the apothecary, his periwig and stock slightly askew from his journey hither, with a courtesy no lower than his, because we are still equals in society, despite my correction.

Mr. Henry slips his hat flat under his arm.

"What, what? I did not realize the girl was within, Nichols." He fusses like a wet pullet, all but scratching at the floorboards. He speaks to Father around me, the ghost in the room.

"It is said that you have been called upon by the renowned physician of Boston, Greenleaf, who is the son of that minister of some repute, is he not? Yes, yes, so he is, and it has come to our attention that the, ah—your daughter, ah, here might have needed additional medicaments or attention beyond what we had attempted in the winter past. We thought perhaps some sack would serve her melancholia, what?"

He presents the bottle with a flourish, speaking as if I am not standing right before him. "Ta-ra—wine, but not too much wine: For some, the heat of the vine helps provide circulation and thus a quickening of the stagnant black humor, while for others, it only worsens the despondent frenzy. Give her a gill of wine in the evening and also at breakfast, not cool but blood-warm, so as not to excite her circulation neither depress it."

He cuts his eyes over at me just once, to assess my complexion. "Less venturing out of doors, and by no means should she cultivate the honeybee. It is fraught for her nerves—a single bee-bite could send her into an incurable malaise. Her blood cannot bear the heat of the venom. I pray you forbid her at once, indeed I do."

My heart squeezes sharply when he says *a single-bee-bite*, apparently forgetting my David. What brutes men are. I could kick him.

"We shall take it under advisement, Henry." My father, always diplomatic with townspeople he depends on for trade, gestures to the door.

"I shall bid you good day, then, chirrah!" Mr. Henry replaces his cocked hat and bows himself away.

Father turns to me with his wiry eyebrows raised. He holds the bottle of sack in his hand and proffers it me. "Did you care to begin your regimen?"

I heave a sigh, irked beyond comment. And I cannot serve two doctors, nor two masters.

"No wine for you, then, girl. And do you wish to continue your solitary walking, per Greenleaf's order, and your bee-keeping? Aye? I thought so. Carry on, then." Father sets the wine bottle on the table and returns to his loom.

I rest on the settle, thinking of the townspeople and how tittle-tattle spreads like disease. The tale of a physician visiting the ailing Silence has no doubt circled the village. They have debated the topic and shared their opinions, which is what brought Mr. Henry to our door—jealousy, curiosity, or professional competition. After a long moment's misanthropy, I return to the cheesemaking enterprise.

Zuriel comes again and helps me butter and wrap the cheeses, running the muslined blocks down cellar afterward. She stays, chattering, laughing, until I shoo her home.

Late afternoon, when Father is having a short rest on the settle to ease his weary back, I take my exercise, walking for my paces up the stony shore, gray-green waves creaming between the rocks, then the hiss and rattle as the water sieves out again. I've always admired what I used to think of as God's paintbox—rocks of every imaginable color, smoothed by years of rolling surf and grains of sand. Dank seaweed lies in drifts at the high tide mark, waiting freely for the first planter to gather it for his garden, or feed it to his goats. The two black-rock islands have withstood an eternal bash of waves, a familiar reminder that tides may pass over but need not drown. The empty ocean before me is quite wild in its beauty. I can hear gulls *breek* and whine, while the gray seals bark on the rocks. Yellowlegs, great and small, run along the waterline, dipping in for their prey.

When I am hale enough for still longer walks, I should like to circle the whole of Hull, stand and look across at Boston

Town, see the new whitewashed lighthouse with its refracting eye, guiding ships around shoals and into safe harbor. I have heard that every ship coming into port pays a penny tax per ton of cargo, which seems a mere trifle to pay for safety, but I do not understand the mercantile of the sea, so perhaps it is a hardship, as it were, for captains to pay.

I walk as distant as the far end of the crescent-shaped shore and then cross over to the Straits Pond side and walk back. Upon my return, another visitor has come, a wain drawn by a gray mule. It can only be one of the Lincolns, who breed mules at their holdings on the western side of Hingham.

My father has been roused from his catnap due to my absence. I hurry in, leaving my straw hat and my gloves in the kitchen, adjusting my coif to meet visitors. I do not want to, but I owe Father my duty as the current mistress of his house.

It is Rebecca Lincoln, the spinster sister, I see, and her nephew, Jacob-Wrestling, as I venture to join them. I enter the room smoothing my petticoats and with a pleasant expression on my face, which I can pretend if I feel like doing so. I only know the Spinster Lincoln by sight and reputation; she is reputed to be eager to please but a little awkward in the execution of pleasing. She is nearer to my father than me in age, in her fortieth year, with a talented mantua-maker; that striped gown wasn't sewn by her, though I know she has the time for such sewing. Her skin is yet smooth, but she is a horse-faced woman, big boned in the wrist and crooked of nose and teeth. She still has them, which says much for the care of her health. Her coif and fichu are both starched well and sit prettily upon her.

"Widow Marsh." She rises from her place on the settle. "I heard you were still unwell and thought some beef jelly might help your constitution." I bow my thanks, accepting the gift, and with a glance from Father inviting me to join them, I also sit.

"Miss Lincoln has been telling me that her brothers' maize crop does well," Father includes me in the conversation.

"The stalks are as high as your waist by now," she says, appraising me. "Mr. Nichols was saying that your maize grows well, but your flocks do better on the harbor land." Her eyes drift across the room, assaying. "Such a nice, bright room. I do admire the windowpanes, when so many have only shutters."

"We have had our window glass for some years now. The sun brightens this room all afternoon; it is the kitchen and bedrooms that take the morning light." Father's workroom benefits with its southern window to have light all the day.

"Window glass in the diamond shape is particularly pleasant," she smiles at Father. "It catches the sun and sets the room with rainbows of light, does it not?"

It does, and I suddenly realize this is not a social call but that I am chaperoning a courtship, although I don't know if Father sees it yet. My father has been widowed more than a year now; it is high time, or past it, if I weren't here to act as help-meet. I gather that Rebecca has come along to adjudge the household and see if Father is a worthy catch for her childless self. No one but Father to please. Her brothers may have urged her to try her hand. And the nephew is along as chaperone.

Jacob-Wrestling is tall and as horse-faced as his aunt, with light brown hair that looks stringy under his farmer's hat. He must be twenty by now; though I remember him as a child behind me in years, assuredly younger than I. His skin is no longer carbuncled but he has not learned the art of growing a beard yet. His is a straggly little swirl at his chin and no more. I feel very old when I look upon him and consider my losses. He must be looking for a wife for himself soon. My father may be as well, whether he knows it or no. I cannot stand in their way.

I stand and gesture around the room, inviting Rebecca to see the rest. Father interprets for me. "Pray accompany Silence and she will show you the rest of the house, if you'd like, Miss Lincoln?" I imagine Father sees us becoming friendly in this way. His bashful smile tells me he is flattered by her attention and thinking of his future.

She flutters as if surprised by the suggestion but follows me with alacrity. Father, freed, returns to his loom—we follow, so Rebecca can see his bright workspace. She strolls through the room, running her fingers across the woolen hanks in red, white, indigo, yellow, black, and brown, different weights and textures to suit his customers' need. The loom itself takes most of the room, and once he begins, she might dislike the noise that we are accustomed to. She wants to sit at the loom and see how the machine works, so Father lets her take the seat and press her feet on the treadle; he tosses the shuttle back and forth to show her how he weaves. Jacob-Wrestling follows, unspeaking, a scarecrow with a pompion's head, as awkward as a newborn calf.

"And there you see how that pattern emerges, mistress, and becomes a coverlet for a bed or a table. Pretty, is it not?"

"It is fascinating to see such wonders—I thought it all done by hand somehow, not seeing the very machine at work. I feel transported to a European capital, where such industry flourishes, I dare to say."

Father accepts her praise and more, while I stand in the doorway, not able to participate or step away from this sudden change in heat.

"Get along with you both so I may finish this in a timely manner, my ladies," he says at last, and I wait for Rebecca and Jacob-Wrestling to follow me out. We pause at the stair and I ask with a gesture if they want to see the remainder of the house. Rebecca does; Jacob-Wrestling follows behind like a puppy. Her eyes feast on the plastered ceilings, the papered walls in Father's bedchamber, fresh summer linen curtains on the beds; her hand caresses the banister of the stairs and the backs of chairs as we return to the main room.

I gesture for them to sit, and lead her to the dining board, set with silver candlesticks and purchased spermaceti candles. I will make our beeswax into candles again by autumn, or bayberry if no wax, but this is beyond my ability to explain. I return to the kitchen hearth for hot water, the teapot and sweetmeats. I pour for them and pass the sugar bowl and milk, tartlets with shore-plum preserves and beaten yellow cream thick as butter, and Charity's squares of nutmeg cake sparkling with beaten sugar atop.

The good blue China tea service came from my mother's dowry, but the candlesticks are from my father's first wife, Mary Wise. This is the way of all spouses—one dies, and another takes their place. I have not the heart yet to consider such a move, but my father's courtship might effect a change in my thinking. Finding another husband is starting over, as if I were a maid again, but such an old soul as I am now, who will want me and my broken self? Who would want this old worn shoe?

I partake of a tart and my cup of tea and quietly stir my sugar and milk. I feel awkward in the extreme, but Rebecca sits at table and enjoys the tea and sweets. Jacob-Wrestling munches his treats and manages his cup without dropping it or spilling. It seems a great treat for him to sit at table like a grown man and eat sweet things while all the world works in the afternoon. My father's loom *thumps* and *thwacks* in the workroom.

"Oh, my days, what a racket," Rebecca says, laughing so that her big teeth show. I can't tell if she is complaining or finds it amusing. I almost do not hear the noise. They say one might get used to anything. Noise, aye.

Silence? I won't say I was used to it, but I endure.

Rebecca accepts another pour and then seems to feel she can ignore me, chatting quietly with Jacob-Wrestling about the weather. In my view, this is not her best endeavor for wooing my father by way of me, the resident daughter, but Rebecca is not subtle. She has set her cap at Father, and I do not doubt she will stick to it a while. She looks upon the many silver tankards and platters up along the dining chamber sill. She can't know that those are mine, my widow's third converted to silver wares for safekeeping when David died. I see her counting it, her lips moving, valuing it in her mind.

I place my cup in the saucer and wait for our caller to come to her senses.

She lingers over her sweets and finally drains her cup, saying, "My days, what a refreshment."

Although I would dearly have rather been in the kitchen, out visiting the bees, or in my own dark cellar counting potatoes, I sit, silent as always, the proverbial bump on the log, until she decides she is ready to leave.

I pass to Father's workroom, knocking lightly. He leaps from the bench, altogether too jaunty for a gentleman of his years, to come and bid them godspeed home to the family at Broad Cove.

"Please give our best to your brothers, Miss Lincoln, and your father, Master Lincoln. I hope the maize continues in excellence. And Silence thanks you for your kind gift of beef jelly."

I hold a hand to my heart, nodding emphatically, though I detest meat jellies; they taste of blood. I shall add it to soup or tip it into the midden, and return the crock forthwith.

"I shall relay that message, Mr. Nichols. Thank you kindly for the tea, Mistress Marsh. It was my honor to have had this time with you." Rebecca smiles her crooked smile and dips a little bow. The two elders almost simper at each other and I feel left out, or rather, pushed aside, more than I have been used to. A new wife, as Fellows had ordered. Was it she?

But when Jacob-Wrestling bows especially to me, holding my gaze for the first time since his awkward arrival, I realize with a jolt that I am being offered up as well. To this pink-cheeked sirrah. A double handfasting may be in our future. I would be speechless, if I weren't already accursedly so.

Feeling suddenly defeated and tired, I bow my farewell and retreat to my chamber. I lie there, while the shadows lengthen outside, and my angled ceiling catches all the darkness before nightfall. A bright pink-orange luminescence hangs in the sky after the sun's setting, and I know I must make the supper board. But I cannot bear to be pushed out from my last haven. Am I the weight that drowns him now?

And whether Father wants Rebecca Lincoln or if she would have him, I will not be tossed to the hungry youth who is too shy and stupid to choose for himself. I cannot go forward like this—tainted and silent.

I return to the kitchen and make the supper, and we say no more of the Lincolns' visit. But he is thinking, and planning, and I keep my eyes on my plate until the repast is done and I may wipe the dishes and the platter, drain the rinsed cups on the linen cloth. I drift upstairs to my chamber like dandelion fluff.

Father pauses outside my chamber door on his way to bed. I know he is weary. I am sorry to vex him with my mortification, the cumbersome problem I have become to him. He is still a virile man, and can yet father children, I warrant. He should have another wife if he wants one, and Rebecca Lincoln comes from good stock. She might not bear young, but she will keep him in a warm cap at night and dry stockings in the winter. She will rub his back and ease his weaver's bottom. I don't doubt her social class or her intellect. I wonder only for myself, how long I will be welcome in my father's house with ere a new wife to pour his tea, or before they push me into the arms of young Jacob-Wrestling.

Father does not knock up my door; he goes on to bed, his candle glow disappearing when he closes his door. I lie in the dark with a halo of moon rising over the sea, winking through diamond windowpanes across my woven coverlet, my walls. If I let the moonlight fall upon my pillowbere, lighting my face as I sleep, will I see my future husband in my slumbers? Will I see a future for myself at all?

Down the shore

I see my little friend Zuriel at Sabbath meeting each week and am glad when she comes down the shore to visit and chatter to me, busy in my chores. I show the girl how to make drop biscuits, rough on the outside but tender within. There are yet no new beach plums or blue whortle-berries to pick in early June. One afternoon at low tide we dig our own clams to save myself the journey to the wharf. I brush her off before she rides home, still sprinkling sand from her petticoats; I shake mine out the window and sweep up afterward. What a bother for such little morsels, but so delicious in the heavy broth. I wonder how the parson's daughter makes away with so much unregulated time, but I have no call to police her. She is safe enough learning housewifely arts from me, what knowledge I have to share.

Some days later, just after nooning, the black mare appears at the post and Dr. Greenleaf stands at the door when I open it. "Good morrow, madam."

I stand back to admit him.

"How goeth the invalid?"

I shrug, my feelings mixed, both pleased at company who will speak at me, and weighted with my sins. But he looks closer.

"I see that the exercise has done you some good." He brushes my cheekbone with his thumb. "Your color is good. What ho, are those pips from the sun?" He then takes my hand and pinches the skin at the back. "You must drink more cider or small beer, or water, if your well is sweet. You are too dry inside. Look how the skin is pinched like a pleat of linen. More liquids, my lady patient, and I do not mean wine or milk."

Father hears the doctor's voice and pauses in his work. "Do I hear the doctor calling for a quaff? Hear, hear—Daughter, pray fetch us a draught of your cider, to slake the doctor's thirst. It is roasting outside this noon. Do sit!"

I take the man's tricorne and go to the kitchen while they sit and palaver about Boston and the roads thereto. I want the doctor to stay awhile, to please Father, and think perhaps some cake and cheese might be better with my light ale. I unwrap Charity's special seed cake, rich with benne, caraway and the black walnuts we had gathered in the fall, then slice and butter it well. I cut a wedge from the white Narragansett-style cheese we made just last month, putting both on a wooden trencher with a small knife. I scoop a spoonful of tart-sweet red quince jelly into a saucer and add it to the tray with a silver jelly spoon. Father's eyes light when he sees the tray.

"Doctor, you must try my daughter Charity's seed cake. It is like no other!" They both come to table and seat themselves, continuing their discourse. "Sit you down, sir. Now, as to the King's tax on the shipping, I think it meet that each *captain* pay his share. But not every fisherman can afford it."

I wait in a chair with my darning needle busy in Father's stockings until he has exhausted his opinion.

"I'll leave you to treat my daughter and thank you for your services. Do leave your bill with Silence, and she will pay it."

I roll the stockings with the needle and thread inside and gesture to the doctor to come back to the settle. But he has a different idea.

"Shall we walk, Mistress Marsh?" He eases his back a little, and explains, "I have sat so much, astride, and in house, and it is a lovely day out. I'd like to catch the sea breeze and march out for a while, if you will accompany me." He glances toward Father's noisy workroom and says, softer, "The air might be a little freer out of doors."

I have nothing to hide from my father, but it might be easier to walk side by side than to have those searching gray eyes diagnosing my every move. I nod and excuse myself to fetch his hat and my own, and my gloves.

"Oh, bother the gloves. Sunshine on your skin, madam, is far better than what the buffle-headed rabble might say," he catches me out. I hesitate, then ball the gloves and toss them back at the coat tree and tie my hat ribbons instead. I lead the way out the front door and head to his mare to greet her. I pet her soft nose and tickle her face following her blaze, brushing back her forelock, stroking her jowl. She nickers a little and tries to nibble my sleeve.

What a beauty is Raven. I long to croon it to her, but I keep her name in my mouth like a sweetmeat I can savor a long while. I lean down to pluck some grass to palm for her, and she takes it with whiskery lips and a saucy nodding of her head. I must find her an apple or a parsnip to crunch before they depart. Smiling, I turn and realize Dr. Greenleaf is watching me.

"Is it difficult, to remain silent?"

I shrug. Who has a choice?

"You have something intelligent to say, on many occasions and subjects. Yet I don't think you are one of those fussocks whose tongue flips and flops all the day." He looks away at the sea. "Shall we?"

I pat the mare, Raven-black, a final time and lead the way around the house, stepping over the stile in the stone wall and head north along the dunes. The sun is quite warm, but a fresh breeze blows in from the water and soothes any heat we might suffer. I pick up scallop shells when I see them, thinking to line my pathway to the bee-yard; I blow away the sand and tuck them into my apron, which makes the doctor laugh.

"With silver bells and cockle shells? Are you also contrary? I believe you are."

I keep walking, irritated. Is every move I made to be thus analyzed and mocked? What is it to him if I gather shells? I have little enough to amuse myself. As a doctor, he seems not to practice much medicine. He rather avoids it, I shouldn't wonder, preferring to lollygag and prattle and visit the outer banks of the great city. Should he not be busier in town? Was the spring fever abated and his time free enough to canter our way?

In a moment he catches up with me, a portion of scallop shells in his hand. "Will these do, my tacit lady?"

I stop walking to look at his handful, blow a little breath to show him to dust them off, which he does. I accept the scoured shells, touching my heart in thanks, but not lingering the way I do with my father or Zuriel. I still think him irritating. *Tacit*—as if I have a choice. We walk, the hard wet sand underfoot noiseless but easier to walk upon than the slick rocks or soft sand.

"I told you there would be further remedies in treating your melancholia. Did you think I had forgotten?" He bends to pick up a flat stone, hurl it out to sea. "No skips," he mocks himself.

I have wondered what his next order might be. I had first scoffed at his command to exercise but I have enjoyed it, and it is neither bitter nor painful. What next?

The man finds another flat stone and flings it out to sea, trying to avoid the curling waves. The stone goes in with a splash, nary a skip. "Hmmph. It works better on still water. Do you read?" He amends his question, "I'm sure you *can* read, as a good Puritan girl, but have you books to read? Aside from your beloved Bible, that is."

I have my Bible and prayerbook, of course, given me at an early age and catechized well. I have read Mathers, both Increase and Cotton, as well as Mistress Bradstreet's poetry, which my mother owned. My father was no scholar; none of my brothers had attended Harvard after their grammar school and Latin tutor. But my mother had been lettered and taught me after the dame-school; she had shown me the beauty in the lady-poet's works, as well as in the beautiful language of the Psalms. My bookish husband had owned *Treatises on the Laws & Equity* and *Statutes in Force Since Magna Carta*, and some others, but they had not held my interest. His brother Ephraim took the law books with the house when David died intestate.

I can't communicate all that, but I mime, *indeed, I can read.*
"Books at home?"

Nay, none. Father had sold the books when he paid his fine last fall.

Dr. Greenleaf bends to select another few stones, palming them, then jangling them like coins. He arises. "I have one in my saddlebag that you might try. Do you fancy poetry? Do you hear it much or know it? Aye, you're a Separatist; I'll wager you've read Ann Bradstreet's work? A fine, upright pillar of literature in the New World. Of course you have!" He tries again with the ducks-and-drakes and manages a single bounce off an incoming wave. No small feat, that.

"Do you know sonnets?" He turns back to me. "Nay? It's poetry, in form. I have a collection of sonnets that you might enjoy. They are neither long nor as allegorical as Mistress Bradstreet's work. They are more grounded in the real world—with an easy rhyme and meter. Try them, will you? They're easy to memorize and it's a pleasure to linger amongst them."

Am I allowed pleasure? No one had said me nay, but I
doubt I should win favor, should I be caught out reading
sonnets. What next, *novels*? Nonetheless, once he mentions
reading, I desire it with a rush, to enhance my little closed-
in world; to fly away into another more beautiful, if only in
my mind, would be welcome relief. Reading is not speaking. Reading can be done silently. It is like listening with
your eyes. Surely that's not forbidden me. I shut down any
thought of sin in pleasure—if it is God's word, it is good,
and if it is of a godly pen, then there can be no harm, I tell
myself, as if I believe it. As if I don't long for escape like a
bird fallen down the chimbley.

'Tis strange doctoring, his, to offer me books and clean
air, tisane and fresh greens. I don't understand it—there are no
bitter powders, nor putrid potions to sip. I am neither confined
to my bed, nor to a dark room with the shutters closed and a
fire smoldering on the hottest day. No leeches, no blood, nor
purges, nor blistering. I wonder what they teach at Harvard, if
this is his lectionary, or if he has learned this from his mother, the apothecaress. Greenleaf's method is quite different, and
though I don't want to unclench my teeth nor my heart, I feel
myself warming to new notions, and to him as harbinger of
this fresh cure. He has new ideas, a freshness about him, like
new green—leaves? He catches me woolgathering.

"Another impertinent query, Mistress. Have you considered remarrying?"

I feel this question like a splash of icy water. Another
espousal, an embrace from another man? I am still faithful
to my husband, until death—but he has died. I have been
faithful. Love another? Or—bed another? The idea itself is
so shocking—I miss David fiercely. I want to kick sand at the
doctor. Throw rocks. How dare he intrude upon my grief? I
wait a moment to try to harness my emotions, to express how

I feel, but finally shrug, heaving a sigh. There will never be another such as David, and I don't care to attempt an explanation in my truncated manner.

"I mean no offense, lady."

I shrug him off, my throat aching, my eyes burning with unspent tears, but Dr. Greenleaf continues in a different vein than I expected.

"'Tis not that I presume you are ready to join in matrimony again so soon. Aye, I know your story. My mother related the tale, heard from your father's own lips, and he told me himself as well. *This village!*" He pauses, his lips pressed together as if to hold back an emotion, or a curse. He sighs, wagging his head in disgust or dismay, I know not.

"In your future—I fear this community is not the best for your health. The atmosphere here—indeed, I say this village particularly—is not meet for a woman like you." His mien is serious. He does not mock nor flirt.

"And I must tell you, Mistress, that your future wellbeing rests upon a soothing and healthful air. In this corner of the world, you will suffer. You are suffering now. Do you not see it? Pray, find yourself a husband who will remove you from the backwaters and take you to a home where you may thrive. If you stay here, you shall wither." His voice carries his concern. "This place may kill you, if I may be so frank."

I believe this prognosis. I don't even mind it; in troth, it marries well the inmost secret voice of my heart. Dr. Greenleaf is not run amiss with his opinion. I expect this village, this congregation to kill me at some time, whether directly, or by a slow smothering of my spirit. I am not made for this place. I run my tongue along the sharp edge of my broken tooth. They may as well kill me the next time.

We walk onward, the hard sand giving way to the pebbled shore, our footsteps crunching in the shingle.

"You might enjoy the doings in a city like Boston and perhaps fare better in a more liberal society," says he, naming the thing I would love most, a liberal society—that which Parson Hobart and most of the congregation would call loose and immoral. I crave such society, if I be truthful.

"Lectures, serious music, lively discussions, intellect, visitors from England, from all Europe. It is very broadening. Enlightening. Rich, in the cultural sense. You would *blossom* there, I believe, not wither." He looks ahead, shading his eyes from the sun, as if he can spot the city from our spit of land. "Can you see it, the sun just hitting the spire of Christ Church on the rise of Copp's Hill? 'Tis our new church, and it is glorious inside. So bright and new. My mother and my brothers all worship there."

He is no Separatist—he is an adherent to the English church, I see. I do not think my face betrays my thought, but he chuckles at me. "I am no papist devil," says he. "We both worship the same Father god, my lady, no matter what your parson says." He chuckles again. "For this very reason, you should get yourself from this provincial bog and get thee to Boston, where you can open your eyes to the world."

I have thought of the town myself but am unable to conjure a Boston suitor at my doorstep to sweep me away, after all that I have endured. Who will want to marry me, thus shamed, broken, jaded, unrepentant and as full of anger as my skep is full of bees? And what will become of me if I do not wed again? My hair blows about my face, shorn in shame and penance, just long enough to flutter in my eyes.

It enrages me that he so glibly asks, as if he has the right to inquire, to judge my situation as lacking, when I have all the seashore and the love of my father, and my bees, and Ginger, and the herbs of Mother's garden—but Rebecca Lincoln flashes through my mind. I stay because I have nowhere else to go. I stay because I must. No matter how much better I might prefer Boston, or London, or the moon, I am a Hingham lass, and the Cohasset shore will be my home for my remaining years, whether I speak aloud again or never.

I am as barren as a cask left on the wharf. I am an empty trap; no bait, no lobster.

I stop and crouch to examine some pebbles that I don't care about, to hide angry tears that wet my eyes again.

"I see I've vexed you." His voice is kind. "I am sorry for treading too roughly in these big feet."

I don't answer but glance at his feet clad in soft black leather boots. It isn't the feet that vex me, but the assuming wit of this doctor. He should go home. I rise, dropping the rocks I was examining, and shoot him a look, a shake of the head. It doesn't matter. *Go home,* I gestured at him.

"Oh, aye, I shall leave you for now. I've right stepped in it. But you'll take my other advice, will you not?" He pulls his gold timepiece from his pocket with an ease that shows his comfort in a world of clocks and appointed hours. He must live well in Boston. He glances at the hour.

"My time is nearly done here, Mistress Tacit; I must return to my steed, the Lady Raven, and my business in town. But aye, I have a book for you in my bag if you'll accompany me?"

I am willing to receive the book if he will stop asking such sharp questions. We turn and let the ocean breeze buffet us along back down the dunes and over the stile to Mother's kitchen garden. I stop at the pathway toward the bee-yard where my one skep hums and flurries as it should and empty my apron of the sandy shells. I shake it out and dust my hands.

"I have heard you are a bee-mistress again," the doctor observes. "Bee-witching swarms of honeybees out on the open highway."

I didn't expected a pun from this fellow and though it is terrible, as puns always are, it is so pert and apt that I snort and clap a hand across my mouth to keep from laughing aloud. I wag my finger at him.

Dr. Greenleaf laughs aloud, a bright, masculine sound I have not heard in more than a year. It warms me unexpectedly, and I blush, feeling disloyal to David.

"Aye, terrible, am I not? I own it!" He leans in. "I am pleased to see that you can laugh. Nothing will cleanse you quicker than merriment. Now, for the cream."

We skirt the house again and return to the post where sleek Raven swishes her glorious tail. The doctor unties the latchet of a saddlebag, buffed glossy brown from wax and care, and struggles to pull out a slim volume. A second book comes with it, their leather bindings stuck together by the warmth of the day.

"Fiddle, what is the hang-up here? Hello, the second volume wants to come along for a visit! I don't know if you are ready for this. You might find it scurrilous. Well, then?" He hesitates, then hands both books to me. "It's a fiction, but it will open your mind."

The books lie heavily in my hands. I feel I am holding treasure. I hardly know what to think; 'tis fortunate I cannot speak aloud. I doubt very much that novels are permitted by the laws of the Separatist congregation in Massachusetts Colony. And I desire to read it more than anything in my life.

"Doctor's order," he assures me. "I have every faith in you. Let me know if you like it next time." He closes the saddlebag with a neat tuck of the leather strap.

"Keep on with the exercise; go a little farther if you feel hale enough, and more liquids. Sweet well water, barley water, light ale or cider, cold tea if you like, but water is best. Greens, boiled well. Fresh herbs and ripe love-apples with vinegar and a sprinkle of ground sugar and black peppers. Victuals for good health, we call them in Boston Town. Fare you well, Mistress Tacit."

He mounts up and Raven lopes away, dust blowing with them and the wind toward the village. I sketch a brief wave before my eyes are dragged down to my treasure: Books. I had forgotten my love for books. I am like a child with a sweet cake.

In my hands I behold a much-read volume of sonnets, *Idea's Mirror*, of the poet Drayton, its binding worn and its pages touched with age. It falls open and delicious words fill every page. Poetry, one per page, in rhyming lines, speak of love and hunger and beauty. I cannot bear to deny myself. My eyes graze the page, my fingers flip the edges and I feel the fan of paper in my face. Poetry. Beautiful words.

What of the other, the scurrilous tale? The second volume smells scholarly and new, and the creamy pages are freshly cut, still slightly ragged. It is indeed a very new volume, bearing just two words, *Robinson Crusoe*, the author's name in gold stamp upon the cover. Later I learn that *Crusoe* is the name of the story of a shipwrecked man, written down by an English gentleman called Daniel Defoe. It looks an adventure, a tale of a shipwreck, of a man in hiding—no, he builds his own palisado, he keeps goats and gathers raisins to dry? He wears a goatskin like a pagan, but he fears the cannibal tribe—what? My cheeks burn. I close the volume and hug it to my breast. What joyful hours I have before me. I am stupefied with delight.

Daniel Greenleaf has neglected to tell me what price we owe for his calls. He vexes me, aye, but he piques my attention as well. He knows how to find me when no one else sees or hears me. I feel my blood stirring. Whatever our debt for this medicine, the fee is too low for what I have gained in the bargain.

A taste of honey

Zuriel is ever at my doorstep now, grateful for attention and soaking up knowledge like a sea sponge. It is time to take first honey from the hive, sparingly, judiciously, and she wants to see all the necessary steps, from smoking and drumming out the bees to filtering the honey and trying out the wax. We'll make candles and balm last of all, in the fall of the year, when the wax will stiffen instead of melt under the warm sun, and the lavender blossoms are gathered in.

I dress in Mother's yellow bee-gown again, after swearing I would never, and I'm glad I hadn't burned the dress as I'd planned to. It somehow still smells of Mother. I had shown Zuriel that if she wants to assist, she must dress in a fair-colored gown, not black or indigo. She appears that Saturday morning in her old rose-colored gown, earlier than her usual afternoon arrival. It is a bright day, perfect for taking honey. Most bees are out foraging on a fine summer's day; a drizzly day, though cooler for the keeper, is the worst time to bother the hive, as they are home and dry, and not amused by our predations.

"I told Father I was gathering berries today." She doesn't seem to mind the lie. I won't advise her how to live her faith, not when I am unable to live out my own, but I raise an eyebrow at her statement, and she has the good grace to color. "I will look for berries and bring some home if there are any."

There are no ripe berries yet, only hard green chokeberries and whortle-berries out on the slopes. Even the Mayapple isn't ripe until August. Zuriel is ahead of herself, but as a town lass perhaps she doesn't know, and if her father has not corrected her excursion, it is beyond me. If a man cannot police his own family, is it everyone else's duty to police them in his stead? Nay, say I, but I'm certain my congregation would avow it. They certainly show no quarter in judging and correcting my peccadillos.

We leave Angel with Ginger on picket-lines near grass and some shade, away from Mother's herbarium. I carry a tin pail and an old pierced-tin lanthorn, rusting but useful for me, no candle inside it, just to smoke the bees. We stoop at the stable to gather dried horse manure, the driest best for our purpose, a handful in the tin pail to suffice. I return to the kitchen and come back with a few embers in a scoop, and carry it out to the bee-yard. In my apron pocket I carry a sharp kitchen blade about four inches in length, with an old leather fire-fan, much used, under my arm. Zuriel totes the other implements.

I don Mother's long kid gloves, stained golden yellow from her years as a bee-mistress. I give Zuriel a pair of my old wool gloves, which will protect her from incidental bee sting but not a concerted effort by aggressive insects. I wrap the fine muslin veil around her hat and across her face, then mine, waiting to pull mine across my face until I have lit the smoking lanthorn. I crush a handful of the dry dung and add a few more solid nuts of horse dung into the lanthorn, then, with a stick, scrape one of the small embers into the open top of the lanthorn. I blow gently, and some of the undigested grass catches and smolders. Very soon, gray smoke filters through the pierced lanthorn, and I snap down the lid. I adjust my veil and proceed as Mother showed me many times before, though I have not harvested by myself before.

I miss you, my Mother.

I hold up my hand to keep Zuriel back. My second empty skep sits on the bench, awaiting its new residents. I smoke the entrance of the occupied hive and then, in a swift move, tip it sideways on the bench, releasing many bees which swirl around me. I snap my fingers at Zuriel to take the smoker and to waft the smoke at the opening with the fan. With my sharp knife, I slice around the propolis and wax at the base of the hive, where the new brood is stored and hatching. With some effort, I pry thick several inches of wax base from the full skep and turn it directly into the empty skep. I see the queen bee, as long as my little finger, crawling and wriggling, upset, and her guards are furious. I want to show Zuriel the queen but the bees are swirling and the girl is afraid. I decide to leave it for now.

I take back the smoker in one hand and begin to drum lightly on the exterior of the old skep, beating my hand against the bulrushes like a Native of the woods, to drive the bees outward, away from smoke and vibration and noise. I tip the new skep upright next to the old hive and continued smoking the bees within the old one. I continue drumming and smoking the old skep, and more bees pour out. They are desperate to find their queen, now ensconced in the new skep, bearded with honeybees. I pass the smoker and fan to Zuriel again.

Honeybees are all over my gown and veil, but they fly off as I walk; they don't bother me. I know they are dismayed, unhoused and desperate to protect their queen. I take the old skep with me, holding it by the top, upside down, so that the remaining bees can fly out, and I back away. I continue backing away as bees fly from the opening. I drum a little more, and most of the bees fly out. They are swirling around the new skep, confused and desperate for order. We leave the bee-yard and head toward the kitchen dooryard, where Father had set a worktable from sawhorses and boards. Father looks out his workroom window and claps his hands in glee at the coming of the honey.

Zuriel follows me, still fearful, and I can't see her face clearly through the veil. I motion to her for the fan and use it to fan bees from her back and veil. I shake out my skirts and hand her the fan. She fans more bees off me. There are still some hundreds of bees in the old skep but I have to finish this part to clear the dooryard of so many insects. I reach into the skep with my gloved hand and the knife, and cut out as much honeycomb as I can see. Honey drips and sticks to my hand and the knife and drips to the ground. I feel a stinger penetrate my kid glove and apologize in my heart to the bees that are dying because of my actions.

The comb falls in slabs into the waiting copper kettle. I scrape all I can, then clap on the lid. I unfurl a piece of linen cloth and tent the entire table, leaving it until sundown. At dusk I will shake out the cloth near the bee-yard and they will find their way home. Any bees left in the kettle will die in a day or two. Then we will begin to strain the honey and crush the comb to save for wax later in the year. Taking a spoon, I scrape the inside of the old skep and fill a small bowl with honey and comb. I hand it to Zuriel and wave at her to wait for me. Then I carry the skep back to the bee-yard, leaving it on its side, where the bees will scour it of its old honey and refresh it for the next time I need an empty skep. We will leave the yard alone, only looking at it tomorrow to ensure the bees stayed in the new hive. I feel certain they will.

I have copied my mother's actions down to the least motion. I had a fine teacher.

I place a cloth over the bowl of honey and leave it on the table. Grasping Zuriel's hand, I lead her past the house and over the stile to the top of the dunes, where the fresh wind blows off the ocean. I turn her around and see just one or two remaining bees on her veil. With my gloved hands, I flick them away and the stiff breeze blows them inland. I unwrap Zuriel's veil from her head and turn about so she can see any remaining bees on me.

"Oh, on your petticoat! And your veil!"

I shake them off and unwind my veil. The breeze feels good on my bare neck. There are still bees in the muslin, but I shake them off and they are also blown away. At last, we are both free of bees.

"That was so strange and wonderful. Almost magical," Zuriel marvels. "Weren't you afraid?"

Nay, not even a portion. I still feel the burn of the one sting in my finger, and pulling off my gloves, I look to see the stinger still there. I pick up a broken mussel shell, dropped by a sated gull, and with a quick scrape, pull out the stinger on the sharp edge. I make a face to show it stings, then bite and suck at the sting to soothe it. I spit on the ground, in case I have sucked out any poison.

"Ooh, does it hurt? I was stung by a wasp last year and it hurt like a red-hot coal for hours!" She puts her bare finger in her mouth, remembering with a shudder.

I smile and shake my head. Wasps are not our friends, but bees are. I dab some sticky honey from one glove onto the sting, knowing that honey hath curative powers, and we walk back to the house. Bees still fly around the covered kettle. I take the bowl from the table. We walk around to the front door and pass through the keeping room, and Father's closed workroom door, where I can hear him humming to himself but not weaving. He is dressing the loom with a new warp, his quietest activity.

In the kitchen I take a silver spoon to taste the new honey. I pass the spoon to Zuriel.

"Mmm, so flowery! It's better than maple sugar sap. Better than molasses!" She licks the spoon like a child. "Better than licking the cone of sugar!"

I marvel at the girl's naughtiness.

Zuriel laughs, her cheeks pink. "Well, I only did that when I was wee. Papa never caught me at it," Zuriel admits. "I was a beastly child. My step-mother hates me."

She falls silent while this phrase swirls around the room like an errant bee.

Is it so bad as that? I wonder. I can certainly believe it—Aphra Hobart hates everyone and everything. It's a wonder she got the parson to marry her.

"I want to go to Boston to live with my mother's sister, but Papa says I must remain. He doesn't know how *she* is with me." Zuriel looks at me, defiant, repentant, both at once. "I honor my father. And my mother. But I don't honor *her*. She's not my mother, and she hates any reference to my mother. The first thing she did when they wed, she took away the doll my mother had made. She burnt it for a poppet. I was just a child! And she won't let us speak of Mother."

I know how it feels to lose a beloved mother, and I had been graced with a full score of years before losing mine. I pity the girl. I lay my hand on her arm, my other hand on my heart, sympathetic. Zuriel winces when I touch her, meets my eyes, and slowly pulls up her sleeve. Zuriel's arm reveals itself under the linen sleeve, an inch at a time, faded bruises, old burn marks, suppurating scars from a hot pan or a poker pressed to skin. Unless Zuriel had done hard labor in a kitchen, she ought not to have such marks. And I know for certain that they pay a kitchen servant, while Goodwife Hobart manages the rest of the house, so it wasn't in the kitchen.

I reach for the other arm, touching the sleeve lightly, *Pull it up?* Zuriel hesitates, then complies, her face burning in her revealed shame. Her left arm, too, is bruised from what looks like sharp pinches, and burn marks that have scabbed over. I realize that two of her left hand's fingers are crooked. I take her left hand gently, seeking her eyes, asking, *These, too?*

She pulls away, jerking her sleeves down. "I should go home now."

She looks at me, a frightened girl. "Pray forget what you saw. It's better to forget. My father would be very angry, and she would—" She hunches her shoulders a moment, then stands tall. "I don't care. I'll stay here a little longer anyhow. I want to stay."

I cut a slice from the loaf of bread and spread it with our yellow butter, top it with fresh honey, still crunchy with comb.

Zuriel takes the bread, awkward and shy as her first time visiting. "I am sorry. I soured the mood."

I hug her and kiss the top of her head, as if she were my little sister. I shake my head, then chuck her under the chin. *All is well. You're safe here. I am your friend.*

After the girl rides away, I flap the sheet of muslin draped over the copper pot. Most of the bees have flown away, back the bee-yard. The bee-yard itself is still buzzing with angry bees, *hot*, as Mother called it. The hive is anxious about the new skep and realize they have been robbed of their honey. Several bees cling to the old sticky skep, eating up the remaining honey, carrying it into the new skep, where they will rebuild their walls of wax, their caverns of honeycomb. I know the hive will be hot for several days. It's best to give them a wide berth while they adjust to their new home.

I cannot get the girl's injuries out of my mind.

Father is delighted to see fresh honey at table that evening. "I have missed this flavor. It reminds me of your mother so much." His voice chokes and he sits in silence with his eyes closed for a moment, in prayer or in memory, I cannot tell. A single tear runs down his red cheek. "I thank you, daughter, for bringing back the hive."

He bites into his honeyed bread with great pleasure, the extra sweet making the meal festive in its own way.

After dark, in my chamber, I think again of Zuriel's wounds, her broken fingers. What kind of mother does such to her child? None that I have ever heard. But a step-mother? I believe the girl. Zuriel could not have burned the outside of her arms herself. The stripes were laid upon her by someone else. She is fiercely protective of her father; I do not doubt it was Aphra Hobart, that malice in her eye, who has harmed the girl.

I question the sense of the parson, who lets such barbarity continue under his roof, even in an age when all children expect to be chastised with rod and switch. A red-hot iron is a different matter. Still, 'tis not against the law. And 'tis not my home, and I, a mere widow, not a beloved acquaintance or congregant who might speak for the child. I cannot even speak. Who is there to speak on behalf of the child? I consider Father, but would he speak to Parson? Father did not see the girl's wounds. Perhaps Dr. Greenleaf? I feel tangled in unknowing what to say or how to proceed, and at last, I descend to the kitchen and mull myself a tisane of the St. John's Wort as prescribed. It is flat and dull in savor, but it soothes my nerves. Yet a cup of tea does not answer the question: What should we do for poor Zuriel?

To the point, what *can* we do? I sit in the flickering light of the hearth fire and worry over my surrogate sister, my young friend. A man's children are his chattel, as is his wife. The girl has no rights, nor does Aphra, nor I. But surely there is something I can think of to stop this barbarity. There must be some way to ease a child's suffering.

A few days hence, I peek beneath the muslin and see that the handful of bees are dead inside the kettle, drowned in their own honey. I start to process the harvest by slicing through the comb with a large knife and sieving it through a colander into another kettle. I make the honey another pass with a loose-woven linen clout, that filters out dead bee-bodies and wings and legs and the occasional stinger. No one wants to eat a piece of bread and honey and find a loose stinger on his tongue.

I pour the new honey into crocks to share and to save for cooking or the table. I start a fire outside with a brazier over the coals, and when the coals are red and covered with gray ash, I scrape all the empty honeycomb and crushed bits of wax from the strainings into a kettle. Slowly the wax melts, and all the detritus of the hive floats on top. With a slotted spoon I scrape off the bits of grass and dead bee bodies, wiping the cooling wax from the spoon with a handful of pine straw. The waxy straw will be used to light fires, so nothing of the bees' industry and the Lord's bounty is wasted.

A handful of bees buzz around me, on the scent of their missing honey, and the air is sweet as a spring garden bower. I take the remaining cleaned wax off the fire and carry the wax-pot down to the cellar to cool and harden. When the days grow short, that is the time to make salve and candles. An afternoon like today, when the sun beats down on sand and sea alike, is not the day for candlecraft.

Before Father drives Ginger to the wharf to pick up some imported hanks and spools for his workroom, he asks, "Might I proffer a crock of your new honey to the Lincolns? I was, er, perhaps, I should like to—" His red face burns like a torch. I would be amused at Father's ardor if it meant not that I might become the third wheel. But I dip a generous portion and tie on a muslin cap to the crock so it mightn't spill. I feel a little out of sorts at playing in this charade.

"Gracious, daughter. I thank you." He takes the gift and looks bashfully at me, his apple cheeks red. "T'would be a blessing if you and Mistress Lincoln became friends. And shall I give young Master Lincoln your greeting?"

I give a small nod. I don't want to be Rebecca's friend, but it is better than being her step-daughter. And I don't want to offend the Lincolns over young Jacob-Wrestling, but until he actually offers me his troth, I cannot refuse it. I feel I am on a danger path heading that direction, and one of these days I might find myself betrothed to that raw youth. I shudder at the thought, but I have no other choices for now. Perhaps life with the Lincoln family would not be so terrible? Rebecca would be here with Father, and I would be closer to the village from the eastern side, and I would have mules to drive my wain.

I think again. Nay, there is nothing there for me—and given the choice, I would rather be a tainted widow than make a miserable second attachment. I consider Goodwife Hobart's sharp nose and eyes that never stop seeking wrongdoing, and the step-daughter who has paid the price of her father's second rush to the magistrate.

But this isn't my house, and it isn't my decision if Father reweds. I have my chamber upstairs, until I want to leave, or until my future espousal. I am like a scantly used spinning wheel to be moved to the attics or given to another when I'm no longer wanted. Still useful, still pretty—but needed not. Oh, what a tangled web, when all I want is peace and my solitude.

As Father jogs away toward town in the wain with Ginger and the crock of honey, I seek my novel and my straw hat, and step over the stile and out to the shore, where I can sit in the cleft of a rock and read undisturbed. No one is watching or waiting for me, and I might take a moment to myself without sinning, mayn't I?

I have got many of Drayton's sonnets to memory, and I like the cadence of the verse. The first four lines alternate rhymes, as do the next two stanzas; the last two lines rhyme, and this simple scheme is easy to learn by heart. I have never tried my hand to write one, but I understand the idea behind a sonnet now, and believe I could if I were so moved. Would not that make my David proud? He had loved the written word. I miss him dreadfully when I cannot read aloud one of these lovely verses to him. But, shoreside, I whisper them, with no one to hear me, just to hear the rhymes fitting together. Of course I know that if I take to writing verse, that would violate the spirit of my sanction. Even if I wrote it only in my mind.

Silence is silence is silence.

So instead, I read *Robinson Crusoe* twice and love it all the more the second time. I am not lost on unfamiliar sands, as he were, the second time through—I know where we are headed and I see more along the way, in a manner of speaking. I wish I could talk of this book to Dr. Greenleaf, but I must await his next visit to at least share my pleasure with the novel. It suits me to read on the shore, wondering at footprints in the sand, and who else walks these stony paths. Who stands here and watches the sun rise, who else greets the morning and welcomes the rising moon? None but the Native folk, I believe. The colonists of Massachusetts, King George's subjects—are too busy working and judging and asking God to save them and eating and sleeping—too much noise in the world, and not enough silence.

Beautiful things are silent: falling snow and roses opening to greet the bees. Butter-flies are silent, unlike blackflies or mayflies or my honey-makers. The sunrise has no song, and neither do trees. The far blue mountains are without voice, as are the grass, the sand, this agate on the shore. Do clams make a sound? Do fish? Do clouds? Do I make a sound when sitting still? Only my breath. Only this still small voice inside me, that only I can hear. My muteness hath no shame.

The sun also rises, and the sun goes down, and hastens to the place where it arose, saith the writer of Ecclesiastes. The shore and the sun and the bussing breeze and the quietest sounds of Nature are a boon and a blessing. In this moment I feel that my chastisement is a grace that no one else can ever share. It is lonely, but it is not heinous. And the magistrate and church elders do not even realize what they have given me.

The silence is a gift.

A blue line

As I have told, in our congregation we celebrate neither birthdays nor saints' days, nor feast days, noting only Election Day, for the gentlemen to vote; Commencement Day, when graduates from Harvard have completed their courses; Training Day, for military upkeep (it's not much of a celebration); and the Thanks-giving Day, when we gather at meeting to show thanks from our humble beginnings in the colony. But I acknowledge my birthday, to myself, at least, as it's the fourth of this month of July. I have completed 23 years on this earth and my life is over. And yet I live on. My baby brother, Israel, had a single year of life. Sister Rebecca died at exactly this age. Why should I be given longer?

The month opens with a heat wave, and an impressive lack of the sultriness we are used to, which sends the squashes and pompions and love-apples wild in the kitchen garden and puts a rapid end to the green peas. Jazaniah says Father's maize is now as high as my chin, though I am but a short woman. No matter what boasting Rebecca Lincoln had done, she was probably fibbing. The sunflowers alongside the hencoop bloom. I haven't planted a thing this year; these are wild-seeded from Mother's last crop. I weed and hoe to give vent to my feelings. Even pounding dough in the trough does not soothe me.

I feel restless now, not so much angered as desperate to be off, to fly away. Poems about love and nature, novels about distant sea voyages and shipwrecks, or mysterious lands in my newest book from the doctor, *Fables Ancient and Modern*, make me long to leave the village, the shoreline, but there is nowhere for a widow to go. I am as useless as a dowerless maid, an unbred heifer.

Even bees can take up and fly away when they want a new abode.

Taking exercise has made me stronger, but I also feel bound to one place, my silence a veritable hobble. Reading makes me long to see other lands, read ever more words, learn ever more ideas. I do not speak other languages so my reading is contingent on English translation, but Dr. Green-leaf brings or sends books that I would never otherwise see, and ideas I would never taste. I read Alexander Pope's *Essay on Criticism* and learn that good taste derives from Nature. I have known this in my bones, despite being told in Sabbath sermons that Nature is a wild monster, akin to Satan, and we are always to be fighting the beast. This isn't true—Nature is of God and God is in Nature—I had already learned that as a child from the bees and the surging tide and the waterbirds chasing the waves.

I read the words of Lady Mary Wortley Montagu, discovering with a shock of pleasure that many women besides Mrs. Bradstreet write beautiful poetry—and even plays, though I daren't read them (yet). Some of the new poems touch me in ways I have not felt since my wedding night—and I am compelled to read those poems over again, then move guiltily past them and find another more spiritually minded. The two ideas play in my mind, the corporeal and the spiritual, the sacred and the profane, and all of this is a sin, and yet I am a punished sinner, unrepentant—I stop trying to understand

and give myself to reading the poems until they move to re-side in my mind forever.

I long to recite these poems aloud, on the shore, to the plovers and sandpipers, to the herons and the seals, like a New World Francis of Assisi. And indeed, I whisper the words on my seaward walks, but carefully. No one must see me speaking, even moving my lips. But with these poems, I long to sing, to shout and laugh aloud. I long, at last, to use my voice, and it is just July, and the year but halfway gone. I would like to retail these ideas and these emotions with Dr. Greenleaf, tell him my thoughts and thank him for his gifts of words. He has passed me a lifeline from the storm to the shore. I tell him in my mind how I feel, and wonder if I might tell him in real words someday.

The doctor has not come this month; he is visiting his father the minister at Yarmouth on the Cape over midsummer and I am left to my own thoughts. Now my silence again becomes an undeniable punishment, not a quiet refuge, when I cannot speak of this new joy—the discovery of words, the enjoyment of literature, the pleasures of the page—when I thought I would never again feel pleasure.

And in this month, past the halfway point of my punishment, I feel truly that the magistrate and the elders have done me a very grave wrong. But still I will not speak. I am isolate as Crusoe on his island, captive as the Widow Reeves with her Native jailers and their blue ink, with nowhere else to go. I shall have to live by their rules as long as they hold me here. I have grown beyond the walls of my prison. How am I to live the remainder of my life this way?

There is no celebration for my day of birth, but I feel myself a year wiser, and see the broken year unspooling behind me as I remain in the silence of my correction. Father does not think to mention it, and there is no special meal planned, as is our custom as Separatists. On a day like any other, I must go into Hingham and pick up stores. Father drives the wain.

Ginger clops along the horse-path toward the village, two grooves making a dusty track for all wains, and the heavy heat of high summer unbroken by cloud or wind. It takes an hour to ride in the wain, or a scant bit over an hour to go afoot, but I won't have to cart anything home in my apron or basket. I might let Father drive home with the goods and walk my legs off, just to burn the restlessness from my body.

The shore breeze is too light to blow away gnats and gallinippers by the time we reach town, and I feel as bothered as the kine in the field, their tails swishing. I should have put a hood on Ginger; her eyes are thick with maddening flies. My shortgown is limp with perspiration, my petticoats beneath also damp. Father streams with sweat, wiping his brow with his linen sleeve. My straw hat, a fan, gloves, a lighter shift—none of these will ease the heat and stickiness of the air.

We pull to before the warehouses at the wharf, seagulls screaming atop each sunken post, their thick white droppings like a coat of paint. Townspeople glance at me and hold their stares. I feel their gaze like the sharp end of a knitting needle, at my back, my face. I am fatigued by their obsession. May I not silently attend to my duties? Must I always be an object of interest instead of a lady about her business? I wrap myself in my invisible armor, my inner shield, as Father helps me from the wagon. He will come anon to answer queries if there are any to be asked.

Basket on my arm, list in hand, we approach the first warehouse, where Father orders his dry goods; Mr. Godfrey the wharfinger within awaits our order. And directly from the door comes the Widow Reeves, her summer hat draped with the lightest of muslin veils, and that thrown across her face so that only her eyes are visible, like one of the woodcut ladies in *Fables Ancient and Modern*. I wish I could tell her that the blue line on her chin doesn't matter, that we are all marked by life in some way. She is older than I by a decade or more; she should know this. Her basket weighs on her arm with a heavy fold of woolen, spools of linen thread, other items I can't see.

I want to help her. I step back as she exits the doorway, and I tap Father—gesture towards the storehouse.

He responds without hesitation. "I shall go in ahead. Don't be long, daughter."

The widow meets my eyes. I gesture toward the wain, and toward her basket, but she wags her head.

"'Tisn't far, I thank you."

I step back so she might pass, but she sets her basket in the wain. She turns on me. "Pray you walk with me this little bit, out of the eye of the sun?" She takes my arm in hers.

We stroll arm in arm, for all the world less like two strangers as two fast friends, toward the lee of the warehouse, into the shade.

She turns to me again. "It must seem peculiar for me to accost you in this way."

I can only nod. What does she want? I am intrigued.

"I have seen you about the town. At meeting. Walking alone, betimes. You are widowed, as am I? I thought so. And no children?"

A dagger in my heart. I drop my gaze and cover my mouth, to hold back the sudden sob that wants to erupt. I cradle my womb and rock, shaking my head.

"Pray forgive me. I thought not." She places her hand upon my arm, her blue eyes deeply concerned and bright with tears.

"My children are scattered," says she. "My husband's family has the elder boys, at the plantation. My two youngest were not ransomed. They stayed with the tribe and live as young children of the Mohican People." She hesitates.

"I miss them. I mean—I miss the tribe. I miss the People who took me captive, and I live every day in rage and sorrow that I can't leave here to go back. It is too far. I don't know the way. I have no way to reach them. I am more a captive here than I was within the woods of the frontier."

I struggle to comprehend all that she says. It's as if she's speaking arsy-varsy and standing upside down. Her pain is as real as my own. She, like me, has no child and no husband, and lives under a garden cloche, where all can see her every move. Her family scattered like a handful of flint corn. I want to ask about her face. I touch my lip and draw downward.

"It is so tiresome, the way people stare. The women— how they stare! The men believe I am soiled and they ignore me—or try to advance upon me." She pauses, as if to name the molester. She shakes her head sharply.

I shape my hands about my head, as if to indicate a periwig, and stroke my invisible minivers. I look at her, my head tilted in query.

"You know him, I see," she admits. "Say nothing. It is enough to know that I am not alone."

Of course, I shall say nothing.

She gasps a moment later, realizing what she has said to me. I shrug it away.

"I mean no harm," says the widow. "The women—I am trapped here. I may not leave; I may not live my life here in peace. I am caught in a spider's web. This line—" she touches her face where the blue marking is visible. "This is all I have left of a time in my life when I was free. I was equal. I was respected. I was accepted. And my 'rescue' took that away. They can't bring back my husband, and they took away whatever chance I had of happiness in a new world. I am in living Hell here.

"If I cover this line with my veil, I keep it for me, for no one to stare at and belittle and fear. It's mine alone. If I show it off, it is to proclaim my attachment to that time. I shall decide—what few choices I have here."

I believe I understand her, and that we are correspondents in our solitude and ostracization. I take her hand and she grips mine.

"I have not asked about your—" she gestures from her lips with her hand, as if to indicate a song. Her movements are elegant, fluid. "The People—my tribe, they sometimes speak with their hands. They taught me many signs. I could show you."

No, I think not. I am not mute. I can communicate. But I will not. As long as I live here in this community, they will not hear my voice again until I am ready, and if that means never, so be it. I shake my head and touch my heart in gratitude. I have spoken more deeply with Mistress Reeves than with anyone but my family, more or less, in months. For once, I feel almost human again—I feel I have a true friend.

"So be it. I must go. Pray, accept my good wishes, Widow Marsh."

She pulls her veil about her face again, but I reach back and tuck it beneath her chin. I stick out my chin and narrow my eyes. *Wear it proudly*, I indicate. To Hell with those squawking Pilgrim fowl!

"Should I?"

Aye, do!

She smiles a little grimace at me, part rebellion, part glee. "The women will fall down dead looking at me."

May it be so, I kiss my fingers and raise them up to God.

Widow Reeve smothers a little chuckle behind her hand, looking young as I am for a moment. "Bless you—my friend." She squeezes my hand, returns to retrieve her basket.

If she can face them all with her face disfigured, so to speak, so might I. I follow her and nod my farewell to Mary

Reeves. She walks taller, and her veil flutters behind her. I enter the warehouse with my empty basket, with my head held high.

On our way from the third shop, with a country ham and dried sausages in an Osnaburg sack, slabs of salt cod heavy in my basket, we come abruptly to face with Goodwife Hobart. She travels without Zuriel, nor their manservant. She jerks back as if lightning-struck or crossed by a striped polecat. She looks cutty-eyed upon us.

Fired by my parley with the Widow Reeves, I hold my station. I have nothing to skulk about. I carry my chastisement like a fire in my breast today. In the meeting-house, Goodwife Hobart holds a scantly superior position; she takes the front chair on the women's side when her husband speaks. On the street, in the world, however, as the widow of the constable and daughter of the webster, I am her superior, and I stand, awaiting her bob or nod to show that she knows it.

We face each other, the seconds stretching out. My eyes catch hers and hold them until she looks away. She sets her mouth in a snarl, the old tabby, though she is but a mouse today, and steps back. I let the tiniest corner of my mouth quirk upward, and nod graciously.

Good morrow, snake. Pray you do not choke on your own venom.

And what if we art blessed?

lizabeth would have made her first birthday, not with a celebration, but with a sigh of relief, and I might have relaxed the tiniest bit, knowing we had passed a milestone, that my child had passed the twelvemonth of infancy. But instead, on this day I walk the shoreline again, thinking on Psalms and sonnets and how words play together in rhyme and reason. Dr. Greenleaf had not brought his mother but a letter in her own hand, wishing me good health and sending a receipt for drinking vinegars and some tart crab-apples for jelly. I make the rosy sweet, stirring it over the fire, with Zuriel's help squeezing the jelly bag. We fill three small crocks, enough for autumn feasting. Angel and Ginger eat the squeezed pulp afterward.

I fill more crocks with black-berry preserves and my brothers reap the maize. I have been sorting the house for winter. I gather black walnuts and set aside the hulls; harvest the thorny black-berries to dry in the sun. I weave new lavender wands and make sachets of sweet rose petals, make rose-water and boil sheep's tallow and lye into soap.

But when the doctor comes, I take my hour for his treatment—which has come to mean walking and listening to him talk about the books he's read, or shared to me, filling my head with ideas and excitement like no other person has ever done me.

I cannot parse the new lesson Dr. Greenleaf has set me. We walk southerly, along the Jerusalem wain road, toward Mink Isle, a full hour's walk against late summer's still warm breezes, while the harvest is got in.

According to all I have ever learned, it is wrong. We are taught as Separatists that pleasure is sinful—to seek out delight is to expose ourselves to sin. Life is work and duty, duty and moil. God asks of us to be attentive to our fragile faith and to pray that we might be elected to salvation. To presume we are already saved, to let up for *even an instant*, is to invite Satan to distract us, to destroy us.

Yet if I understand Dr. Greenleaf aright, he says that God did *not* ask of us to be so dour and so vigilant against happiness. And this fit not with any lesson I had ere beheld.

"The Good Lord doesn't expect you to live your lifespan in misery."

I swing toward him in disbelief, my lifespan's learnings almost upon my lips to argue him from this nonsense.

"Nay, hear me out, Mistress Tacit. Have you heard of the ancient Greeks? Of course, you have—any educated creature has. Hippocrates, yes, in my mother's shop? Exactly thus, and so—prepare yourself, Mistress. You won't like this a bit." He glances at me, then plunges forth with shocking words.

"The Greek philosopher Epicurus asks, is God willing to prevent evil, but not able? Then he is not *omnipotent*. Is he able, but not willing? Then he is *malevolent*. Is he both able and willing? Then whence cometh evil? Is he neither able nor willing?"

The doctor ambles on a few paces. "Then why call Him God?"

The blasphemy in this statement—I almost choke with fear and wonder. I nigh expect a bolt of lightning to strike. I cannot even look at him but trudge ahead in the sand, then turn suddenly and look out to the billows of the sea, toward Barrel Rock and the other rocky outcrops.

Our God is a mighty God. A good God. Is He not? And yet—the Lord prevented not my beloved husband's demise, nor my infant daughter's. Nor my dear mother's, my infant brothers Israel, my elder sister Experience. He rather took them for reasons yet unknown to me. I have been angry, woebegone. I still do not understand, and wonder by night, watchful, wakeful, how my life so changed in an instant, and I follow still a path that no longer exists. I am rudderless in the storm.

And, I must own, I do not find solace and strength in my fear of God.

The doctor catches up with me, the wind blowing his words away. "Don't take offense at what I've said of Epicurus. He was wise before his time—and solemn. He maintained that a person can only be happy and free from suffering by living wisely, soberly, and morally. The faith of your childhood has also told you to live wisely, soberly, and morally. But has it never offered you *happiness*—? Nay, only fear."

This gentleman is not wrong. There is so much right in his words that they surely must be blasphemous. I feel I am hearing my secret sinful truths spoke aloud for the first time. I glance up at him and meet the gray eyes squarely. They hold wisdom, good humor, and—something more. He makes a wry face and continues.

"Hear this, then. Why not live as you have done, and—rather than expecting the worst—*damnation and doom*—live with the expectation that *all will be well*? Does not the Lord have that power? A wise woman of the Lord once said, 'All shall be well, and all shall be well, and all manner of things shall be well.'"

Which woman had said that? I shrug at him, querying.

"Julian of Norwich, aye, a *woman* of England, from before the Great Reformation, who prayed and taught and sat with the Lord. There is much wisdom in the world if you will not hate it as 'Popery' or 'pagan,' Mistress Tacit." He makes little mincing fingers at the offending words.

How dare he mock these beliefs? And yet, he mocks not at me—just the ideas.

If all should be well, then—all would be *well*? I feel something form together in my breast that I have not hitherto known—that the world is meant to be something beauteous, not always so terrible. If I can but see the beauty, the joy of living, might I not be more reverent of the Lord and His world? What if we are not doomed, but blessed? My mind cannot embrace this. Or can it? I need more time to consider this perspective, mull it like long-stirred wine.

Can we live in this world without a black cloud hovering overhead? Is it possible? I am curious. I am willing to try. I sense the stain of my melancholy fading, and a thing akin to hope begins to rise.

Dr. Greenleaf smiles down at me, the wind pulling his brown hair from its queue. "There are more ways to see the world than through the myopia of this tiny hamlet. Come. Let us find more of your shells."

We walk again, picking up scalloped shells as I find them, lading my apron.

"Did you know that the thinkers of the world, the learned men, have begun a taxonomy of creatures and of plants? In Europe, there is beginning a great age for knowledge. I should like to be there to learn it at their feet. All things will be classified according to their type—not unlike Noah and his ark—you've heard of *him*, I presume?"

I snort. But of course, I have. Every child learns to count by pairs with that beloved story.

The doctor bends to pick up a whorled snail shell, glossy and iridescent, and an indigo mussel. "You see that these mussels are akin to the scalloped shell—both are two halves of the whole. They come in pairs, like Noah's animals. But this whelk—this sea snail—it is a singular shell and has no other half. It grows in a circle and ever larger the longer it lives, like a tree. We say that they are both seashells, or a kind of sea-*creature*, if we are exact, and yet they are different.

"See here the razor clam." He picks the straight, finger-shaped clamshell from the wet sand. "It also grows in pairs around its creature, and yet it is a different shape. We can also eat them, so it's like, and yet not alike. And all of these shelled-fish are sea creatures under the ocean, under the orders of the Lord God. There is a taxonomy, an order, to all that seems random, that seems chaotic. And it is good.

"And there are the birds, the fish, the furred beasts—cats, dogs, horses, cattle—and mankind—we who people the earth. There is a taxonomy, an order to it all. God in His heaven, we down below, insects and reptiles beneath our feet. Each in its place, with its mandate and its duty. The cat to its mouse, the mouse to its grain, the grain to grow another sheaf of corn, to feed the birds of the field, to feed us."

He offers to me the three shells, and though they aren't scallops, I open my apron, and he drops them in.

"As many different shells as there upon a shore-strand, there are ideas about God, and what He wants of us. Your scallops are not the only shell. There are others—equally as lovely and as useful, or just plain pretty to look at. All made by God. All to the good. '*And we know that in all things, God works for the good of those who love him, who have been called according to His purpose.*' Do you recall that verse?"

Of course. I have read it, though Parson rarely preaches the *good* news from the Epistles.

"It is in the Epistle to the Romans. Ah, you do know it! The Apostle Paul has many wise things for us to hear—and he does not speak of Hell and Damnation. He speaks of Love. And again—'*God is love; and he that dwelleth in love dwelleth in God, and God in him.*' The Gospeler John tells us that. And I believe him with my whole heart."

I am the Wanton Gospeler.

We pause at Sandy Beach to look out at the swept grains of sand and the dome of pale blue sky. A few scattered board houses dot the dunes amid the scrubby pine trees. Behind us lies the quaggy bog of the Little Harbor, mete only for small craft. Over the shallow water, a line of geese arises, honking to their destination southward.

The doctor turns to me, and I feel he is going to reach for my hand. He almost does, it seems, but dusts his hands and folds his arms instead.

"*God is love,*" he says again. "I believe in that, and I believe in you, my good lady. You have grieved, you have been punished for *expressing* that grief, and *that*, in my learned opinion, was wrong. It boils my blood to think on it. I wish for you good health and a whole heart, and I—."

He stops suddenly, and whips off his hat, rubbing a hand through his wind-blown hair. He coughs and does not continue.

I feel the truth deeply wedged in his words, a recognition almost of something I had wondered, had secretly thought for years. I have never doubted the religion of my father and mother, but why must it be so dour, so drab, so punishing, so lacking in ruth? When the Savior told us that God is our Father, the Bible did not show me that man—I see that my own father is kind, forgiving, loving despite my many faults. But God-the-Father in the Bible is a terror, if the Separatists are to be believed.

What kind of God silences a person for a twelvemonth? What kind of church believes its god requires that? I no longer trust the elders and their decisions—they serve themselves *(silence that troublesome woman!)* more than the Father God I long for, as kindly as my own dear papa.

What, then, should I do—believe against my better judgment, or disbelieve and risk Hellfire? 'Tis a dilemma I do not wish to explore, not yet. I am still broken. I am—but what was he about to say when he stopped? What other path does he tread?

"Shall we turn about? Let the wind buffet us home? Tally-ho, then, good Mistress Tacit." He shakes back his windblown hair and claps on his tricorne again, giving me his sidewise smile.

My apron is heavy enough. The razor and whelk lie brightly among the brown scallops. I shall keep them to think about his lesson, and mayhap there is a declaration underneath it all.

Mayhap I am a goose-girl with a broken heart and empty arms, but methinks he might be a little in love with me, and I had best stop it where it stands.

The fruit of the tree in the garden

I try to tell Father that I have no need for the doctor anymore. When Father asks me how goes our meeting, I shake my head and draw my finger across my throat, wave my hands and wash out the conversation. I want no swain, neither Daniel Greenleaf nor Jacob-Wrestling, and I am over my head in philosophy for now. I enjoy the doctor's company, tis true, and he is a clever—and a not unhandsome gentleman. But though a Protestant, he is not of our faith, he is not of our town, and I am not for him. Certainly not.

Mayhap after this penance has passed over me, there is such an Ebenezer or Ezekiel, some George or Zebediah, who knows the ways of our congregation, who seeks salvation the same as we do here in Hingham, who will desist in speaking of grand cities and taxonomies and God as love. My God is righteous and strikes fear where He finds sin.

There is no other way to believe. I am living proof of what happens when joy is the goal, and love is the lubricant. May my husband and daughter rest in salvation, and may God have mercy upon me.

But my own father, deliberately or perversely, does not understand, and he disregards my plea to be let alone.

"Has he got your goat, daughter? He is only teasing you. Behold your cheeks—they are full, bright apples. Your skin is bright and smooth! Your eyes are sparkling! You are the picture of health. Dr. Greenleaf does you good; he does you very good indeed. Let us have no more of this charade and mum-show, my child."

So I may not resist, it seems. The good doctor shall come a-visiting again.

Father laughs and pulls on his skullcap, newly knit by his special friend, Rebecca Lincoln, worsteds of yellow and red knit together that look clownish to my eyes, and a tassel at its end—a tassel! Rebecca Lincoln entreats us to join her on Saturday nooning at her brother's house for a meal, and we go, and there is so much laughter and cooing that I am enraged, and stew in my own juice. But no one notices, because Silence is golden, is she not? Jacob-Wrestling joins us at table and says not a word to me but gazes upon me with calf-eyes and I feel an hundred years old. Lord, save me from the green yearnings of puppies and bull-calves.

And just as perversely, I long for Dr. Greenleaf's sensible discourse again. Who is the moon-calf now?

*　*　*

IT IS TIME FOR PICKING APPLES, and so to the harvest under a rippled light cloud overhead. *Mackerel sky, mackerel sky—never long wet, never long dry.* But toward the orchards we go, Roger and Bethia, Jazaniah and Nathaniel, all of my sisters, and even Father comes for an outing away from his loom.

"I' truth, it eases my bottom," says he, clowning to rub the ache out of his seat. But the malady pains him, and Mr. Henry prescribes more wine and an occasional tot of rum, with bleeding or leeches to follow if no improvement. I shall ask Dr. Greenleaf to see him next visit, I vow, before the old apothecary kills my father to heal him.

My brothers have delivered a wain full of fresh pine-straw from our woodlot to the neighbor's orchard up at Turkey Hill, and it awaits; Father drives our wain, full of our newly scoured apple barrels. This first load is for eating apples. Bethia and I will take turns picking or laying the apples in fresh straw layers in the barrels, with nary a bruise, or they will rot. These apples must last us the winter, firm and juicy. The next load will be for drying, and the last loads, bruised or not, for the cider press. Father has traded a set of new bed coverlets for five wain-loads of apples, however we choose to take them.

We are not the only neighbors come to pick apples this bright morning. The young Henrys are picking, as are the Hobarts, all my little nieces and nephews, the new constable and his family, and several others from the congregation. All of the women have rucked up their petticoats and sleeves to the elbow, bent to the work. Even the magistrate, Sir Fellows, is come to pick apples, or leer at the young women, perhaps to politick among his constituents, such as we are. He has a lifetime appointment so what we think matters not; however, he has made a showing, which is something, is it not? I turn over these thoughts as I lay apples in pine-straw at the bottoms of each barrel.

Roger has pitched several forks of straw into the wain and I am stooped, setting each apple as carefully as an egg in its nest. A bruised apple will spoil the entire barrel, and Father's apple and cheese at nooning or before bedtime will not last beyond the first month of true winter. It is hard work to bend and stoop over the rim of the barrel so many times, and I am grateful to stop for a dipper of water when the boy comes around with a yoke and two pails. I smile at him and then at Bethia, coming with a full bushel. She sets the basket gently in the wain.

"Take a turn at picking, sister. I'll take your place."

I put out my hand for her to grasp and she climbs up into the wagon-bed. I have half-filled the two barrels already, so her job will be easier, less stooping. My back aches but I ease it and twist a little before climbing down to earth. I stack two empty baskets, sturdy willow bushel-sized, woven by the Natives down Scituate way, upon my hip and pass through the cheerful crowd.

My little nephews run past, shouting, "Worms, worms!" They are barefoot, their legs brown with dirt, and the boys hold bitten apples in each hand.

Someone takes up singing, the Negro servants and slaves joining in a rhythmic song, breaking into harmonies that sound as rich as a choir of angels.

> *Who's sitting 'neath the apple tree? Who's sitting 'neath the apple tree?*
>
> *Adam's underneath the apple tree, all day long.*
>
> *Who's sitting 'neath the apple tree? Who's sitting 'neath the apple tree?*
>
> *Eve is underneath the apple tree, all day long.*

Their voices buoy me down the leafy rows to a quieter stretch of laden apple trees whose boughs are bent and sway-ing over the ground. Round, red-striped apples fit into my palms, juicy, ready to bite, though the air is vinegar-sour with spoils, crawling with ants and yellow-jackets, on the ground. I fill the first basket and lading halfway up the second when I hear my name.

"Widow Marsh. Imagine finding you out here, in com-pany." Sir Fellows, his face damp with perspiration, stands aside, hand on his hip, fanning his face with his plumed hat. When I see him, he sketches a little bow, mocking me. "You make a pretty farm girl. With a lamb and a crook, you'd be the ideal shepherdess."

What tripe. Why should I not be here, working? I cannot believe he is come to make merry with me when I am at my duty, laboring for the family, like the rest of the townsfolk. I keep to my task.

The magistrate takes a lace-edged kerchief from his pocket and pats his damp face. He steps forward now, playing the rogue. He looks all but a pirate today, without his periwig and minivers.

"Cat got your tongue, Widow? I believe you caused a *foxpaw*, as it were, deprived me of my little game, when your husband was nigh, last Election Day. But he's no longer constable, is he? Laid in the ground this twelvemonth or more. My condolences, goodwife."

I stop picking apples. I look straight at him fanning his pink pockmarked face, sick rising in my gullet. I step out from under the overhanging branches. How dare he speak of David? The stub-faced worm.

"What, not a peep? Oh, indeed, the hen has been silenced. Not a cackle, nor a crow from thee, not a feather to fly with. Eight months now, by my reckoning. Whither goeth your pride now, my fine lady?"

I could spit at him if I dared. Indeed, I do dare. But I won't give him the satisfaction. He is desperate for me to squawk, so he might have the pleasure of punishing me, loudly, and in public, again. What I wouldn't give to smack his pompion face.

He steps nearer still. If I were a shy girl fresh from the dame school or off the boat from England, I might be caught in his claws. But silence has taught me a few lessons. No one hears what you do not say. His hand reaches for my waist, my elbow, as if to help me along, right into his arms. He means to disgrace me while giving pleasure to himself.

I step into the lane between trees. I can see our wain and Bethia in it, far down the end of the row. I could cry out and be contemned.

But instead, I clap my hands together, sharp as I would chase a loose hen from the peas, and it echoes down the row. I gesture and wheel my arms, describing nothing, gesticulating with fingers and making such facial expressions, which all amount to nothing. I have no silent language, just a few simple signs. What need, when I have speech? But for all appearances, it looks as if I am giving the magistrate a piece of my mind, or casting up a spirit upon him. Bethia looks up from her labors and climbs down the wagon.

I point at Sir Fellows, then finger sign into my palm, as if writing something, smack my open hand against my inner wrist, snap and then sweep my arm around. I am pantomiming a screed at him, bringing down the imagined insults in my mind, and blowing them toward him. Mayhap it looks as if I am bringing down a magical spell upon him, a curse. Mayhap I am.

"What, you are mad? Lunatic! What say you?" The man's face grows pink again, as Bethia and Roger approach. My father follows.

"What ho, Sir Fellows?" Father dabs at his brow with his own plain kerchief. "Daughter, what matter?"

"Your daughter is touched by the heat," Fellows tells him, his disgust evident. "She is raving with her hands at me. Take her home, out of sight, before someone calls her possessed, or worse!" He claps his plumed hat back upon his head and kicks dust as he walks away.

Father takes my hand. "Pray, sit you down. Are you quite well, daughter?"

I pull a linen kerchief from my pocket and dab the perspiration from my face. I can hardly keep from laughing. A cat may look on a king, and a silent woman may best a magistrate.

I am quite well indeed.

Tongue-tied

Withal, the apples have been cut and dried, the apple-butter crocked, the cider pressed. Crane-berries and wild grape are gathered and dried. The pompions are rolled into heaps in the stable, and my onions cured, braided and hung. It is cold enough to slaughter the hog, and we share in Roger's beasts. I spend a week with sweet sister-in-law Bethia at her kitchen, chopping the meat fine, mixing the spices, pounding the peppercorns and bringing along herbs from Mother's garden: marjoram, parsley, rosemary, sage, summer savory and dill. We brine the haunches and the bacons, and smoke the hocks and the ribs. In the end, we have enough smoked meats for a winter, and we have a share of Nathaniel's beef as well.

Ginger will be snug in her stable with haystacks blocking the wind, and the hens make a home for themselves in the rafters, where the air is warmest. The cow's milk grows thinner and we stop churning for butter. I have salted away many green beans, and pickled and crocked dozens of eggs. When hens are cold, they stop laying until spring.

Zuriel has been my shadow over the summer months, as the sun has shone, but as the days grow short, she has been kept close to her own hearth, for study and sampler-work, and to curb her wandering ways, I imagine. I espy her at

Sabbath service and she comes to find me as I go to the wain after service.

"I wish I could come out to see you. It's hateful at home." The girl whispers to me under guise of petting Ginger's cheek. "She won't let me out of her sight. She is a witch!"

I step back, shocked. I wave my finger at her. *Don't say that! It's dangerous to mock such things!* I glance around to see if she was overheard.

"I don't care. She is. She hates me, and she—she hurts me. I hate her." Zuriel has tears in her eyes, and I look at her hands. They seem fine, but—I stroke my own arm, and point to Zuriel's. She nods, then shakes her head fiercely. "I want to run away. I can't stand it. She's evil!"

I hold my finger to my lips. Evil? Mayhap, but in this church, in this town, accusations may only earn you punishment. Speak the truth at your peril. I hate that Aphra is hurting my dear friend, but I don't know what to do. With my hand on my heart, I look Zuriel in the eye. *I will try to change it, see what I might do for you,* I mime, but she doesn't understand, and I am helpless in the vise of my punishment, and in the law that says a man's family are his property, and he might do what he wish to them. Even unto their deaths, per the command of the Holy Bible.

And her step-mother comes a-looking, with a face like a red lobster, and away they go, punisher and victim, and me helpless as a babe in a cradle to aid her.

On the way home, the wain rattles and Father remarks, "I see your little friend the Hobart girl bid you good morning."

I look around. No one can hear me. I pull my shawl over my face so no one might see my lips move, and I softly utter the first words aloud in some ten months, "Father—." My voice rasps as a crow caws.

"Dear Heaven, girl, hold your tongue," he hisses between gritted teeth. "Don't you know what you are—"

"The Hobart wife—Goody Hobart. She beats the girl," I murmur behind my shawl. My own voice sounds as strange as foreign music to me.

"Not your concern, nor mine!" His tone, between teeth, is a slap of rage and pain. "And if I hear another word from your lips, I shall set you out in the roadside and leave you to the world. Mercy, daughter, what you have already cost me— not another word. I pray you *silence*." His words cut me like the pillory-lash a year ago this month.

I sit tight and bruised next to him on the jouncing seat of the wain in silence the remainder of the ride. *Zuriel, my poor little friend, there is nothing I can do to help you. I am as much a prisoner here as you.*

I hold Father's hand as I climb from the wain and show him I am sorry, holding my heart and making a sad face.

But he misunderstands me. "I can't help her. I can only help us, and I can't protect you the next time, girl! Be still, for once, take your medicine, and let it come to an end. I pray you, leave it!"

He turns his back to me and unbuckles the harness, muttering gently to Ginger, ignoring me.

I retreat to the house, tears falling unchecked. My words hold no power, and again I have been told: *No one wants to hear you. Be silent.*

It is a year now since my daughter's death and my trial for blasphemy, and the tenth month of my silence. As I feel at this moment, awash in the memory of my beloved dead, and in the shame of failure in this one additional transgression, I could stay silent forever. There is nothing I can add to conversation, as my father has told me, and, I firmly believe, no information anyone could possibly want from my lips.

But, it turns out, there I am wrong again.

A summons

November last is best forgotten. For months I have felt mortification when villagers see my shorn hair, who saw me publicly whipped like a felon, my bare flesh exposed to any passersby. I know the Pilgrim fowl clucked and whispered from the crowd, come to witness my humiliation as a *Blasphemer* and a *Wanton Gospeler*, and to jeer from behind their cupped hands at me; the cleft stick was forced into my mouth as if I were a spitted hare. I bore the humiliations because I had nowhere to go, and I owed my father the duty of seeing it through. I embarrassed my family, cost my father real gold, and spent a portion of my widow's third on fines, for expressing my anguish aloud.

A good wife holds her pain in her heart. She does not dare to speak it aloud, or question God.

I had been disobedient.

But the year has turned, my wounds healed, though my tongue is still bridled. I have broken my silence for only one request, and it bore no fruit. I can now count the days remaining in my sentence, but as the year wanes, I find I have become so accustomed to my silence that I do not really mind it, and I no longer carry the sentence as a burden; rather, I embrace my world, and no one expects me to opine. I swim through, silent as a fish. I have imaginings, but I needn't share what I think. I have found that my eyes may flash my meaning well enough; a single eyebrow can tell an entire tale.

And perhaps I will keep my silence from choice for the rest of my days as a *feme sole*. At least as a widow, I may own property and sign contracts, unlike when I was a girl or a wife, *feme covert*, chattel of my father or husband. I have my remaining widow's third in silver, and I can live on it a long while. After a score of months grieving, I am no longer the broken widow, and though my losses will always cut me close, I find I can breathe again, sleep again, and even, by this stage in the year, gather my jaw-length hair into a small queue like a man. Time does heal, and this, too, shall pass.

I have read books aplenty this past year. Since Dr. Greenleaf delivered his books to me, I am a more thoughtful woman. I think deeply on many topics, and have given the faith of my childhood serious contemplation—and, I must own—found it wanting. I have no plan to make a change, not yet, but as I sit here, my knitting needles flashing in candlelight, I begin to think I might want to see Boston Town, I might want a fresh start in another village, or a city this time. My beloved husband and my daughter will lie forever in Hingham, but I might lie elsewhere, when my time comes. Mayhap in England, or on the other side of the blue mountains.

Upon the Sabbath next day, I see neither Zuriel in her new black gown, meet for Sabbath days, nor her step-mother; I don't miss the latter, feel only relief that her eyes do not contemn me as usual. Nonetheless I miss my young friend, one of few folk I genuinely care for in the town, and I worry lest more poker-burns or pinch-bruises appear under the girl's sleeves.

The new week surprises us: Hooves on the road, a message for Father. Without declaiming the message to me, he dons his warm cloak and stocking cap, gloves himself in warm wool, and rides away on Ginger in the frosty air, both their breaths puffing like white smoke. I tarry in the keeping room by the fire with a shawl and the poems of Elizabeth Thomas, a literary woman whose long verse sets me adrift in a daydream of English towns and country-sides. But it is difficult to pay it the attention the verse deserves, whilst wondering at my father's secret errand out in the cold day.

He returns as the light is fading and I have just lit the lanthorn and candles in the keeping room; my sage and butternut pottage and Indian-corn bread are prepared and waiting to serve after evening prayer. Father turns in at the post and takes Ginger to the stable for her rubdown and a bait of summer's marsh grass. He bustles in and hands his garments to me, coming to the fire to warm his chilled hands, toes, and red nose.

I long to ask him what is amiss but bide my time. He will tell me if he pleases.

"I hardly know where to begin, daughter," says he at last, turning his back to the fire. "Only this—Goody Hobart has been accused of *witchcraft*—by her own daughter! Aye, *Zuriel*, the very one. The girl shrieks and babbles and claims she has been tortured by the great Satan—and put the house in an uproar. It is so very like the old Salem business of '92 that I cannot know what to think. Can it be troth?"

I would have been speechless had I speech, but I put my hand across my mouth in case I blurt out. I have seen the burns, the scars. Torture, aye, but not by Satan. Is Goodwife Hobart a witch? I have many unkind thoughts about the vindictive woman, none that I would venture to share. My own grievances are my private thoughts. I believe her a terrible, spiteful woman, a bully, a shrew.

I have some inkling of Zuriel's actions. I always thought the girl a sensible one, for all her rebellion against her step-mother—in spite of it, or perhaps because of it. Zuriel must be wise if she dislikes her sharp-beaked step-mother.

But the cry of *witchcraft* is chilling.

Locals have not forgot the terror of 1692 and 1693, though it was before my birth. My parents lived through it; my brother Nathaniel remembers from his boyhood and has told me tales that curl my toes. All the citizenry older than thirty years remember where they were when the cry went up, when the perch snapped beneath the gallows, their neighbors or kinfolk swinging. Every adult here recalls how anyone could be impugned, suspected, and how quickly the accused met the scaffold. How honest Judge Sewell apologized afterward, saying that they'd been wrong, too quick to contemn. How the ringleader recanted some years later, still claiming Satan worked upon her to fabricate her tales.

The other girls have never recanted nor admitted their enchantment by the ringleader, and have lived lives pretending the terror never occurred. Those trials and hangings left a black smudge over the village of Salem like a swamp-reek they can never vanquish.

The Rev. Hobart was one of those elders on the panel and has styled himself an expert on demonic possession. Could he mayhap see evidence of that in his wife, or in the symptoms of his own daughter?

I gesture, *How? What?*

"There is to be an ad hoc meeting tomorrow of the council of ministers. Hobart will ask for another to take his place at meeting while this issue continues. He feels he cannot separate himself from the investigation otherwise. Under his very nose! He is personally inveigled into this, and though he is thought an expert on the matter of demons and imps, he is overwrought by his wife and daughter's involvement. He called in Fellows to oversee the matter. So we shall see.

Hobart asked the goodmen of the village to support him in this recusal before taking action. That was the up and down of today's assembly."

The news is shocking. Who would have expected witchcraft to reappear, when we are churchgoers and good citizens of the Crown, and wise to such dramatic demonstrations? Who would have thought of such a fantastic slip to superstition and fantasy, after tearing the colony apart just thirty years ago? People forget, or have never known, and so, it seems, we must fear and pray and hope wiser heads and real proof will prevail this time.

As for myself, I don't believe it. Goodwife Hobart is a terror in her own way, but maleficent? And Zuriel possessed? I do not credence either report. Knowing her as I do, more likely the girl is sulky and rebellious. I think to visit Zuriel in her bedchamber, to see the child and learn what she means by this, but when I wish to accompany Father next day, he refuses me.

"I don't want you anywhere near this, hear? They got you last time. I'm not going to let anyone near you, and I don't even want you in the village until this passes. Stay home, and if anyone comes by, look away, go inside, do not even look in their direction. This frenzy—this contagion—I can't bear it again, daughter." There is real fear in his eyes, real agitation in his voice.

I beat my breast lightly and nod to show I understand. I will stay away in case this panic taints me and my family as well. Once called to the floor before the Magistrate is enough for a lifetime.

It is a long day of waiting, mending cloth and working the dough, but outside the hoar is creeping and it is sore cold abroad. I stay by the keeping room fire hoping for good news, and I long to put a quill to paper to write to the doctor, ask his thoughts. I miscount my stitches and worry the day through until Father returns by candle-lighting. I bring woolen house shoes and a fire-warmed cap to him upon his arrival.

"Pour me a stoup of spiced wine, daughter, and I'll warm myself before I commend my tale to you." He is the picture of a cozy man, his Rebecca-made tasseled cap jaunty, but for his face—drawn, tired, pinched from the cold, and deeply concerned.

In a few moments I bring the winecup, and Father warms his hands around the flagon before taking a sip.

"It were a right pickle today, Silence. It were Bedlam. The quidnuncs of the village gathered to gossip and scold and shriek and sniff at brimstone, bruiting about the Devil and the preacher-man. It turned my gut. Half the congregation ready to swear that Goody Hobart is a scold and a huzzy, and the other half preaching her an angel sent from above and the daughter is the perjurer. Then the goodmen of the village try to settle the business, with their scolding wives overleaping the discourse, as if they had a say in the matter. It were a circus and a shambles, and I don't want any part in it."

He sips his wine. "That warms a man from the inside out. I thank thee, daughter." He sighs, a long, tired sigh.

"And when there were another debate; they were calling it retribution on the town for the last go-round with the Devil. 'Salem's vengeance.' And the other half of those folk were calling it Parson Hobart's fault for bringing it to our village. It's a right tangle, daughter, I'll not deny it."

I had not shewn the girl's wounds and bruises to Father. I wonder if it matters. A parent may discipline a child; spare the rod and spoil her, saith the Bible. But Zuriel's wounds were too severe for my taste. The finger-shaped bruises, the bubbling blisters haunt my heart.

"The council has set it back a sennight to gather evidence and witnesses, and set the court of the magistrate and elders on notice." Father tips his flagon back and swallows the rest of his wine. "That will do, girl. Let me have a basin of pottage and I'll take myself to bed soon."

I carry his flagon to the kitchen, and fill the redware bowl for Father's lentils. Trouble is nigh and it causes alarm for all of us. I take his basin and spoon to Father, and caress his shoulder when I serve him. Poor man. He has suffered enough without having to face this ugly scene again.

Holy orders

I hear the hooves approaching and hope it is Greenleaf the doctor, but it is messenger Neriah, the wharf boy who sells clams, on a borrowed horse. The sealed paper is addressed to me, *Mistress Silence Marsh*, not to Father. My hands shaking, I pick open the wax seal and unfolded the thick paper.

> *Mistress Marsh ~*
>
> *You will come before the Magistrate and elders on Tuesday, the 13th of November, forenoon, as witness in the discovery and prosecution of Goodwife Aphra Hobart, accused witch.*
>
> *By order of Magistrate George Fellows, Esq.*
>
> *~GEF~Esq.*

It feels as if I am the one called to account again. I am weak in the knees, heart pounding, head throbbing, all my well-being flown up the chimbly. I am sick in my middling, and sit upon the settle quickly before I faint. Father comes from his bench at loom to see who had knocked up the door. I hand him the summons forthwith.

"What is this? How can you witness when you are under an edict of silence? What freak or fandangle is this?" he asks, saying aloud what I feel. "What make you of it?"

I cannot answer, gesturing helplessly. I will neither witness for nor against the woman, witch or no. I am peccant, unable to give voice. Fellows and the church elders have sentenced me thusly; they have contemned my words.

But my ire grows by the moment. They have taken away my instrument of communication—my voice—in their haste to punish me. And repenting at their leisure, they now recall and expect me to sing? To assist in their prosecution? I will not.

I take the twelvemonth of silence seriously, if they do not. I own my portion—I broke the peace in the sermon and in the church; verily, I did question my faith, ranted at God. I was guilty. I admit it freely now. Let me serve out my sentence without this noisome request. It is beyond the pale to even consider.

Nay, Lord Magistrate, I shall not speak.

I rise from the settle to face Father, my knees no longer weak. I wag my head emphatically. *Nay.*

"I haven't an idea on how to proceed, daughter. They must release your voice if they would bid you speak."

Nay, I shall not. I wave my hands to erase the tableau. I shall not speak, not under pain of fire. His Worship Sir Fellows and the lords of the congregation have played with me and found me wanting. And I will be their plaything no longer. If I do not respond, I know they will come for me. If I do not attend, they will come. Powerless I might be, and voiceless, but I am not brainless.

I mime to Father, *Will you write for me?*

"Sweeting, I know not if that will help. Why do you not write it yourself?"

Nay, I cannot speak. You will write it?

Father sighs. "Daughter, you would tempt the very Devil. Stubborn as one of Lincoln's mules."

He goes to his writing desk and opens the front, finds his quill and mends the nib, opens the stopper to the ink, and sets his writing paper at an angle.

"Very well, daughter, let us begin with,

> To the Lord Magistrate of Massachusetts Colony, Sir George Fellows, Esquire, and Elders of the Separatists Church of Hingham,
>
> I bid you Greetings.

"How does that for opening, daughter? They cannot fault us there."

I agree.

"What next?"

I cannot speak. I will not go. Nay, I shall not go! I mime this.

"Very well, calm thyself, daughter. Fear not—I shall leap directly into the fire and say him nay, shall I? On I go." Father dips his pen again and continues, speaking the words aloud as he writes.

> "In writing a response on behalf of my daughter Mrs. Silence Marsh, widow, she must respectfully decline your summons..."

"So far, very well, aye? Carrying onward.

> "...as she is under a penance of silence for a twelve-month, under your own jurisdiction, and may not speak aloud until her sentence complete, December the 31, at midnight, or dismissed altogether.

"Does that suit you, daughter?"

It does not. The entire situation is preposterous, has been from the beginning, and yet I have no choice, swept along like last year's leaves in the spring freshet. Nevertheless, I nod to Father, for he has helped me keep my silence by writing for me.

"They won't countenance it, you know," he says, his expression grave. "They will take you bound in a wain to the meeting-house to make you speak. They might bring out the cleft stick again. Are you very certain this is what you wish to convey? 'Tis? Aye, I thought so. You're a bushel of troubles, young miss, Lord help us all. I'll close this and let it fly."

> "...*Respectfully written by*
> *Yr obt svt,*
> *~Isrl. Winslow Nichols,*
> *Weaver~*"

He sands the page and leaves it dry, then carefully makes the folds and seals the missive tightly with a blot of our yellow beeswax. He impresses it with his signet ring, IWN, and blows on it to harden the seal.

"Mistress Marsh, you are in God's hands now. Let us pray for your deliverance from this new evil."

Before the court

I have refused the summons, but I know I shall have to attend. I don my warmest gown and woolen petticoats and prepare early this Tuesday morning, with an extra shawl for the cold meeting-house; Father stokes the portable foot-stove with hot coals when we see the King's men arrive. I have packed a cold meal of apples, cheese, and some buttered bread in a folded cloth in a trug. I carry my prayerbook and kerchief and nothing else, my blue woolen mitts for my hands.

I shall end the day in a prison cell, likely, not for anything I've done, but for what I will not do, in the name of God.

An ensign of His Majesty's Army in his scarlet jacket raps the door. Father opens it.

"Good day, Weaver Nichols. Is your daughter the Widow Marsh within? We are come to escort her to court. She should come along prettily, or we shall have to bind her."

"Indeed, she is. We expected you."

"Then why didn't she simply go to the meeting-house, sir? Saved us the trouble?"

Father sighs. "She is a grown woman and is following her conscience, sir. I cannot force her to go against the previous ruling by the Magistrate."

"He'll sort it out before the court. Come along, mistress."

I fasten my cloak and take up my trug-basket and shawl. I nod a brave "very well" at the soldier, and Father follows me to the wain with the footstove. They allow him to place it up in the wain on the floor, and one of the soldiers helps me up to the bench behind the driver. The soldiers take to their mounts as the driver chirrups the horses onward. We turn about and the team begins a slow jog toward the village. Father catches up soon after on horseback.

There is a crowd outside, hoping to hear what goes on within. Nothing so exciting as a witchcraft trial has happened in our hamlet in many years, discounting my own trial. I do not recognize many of the faces and wonder whence they've come. The wain stops and a Redcoat helps me down. I am no prisoner but feel like one. The crowd, staring at me, feels more frenzied than last year when I was sentenced to silence.

They part to let me pass. The meeting-house is full, each bench jammed with congregants and townspeople, faces I know—my sisters Charity and Thankfull and their husbands; Mr. Henry and his wife, even the Widow Reeves—and many I do not know. The murmurs rise ever louder as townsfolk crane to look at me and opine.

The ensign leads me to the front and bids me sit and wait my turn to witness; a second Redcoat brings forth my foot-stove. The room is frightfully chilly. We will need the heat.

"Oyer, oyer, this tribunal is in session. Oyer, oyer."

Magistrate Sir George Fellows comes in wearing his long white periwig and his winter gown, black with white miniver collars. Four ministers follow him, similarly wigged and robed in their Sabbath black; one is familiar from Scituate's meeting-house, the other three are strangers to me. One is quite elderly, almost doddering. I wonder if he were present at the witch trials of '92 and '93.

A local nursemaid, a white woman I know only by sight, comes in with Zuriel, the girl looking distrait and younger than her fourteen years, her hair braided long like a child's. Her sleeves hide her wounded arms. The pair come and sit next to me on the front bench. Zuriel turns to me, teary. I take her hand gently, wary of her bruises. She takes mine up and weeps silently against the back of my hand. Poor girl. I pity her. She does not seem possessed to me, but sad and over her neck in excitement. I want to ask what brought this to a head. But I should hear soon enough.

"Let the accused be brought in," Fellows calls, and a soldier brings in Goodwife Hobart, dressed in her black, wrinkled clothes, none too fresh from a week in the straw and dirt of the prison cell. She is a pitiful sight; the once-proud head of the accused no longer holds its superior tilt. They bring her to stand, front and center, before the board of judges and elders. She looks pale and afraid despite her sour expression. I like it not.

"Goodwife Aphra Hobart, born Aphra Hawkins, you are hereby called to answer the accusation of practicing sorcery on your step-daughter Zuriel Hobart, daughter of your husband the Rev. Ezekiel Hobart, and upon the Widow Silence Marsh.

"On the day of Saturday, October the 26th, you did curse the Widow Silence Marsh, born Nichols, in your home, before your child and husband. You did utter a curse toward Widow Marsh and accused her of charming your daughter away from her home.

"On the night of October the 26th, you did burn the skin of your stepdaughter with your red-hot fingers, as Satan's instrument of torture, cursing her.

"On the Sabbath day of October the 27th, you did miss Meeting and instead placed diverse satanic curses upon your daughter and Widow Marsh; your daughter by law was forced to skip meeting and was found beaten and hysterical in her chamber by her father after service had concluded, saying that you had joined with Satan to beat her.

"You were heard on several occasions to be repeating Widow Marsh's name and cursing her by diverse witnesses thereof.

"Aphra Hobart, what say you to these charges?"

"I call them untrue, your worship. There is not a shred of truth in the girl's words. She lies. She does not honor her mother." She looks over her shoulder at Zuriel with venom, and next to me, Zuriel immediately cries out.

"Oh, nay, I pray you believe me! She hurt me, she hurts me—"

Behind us, around the sides of the meeting room, I hear the cry rise; other women join in, filling the air with shrieks. I sit mutely, of course, but stunned into shock by the howl of noise. I cover my ears. Eventually Zuriel and the others settled down.

"Order, order, order," Fellows calls out, his voice booming. "Goodwife Hobart, I will not allow you to cast your eye on the victim. Pray do not attack her again! You are on shaky ground, woman. Ensign, ensure she does not cast her gaze at the girl. A blindfold if she do it again."

Fellows looks at his papers and coughs. "Let us call forth the first witness. The Rev. Ezekiel Hobart."

The parson steps forward, not six feet from his wife, but does not look upon her. "Aye, your worship." He stands erect, but he has lost his righteous expression.

How humbling is the Lord. These two are in the place of shame this time, and a part of me feels grim satisfaction that they can see how quickly the fickle crowd shifts. But I like it not; the room is filled with a dangerous air.

Fellows does not mince words, even for his longtime peer and friend. There is no mercy in a court of witchcraft.

"Did you witness the accused cursing the name of Mistress Silence Marsh in your home on October the 26th?"

"I did, sir."

"Can you repeat the words she said to us?"

"I prefer not to repeat such language, but as it is the wish of the tribunal, I will." The parson hesitates and shifts his feet in clear dismay. "My wife said, 'Damn that woman to Hell.'" He covers his face with his hand. "In my own home. I am most heartily sorry, my brothers."

"And in your Christian home, your holy and sacred home where you keep the spiritual health of the congregation in your own two hands, did this not seem to you as a stroke of evil?" Fellows bores in, trying to find the proof.

"It seemed an indication of a great stress upon our home, a great stress indeed." The parson stumbles over his words, unwilling to call his wife a devil. He seems to own it as his own spiritual failure.

"Why did you not correct this, as husband and father to the two parties?" Fellows loves to browbeat the husbands and fathers of this congregation, it seems, though he has neither wife nor child.

"I did not feel I could control her rage. It seemed—outsize for the crime." Parson Hobart coughs. "Pray pardon me."

"What was this domestic 'crime,' as you call it?" The magistrate's voice cuts to the quick of the problem.

Parson Hobart coughs again, a nervous habit. "My daughter rides her pony on solitary jaunts through the countryside; she is not wild, but she takes her exercise by horseback, and I believe she sometimes calls at the Nichols home for a dipper of water before returning home. My wife was distressed at the state of the girl's clothing after such a jaunt, at the wasted idle hours, and at the blowsy appearance of the girl's hair after such a ride."

"And did *that* strike you as unnatural?"

"My daughter's appearance was as it would be expected after such a ride. Ah—I felt the reaction to my daughter's coming in was outsize. When my wife learned that Zuriel had stopped at the Nichols house, Aphra became like another person. She fell to cursing the girl and the Nichols house and Mistress Marsh in particular." Parson Hobart, unable to lie, rises on his toes when he doesn't want to answer straightaway. "It was, ah—not what I care for in a wife."

"So you would call it *unnatural*."

"Mayhap, mayhap." He rocks on his toes again.

"That is a failing of your duty as husband and head of the household, minister, to stop such malapertness, and we shall treat it accordingly. Thereupon, did she afflict your girl, with the Devil's help?"

Hobart visibly winces. "I know not how she did it. But she afflicted my daughter with red hot coals."

"In what manner?" The sharpness of Fellows' tone with the parson I have known these many years hurts me almost physically. I am knotted as an old handkerchief inside, recalling my last venture before the court.

Parson Hobart clears his throat and stumbles onward. "Great burns upon the girl's arms, and great purple and yellow bruises, your worship. I did not see Aphra anywhere near my daughter, but Zuriel began to scream, and she pulled at her sleeves and showed me. My wife does not deny doing it. She full admitted to me she had burned the girl as punishment."

"Are those wounds still present?"

"They are." The parson looks not upon his wedded wife. Goodwife Hobart crosses her arms and harrumphs but does not speak out in denial.

"Let us see these wounds." Fellows knocks on the board. "Girl!"

Beside me, Zuriel startles, scrunching down as if to hide. The nursemaid whispers, urges Zuriel to sit up straight.

"Come forward, child. Zuriel Hobart." The magistrate's tone is not softer for a child, but just as sharp. I expect he is waiting for her to appear before him newly married, so he might jeer and leer at her. Zuriel shyly walks to stand before the board, close up next to her father.

"Stand back, Parson. Show us your wounds, girl," Fellows says. She steps forward to show the poker burns and the thumb pinches. Some of the burns are oozing and crusted, while others are dark red scars, puckered skin. Zuriel's hands shake and she presents a tragic figure, her small form trembling before the tribunal and between her parents, one for her and the other against her.

"Doctor," the magistrate calls aside.

I hear a bustle in the crowd off to the side wall, and, to my surprise, Dr. Daniel Greenleaf comes to the front and examines the girl's wounds. He seems different to me, in this house of worship; taller, older, wiser, not so boyish as he appears on the shore, neither so rakish as he does astride a horse or casting drakes into the surf. His glib philosophy and subtle mockery are absent. In their place I see the man the rest of the villagers of Hingham town see: A learned man of Harvard, with family and breeding, his back straight, his mien sober, and his reputation unblemished. When Dr. Greenleaf speaks, the people listen. He looks over Zuriel's wounds gently, front and back of her arms, then straightens and addresses the board.

"Lords, I can assure you as a doctor of medicine that these are indeed burns and brands, and the bruising looks fresh and inflicted by a pinch or harsh seizure—the finger marks are there, and there," he indicates. "I cannot say by whom—," he raises an eyebrow. "Only that they are not self-inflicted."

"So you cannot say that these were inflicted by Goodwife Hobart or by a demon or an imp?" the elderly Scituate minister asks.

"The injury is the same." Dr. Greenleaf answers carefully, but I know how little he credits the idea of witches and demons. "It is impossible to tell by what means she was injured, but I ask leave to treat her wounds as soon as possible, so they do not suppurate. The girl needs care."

Turning to Zuriel again, Fellows asks her outright. "Who gave these wounds to you?"

"My step-mother did," Zuriel says softly, sniffling a little. Goodwife Hobart scoffs and huffs and tsks.

Fellows looks not askance at the fuming step-mother. "And has she done this before?"

Zuriel nods.

"Speak up, girl," one of the ministers barks.

"Aye, many times."

Dr. Greenleaf speaks again, unprompted. "I concur with that statement. The girl has many old burn scars. There is evidence of repeated burns with a hot iron or poker." Although he has never turned to look at me in the meeting-house, I feel he avers this as a gift for me. He is protecting Zuriel as I would. My heart warms to him.

"Sit you down, girl." Fellows dismisses her with a wave. Zuriel comes back to the bench, curling against me, sniffling softly. I wrap my arm around, as safe as I can make her, press a clean kerchief into her hand. As he also turns to retreat, Dr. Greenleaf meets my eyes but there is no wink or playfulness in his face. He is deadly serious. He holds my look long enough to assure me—of what? That he is here, that I am not facing the court alone again, that I might not be in the danger I feared. I cannot know without more time to ponder.

The trial continues.

"Aphra Hobart, did you attack your step-daughter Zuriel Hobart with a hot poker or iron, in the duty and throes of Satan?" The Scituate minister takes the lead.

She does not know what to say, I see, and she is caught in their trap. If she acknowledges she has done the deed, then she implies she has used witchcraft, and she is contemned. If she denies it, they may prosecute her as they had done the accused witches of Salem. Those who confessed to witchcraft back in '92 and '93 tended to survive, while those who resisted the accusation fought it to their deaths on the gibbet.

Goodwife Hobart twists her hands together and shifts her feet, appearing guilty as any convicted criminal. "I cannot say, your Worship. I cannot say."

The room erupts into shouts of, "Witch! She is in Satan's throes! Witchcraft!" and calls for order. Zuriel covers her ears, as do I. I have become too used to silence, and the crowd's noise distresses me.

Fellows lets the hubbub rage, perhaps all to his own purpose, while referring to his papers. I see him look about the room, and the glitter of excitement in his eyes. I watch too long, however; suddenly his eyes lock to mine and I see him, into his core. Though his mouth quirks not the slightest, I see his almost sensual arousal. Fellows enjoys the hubbub. He holds the power of the fickle crowd in his hands, and he savors it. I realize all of this and see my peril. He sees me watching, knows that I know. His eyes pierce me.

I have been angry, but now I'm afraid. I break our gaze and tighten my arm around Zuriel, then realize that if he sees this warm affection, what might he do to her? What might he do unto me next? I have scorned and bested him thrice at least, and he won't suffer it again.

Fellows snaps his fingers at the Redcoats to shush the crowd. They move about the room, calling, "Oyer, oyer!" It takes some moments to calm the crowd again.

Fellows assays another tack. His voice is firm but soft now, as if merely curious. "Goodwife Hobart—you have been heard cursing the name of the Widow Silence Marsh and muttering her name like a charm or curse on many occasions, by your husband, daughter, and people of the town. What say you to this charge?"

"I say nothing. It is true but it was *she* worrying at my mind, not a curse. It is she! She's the witch!" Goodwife Hobart turns and points at me, her voice shrill as a proud hen after laying. "She's the witch. She has charmed my daughter away from me. Burn her! Hang her! She's a witch!"

The hungry crowd takes up the cry as quickly as a flame eats paper, and at once the chamber echoes with cries and shouts of, "Witch, witch! Hang the witch!"

"Silence," Fellows shouts at her, at them all, but that is my name, and I startle like a new lamb, spooking Zuriel under my arm as well. My reflex draws the eyes of Fellows toward me again. Now he smiles, just a flash, like the crazed faces that the harbor boys carve into pompions and light with a candle-stub at All Hallows.

"Sit you down, Goodwife Hobart. Widow Marsh, pray you step forward." His voice curls toward me like smoke.

Zuriel squeezes my hand and I rise, my stomach fluttering and my legs aquiver. I fear now, for Zuriel, for my father, and for whatever pain lies ahead of me. But also, the quiet voice inside ponders—what matter? Why not be a witch, aver it and let them hang me? What matter after all this? I long for release.

Goodwife Hobart glares from her bench at the side. Her eyes prick at me, but I have nothing for her—neither contempt nor pity. Just—nothing. She has made up her own bed.

"Widow Marsh, setting aside the issue of your written refusal to come willingly to testify," Fellows digs in. "You are the target of Goodwife Hobart's curse. Young Zuriel Hobart has charged Goodwife Hobart with cursing and afflicting you. What say you?"

I look directly at him and spread my hands in an *I don't know* gesture.

"Come, come, speak up." He snaps at me, laying his trap for me as well. "A very serious charge has been made against Goodwife Hobart and your testimony is necessary. Speak." He pretends to have forgotten the very edict he laid upon me a scant twelvemonth ago, waiting for me to fall into the snare.

I look back at him and point to my mouth. I put my hand over my mouth, and gesture at the tribunal, then back at my mouth. I shrug. *I cannot speak aloud.* The buzz in the room grows again, the fickle crowd restless for blood.

"She is correct, your Lordship," Parson Hobart says in my defense from his bench. His wife hisses at him from her place across the room. The other ministers discuss among themselves, murmuring.

"Precedent," says one, and "only a woman's testimony" and "but circumstances dictate," quoth the others. Their mumble joins the hum of the crowd. If these were my bees, buzzing about the skeps, I'd call them hot, and wait for a sunnier day, a calmer hour, to approach them. I'd wear my kid gloves and muslin veil and smoke away the more aggressive scouts. Here, I have no such armor.

Fellows acknowledges the paradox to his brethren. "I realize, Widow Marsh, that you are under a twelvemonth penance by this tribunal, through the end of December, but with this grave case before us, as magistrate, I insist you answer me."

This will not stand. For me, now, it is a matter of principle. They had insisted. They stripped me and degraded me on the village green, cut off my hair and clipped my tongue; they made the entire village sit in a solemn day of humiliation to pray for God's mercy and help because of me. We had fasted, all of us, on scant sips of water and dry bread, and listened to the jeremiad of my sins.

And now, when 'tis inconvenient, Fellows would simply erase, or even merely pause, the conviction? Does that not mean the penance was of Man after all, and not of God? And these are men of faith?

I stand taller. *Nay*. I will not speak.

The villagers burst into noisy confusion again. Onlookers debate my silence, some with ribald laughter, and others with genuine astonishment.

"Oh-ho, who shall wear the miniver now?"

"Speak up, woman! Cat got your tongue?"

"Get the branks—that'll teach her when to speak and when not to!"

"She cannot speak until the twelvemonth is up! It's God's will!"

"She's been bewitched and cannot speak! Goodwife Hobart has cloven her tongue!"

"Let her alone—can't you see she's been punished enough?"

"Send her to the ducking stool! She'll speak up!"

In the hubbub I stand firm, afraid of what is to come, but certain I am in the right, even if it means something worse than a year of silence. Even as I've questioned my faith, I know what God asks of us and what Man desires, and they are two different demands altogether. Noise swirls like a winter sea, threatening to submerge me. In the storm, amid the shrill voices, I see Dr. Greenleaf approach the board and speak quietly to the magistrate. Fellows listens, considers, and nods, then turns to the others at the board and they confer beneath the hurly-burly and confusion.

"Order, order!" Fellows cries out, and the Redcoats stand to attention, which helps calm the room. "We will have order here!" He condescends, as if suffering a great patience with me. "Now Mistress Marsh, I have a word from Dr. Daniel Greenleaf, who is your physician, is he not?"

I nod agreement to that.

"He tells me we can ask you yea or nay questions and you will answer, thereby honoring your sentence and yet assisting the tribunal at its decision. That will satisfy the board, and mayhap it suit you as well?" He speaks with a nasty sneer but I have won the point, fair play to Daniel Greenleaf.

It does not suit me; all I want is to be let alone, and not dragged into further bedlam, but I agree: *That will do.*

"Very well then. Did Goodwife Hobart curse you?"

I don't know if she did. I wasn't there. I gesture to show that I do not know.

"Have you been afflicted by mysterious pains, freaks, ailments, or foul dreams and imaginings?"

Nay, other than my melancholia, which has all but dissipated through the year, with thanks to Daniel Greenleaf. *Nay,* I gesture that I were not so afflicted.

"Have you been afflicted or visited by Satan in any of His forms?"

Nay.

They speak among themselves again. "So it seems you have *not* been afflicted nor affected by curse?" Fellows seems not to believe me.

Nay.

"Even though your mother, your husband, and your infant all died last year within a sixmonth, you would not say you were cursed?"

I so utterly do not expect that—my knees crumble beneath me and I fall to the floor, gasping. I stare at the floor, then up at the magistrate and his board. *I don't know.* Mayhap. I never thought it anything other than mischance and sorrow. The nursemaid comes forward to help me to my feet and stands beside me lest I faint again.

"The board is of a mind that even your outcry in the church last year was arranged and impressed upon you by Goodwife Hobart. If you do not understand it, I think the board can decide that for you, Mistress. We have seen demonic possession before." Fellows and his brethren speak again to one another under their hats and shuffling papers.

I cannot process what I'm hearing. It was not witchcraft. She is a cruel woman, but I have acted of my own accord. And I have been punished for it. So how can they call it witchcraft now, after I have suffered a year's worth of punitive recourse? And if I had been Goodwife Hobart's *victim*, why was I singled out for penance? It is a terrible conflation of disparate concerns.

No, I don't know, it can't be! I try to express it—but I will not speak. If I let this go on, if I speak aloud, I will wipe away the vestiges of my faith, what little I have remaining— if my sentence were the result of something else and I were punished for naught, if my censure could have been given with so little forethought as to the cause or result. 'Tis wrong in every manner. And without speech, I cannot voice these thoughts—I won't.

Further, the Hobart woman is not a witch—she is a vicious, insecure scold. She burned, shook and pinched her step-daughter out of jealousy and spite, and if the girl remained in the home, one of them would end up dead.

Yet if no one clears the air, Goodwife Hobart might be hanged as a witch. What can I do that will stop these proceedings?

"If you will not answer us clearly, then we are again at a standstill. How can you witness if you will not speak? If the yea or nay response does not suit, then pray speak up!" Fellows, pretending at the serious nature of the case, taunts me.

Nay, I shake my head again. I will not answer aloud. Our eyes hold. I will not break before him. He silenced me, and now at a whim dares me to speak. He is not my master. Only God, if there is one, will master me, not this self-important power-lord.

Fellows cannot break me. He hasn't yet. His eyes narrow. He knows my mind. He counts the times I have bested him, cheated him of a slap and tickle, a public or private humiliation. He will not brook it, I know.

"Enough!" he pounds the board. "Mistress Marsh is withholding information and refusing to speak. You are in contempt of this hearing! I order a thrice-ducking at the stool, immediately."

"Ha!" Aphra Hobart crows from her place at the side, forgetting her peril. "She's a witch!"

"You will join her for a thrice-ducking, Goodwife Hobart. Immediately. Perhaps it will loosen both your tongues." Fellows slams his hand on the board again loud as a drum, and the meeting-house erupts in shouts, wails, crying aloud, and pandemonium like to Babel.

Accursed with spitting and shame

Fellows calls the Redcoats, who come forward and bind Goodwife Hobart's hands, then mine, a leathern strap bound around them in front of me.

Daniel Greenleaf is before the board, arguing in his firm voice. "I urge you to reconsider, Lordship. There is no cause for such primitive treatment of a recalcitrant witness."

"Are you a Doctor of Law as well as of medicine, sir? What a blessing we have in the college at Harvard, that a fellow might get two educations for the cost of one. A pettyfogger as well as a leech-master." Fellows snaps his fingers at the Redcoats to carry on. "Thank you for your service, Doctor. You are dismissed from the court."

"This isn't over, sir." Daniel is lost in the wrangle as Goodwife Hobart and I are jostled through the shrieking, shouting crowd toward the double doorway.

I catch Zuriel's eyes, her face pinched white with panic.

"Nay, nay," she sobs. "I'm sorry, I'm sorry! I take it back, I take it all back!" No one listens to a mere girl.

I know Zuriel did not intend to make mischief for me. Her step-mother has not liked me since I came of age, equal or higher in status than she, and being caught out publicly as a storybook cruel step-mother has not appeased the woman's wrath. Anyone who burns her child with a red-hot poker, repeatedly, intentionally, deserves and has earned the label of wicked step-mother. I have no blame for Zuriel and hope she can read my face and know that I care for her. The girl broke when she was pushed too far, and this helter-skelter has been the result.

The girl takes up my cloak and holds it tightly, like a small child with a favorite blanket.

We are buffeted out the doors amid the clot of villagers. Both of us women are roughly pushed up into the back of a hay-wain, where we must stand and hold the wooden stakes with our hobbled hands. I cannot even look at Aphra Hobart, who has made a muckle of her world as well as mine. Cruel scold, who hurt my sweeting friend Zuriel and cares not what havoc plays out. I almost pity Parson Hobart for his poor choice in wives, but he deserves what he has got. Zuriel, my little friend, is the bearer of the consequences between us all.

In the bustle is my dear father, in consternation with Parson Hobart and Sir Fellows, the three arguing over what is to become of us women. Brother Nathaniel fights his way through the crowd like a swimmer crawling upstream to join our father. Redcoats surround the crowds, with bayonets and blunderbusses at hand to quell the shoving mass. I try to find Daniel Greenleaf, my physician, my teacher, my book-bringer, my catechist on the shore, my spyglass upon the greater world, but one tricorne looks as like another from here.

The November air is frigid. I long for my cloak but I doubt I'll be given even such a mercy now. To the ducking pond—I'm sick at the thought. I cannot swim and I cannot breathe underwater like a fish. I cannot cry out or be found in breach of my punishment. I shall surely drown and be found silent still when all's over.

The sky clouded over whilst we were in the meeting-house, and now it smells of coming snow. The soldier who drove me here this very morning again chirrups the horses. The wain rattles down the slope toward the Home Meadow and its pond, where the ducking stool awaits malcontents and tale-bearers and married couples who cannot get along.

The crowd jeers us as we pass, and now harbor boys and loafers follow along behind, as if at parade for a pagan holiday. Sailors off one of the ships have come up to see what the fuss is, and they join the throng following, with a pair of rattling silver spoons and a Jew's harp twanging for our procession. A harbor boy bangs his tin bucket as a drum.

"Constable's wife in trouble again! She deserves it!"

"He broke my nose with his cudgel, I'll get her good for that."

My father-in-law Ephraim Marsh's rough ways with the yobs has festered all these years, and revenge is in their hearts. It is cold comfort for any of us. I'm shivering, with chill and fear.

"It's your fault," Aphra Hobart snipes as we rolled along the wain road. "If you had let that girl be, none of this would have happened."

I refuse to look at the woman. She is poison. I pity Zuriel her father's household arrangements. We are all wounded when our mothers die.

"It's your fault." She says it louder. When I still do not respond, she shouts, "Witch, witch, she's a witch! Silence Marsh is a witch!"

The followers raise the shout—"Witch, witch, in the ditch!" They hurl objects at us: dirt clods, rocks, clumps of wet horse dung. I duck my head and try to avoid the missiles, but I feel a clod hit my shoulders, something cold and soft like mud hits my back, and a stone cracks at my head, cushioned by my coif, but painful, nonetheless. I hide my face behind the hay-slat, anxious I should not lose an eye or another tooth. I know Aphra Hobart feels the sting; she cries out whenever they hit her, and, for entertainment's sake, she becomes more the target than I. *The squeaky wheel gets the grease*, say the sages.

We ride through the village and inward toward the pond, passing a little saltbox house with smoke drifting from its chimbley. A woman stands before its closed door, a broom in her hand, her thick shawl pinned at her throat. She neither waves nor shouts, but I hold her sympathetic gaze—my friend Prudence Henry, as I am carried past in infamy. But soon she, as helpless as I am, is lost to view.

Suddenly the wain halts. I feel the sharp jerk against the rough wooden spars and hear a voice I recognize. The crowd drops into eerie silence. I crane to look.

"Leave her go. She is neither witch nor sinner. She has already done your bidding. Leave her go."

The Widow Mary Reeves stands in the middle of the road, her arms spread wide, to halt the procession. She covers not her face this day. The sight of her, fully revealed, unashamed of her marks—she stands like some kind of pagan queen in the road, her blue-marked chin some sort of mark of faith, holding the assembly. The proverbial pin could fall and we should hear it land in the dirt.

"Leave them go. Settle this in a civilized manner. Are you not civilized? Can you not proceed without superstition and fear? Are you *savages*?"

I don't know what I expect, but it is not this lone woman holding up the train. One woman facing down the Redcoat army, a Magistrate of Massachusetts Colony, and a slate of ministers from the Separatist Church, like some holy woman of Bible times, a modern Deborah facing down 900 chariots of iron.

The only sound is a horse stamping its foot, the creak of the wagon. The moment seems endless. Am I to be set free? Am I—

The ensign slaps the rein and the horses move forward a step, another step, right up to the Widow's breast, and it seems she will be run down, but someone pulls her roughly from the side, she is pulled into the sideline, and a roar goes up. The pail-banging drum begins again, and the jeers continue all the louder. "Witch, witch, in the ditch!"

The train continues toward the pond, unabated and without further contest.

My gloved fingers, my toes in thick stockings and shoes, are already numb before we arrive at the little pier built at the edge of the green pond, with the stool's thick beam and arm over the water. The wain halts, the horses rattling their harness, His Majesty's soldiers sitting in wait. There are still chunks of dirt and stone flying toward us from the hands of bait boys and fishermen's children, until a stone strikes the ensign; with a sharp whistle between his fingers, he calls the Redcoats to face the crowds.

Fellows and his court of elders arrive horseback. "Get these people back," he scowls at the soldiers. "They are interfering with court business!"

Using their horses as shields, the handful of soldiers pushed back at the crowd, their red coats blazing brightly against the drabs of the citizenry. Out in the mix is my father, my brothers and brothers-in-laws, the Lincoln brothers, though I hope not their sister Rebecca. Perhaps Zuriel, and I hope, mayhap, Daniel Greenleaf. Perhaps Widow Reeves followed? My time for pondering is suddenly over.

I am slipping from the hopeful place where I have dwelt these past few months, under the doctor's care, and this day I might lose what is left of my life. I have done my duty. I have done their bidding. Why take every last morsel of dignity and worth from my person? I am holding on; I am trying to hope.

But when I see Fellows' face, when I see the men in the crowd jeering, I see their wives' faces, too, and the young boys learning from their elders, and the young wives like Prudence, and the older women like Widow Reeves, the girls like Zuriel, and younger, know it as well—this is how they teach us that women are worthless. We are here to make babies and scour and cook. Our pain is nothing to them. Our losses. Our hopes. Our dreams are for crushing. Our personal desires are evil. Our lives are meaningless to this church, this town, this people.

And this is why I will not give in.

I could have spoken up, at any time, and said my piece. I could say it right now, whatever they want, but I am just too stubborn, I suppose. And this is not even *my* trial. Aphra Hobart, child-abuser, scold, I must own, is as much a victim of this woman-hatred as I, but it were *her* trial, her misdeeds, not mine. Yet all of them are content, it seems, to watch me swirl down the millrace as well. I am between my headstrong will and the village's utter disdain for any woman's being— our thoughts, our hearts, our fancies.

We are bundled off the wain by two soldiers, pulled up none too kindly when we stumble, and hauled like balky calves across the grassy banks of the glebe to the pier. The wife of one of the elders takes away our hats and coifs, showing our hair like common guttersnipes. Mine is short, of course, but Aphra's is long and stringy, a thatch of mud-colored hair. The crowd begins to hoot and whistle at us as if we are cheap scuts. The wife takes our shortgowns and petticoats, our gloves, shoes and stockings, leaving us in our shifts, unshod. The villagers hiss and clap and hurl base insults, forgetting that they are Christians and I am one among them. Mud is cold beneath my feet, the stones sharp.

"Turn her away," Fellows orders the soldiers to put me, reluctant witness, in the seat facing away from the hectoring people. They tie my hands at the wrist to the arms of the chair, my feet bound to each leg. Her back to mine, Aphra Hobart, accused witch, is bound, the like as I was, her feet as well, but she faces the crowd, who still throw stones. She cries out when their aim is true.

Deshabille, we wait, shivering, while the half-dozen soldiers spit on their hands and begin a singsong shanty:

Then was the Scold herself,
In a barrow brought,
Stripped naked to the smock,
As in that case she ought:
The neats' tongues about her neck
Were hung in open show;
And thus unto the ducking stool
The famous Scold did go —
And thus into the ducking pond
The famous Scold did go!

The pail drum-beats and the Jew's harp and spoons keep time. The sailors have joined the song, and it becomes a festive air.

Sometime before the verse ends, the chair rises into the air on the crane and swings out over the water, to great jeers. Stomach turning, I look at the gray sky, and over the greenwood at the water's edge, wishing I could fly away, wishing I could run into the woods for safety like a fawn. The water rises beneath me and down we plunge, into green mucky water fouled with duckweed and goose manure, icy, so cold my head throbs, and just when I begin to panic for air, the chair comes up out of the water, with a roaring shout at the banks, Aphra Hobart coughing and blubbering in the seat behind me.

I breathe again, once, twice, then down again, the green horizon obliterated by black water, slimy reeds and old feathers, dead leaves, a smell of rot and—up again, half-frozen, water streaming from my shift, and Aphra Hobart sputtering behind me as she struggles for breath. Harbor boys and goodmen and fishwives hoot and screech like hounds at bay. I might screech myself, but there isn't time.

The last plunge gives me almost no breath of air, and with half a breath I hold it. But the last dip is the longest, and I cannot hold my breath; I cannot stop myself, silver bubbles slipping from my mouth and nose, the lambs in their little postholes, Ginger's trough, the rough waves, my hands tied away from my mouth, unable to stop the scream that would kill me.

I lose my vision then; my ears fill with roaring, and I am weightless, rising into the sky, colder than a body should be, my ears and eyes full of the stink of pond water, my mouth puking and belching it out, the taste of frog spawn, duck shit, mildew, damp rot. It's in my hair, in my nose and my teeth. I fall from the chair when untied, my face in the mud. Someone wraps me in a blanket and carries me, witless, to a horse, bundled up across the lap of someone I know not, an arm around me, a swift trot jarring me, my feet like ice; I retch over the horse's neck, gasp to get the taste, this poison, this injustice, from my lungs, my very gut, until I taste only sour acid and bile.

In a strange bed

I wake some time, mayhap even days later, in a fresh shift, in a bed and blankets I know not. The chamber is very small, just a bed and a chair with a small table between them. Next to me a strange woman, yet somehow familiar, nurses me with tisanes and bone broth, a hand on my fevered pate; sometimes she croons a sweet lilting song under her breath. Where we are, she will perhaps tell me, but I care not. The rest is but a blur, and I'm content to leave it. I close my eyes again and dream of a long-necked bird like a pheasant or a pea-hen fighting a great serpent, and wake when the morning sun comes through the east window.

It has snowed, and the brightness of the sun outside makes me squint my eyes, closed for so long. There's a ruff of snow on the windowsill, and a cold, fresh breeze comes in through a finger-width gap where the pane is pushed open. This cannot be Mr. Henry's house, and I am surely not in his care; a closed-in room with a fire that fogs the windows would be his preference. I feel weary, and my chest hurts from coughing, and it feels heat-flushed as well, no doubt from a hot mustard plaster. Indeed, I see the now-cold cloth, stiff with mustard and flour paste, in a wooden bowl on the table. No bleeding bowl and fleam to be seen, for which I am grateful.

I blink and focus on the chamber wall, papered in a green stripe, plastered at the ceiling. The base-board is varnished a glossy red maple color, and the furnishings are costly, imported from England or beyond. A small wooden box on the table has an Oriental design of a dragon and a bird of fantastic imagination, something out of my fever dreams; I must have seen it while waking in the night. The eyes of the dragon are small green stones, and the bird has red gems for eyes. Every feather and scale on these beasts is carven. I wonder who has been to the Orient for such a treasure?

I linger for a while between waking and sleep, recalling how I have come to this place. The chair is empty now, but a half-knitted stocking lies in the chair, needles akimbo, poked into a skein of fine creamy wool. I like well the soft feather-bed, the pillowbere as smooth a linen as ever I've slept upon, hemstitched linen sheet edged as neatly as a bee makes her comb. I cough, a deep, brassy note.

The door clicks and swings open on smooth iron hinges, and a tray appears in the arms of—Mistress Greenleaf, my distant friend. Tears spring to my eyes on simply seeing her face, her dimpled cheek and her warm smile.

"Now you're awake," she says, playfully scolding in her tone, and glad to see me, I believe. "You have come through the worst, I believe."

"Whe—" I stop myself with a cough. My days, the silence! I look up at her, my hand across my mouth. *Where are we?*

"We are in my daughter's house." Mistress Greenleaf sets her tray on the little table and feels my pate with her warm, smooth hand. "Mistress Richards is sister to Daniel. He brought you here on his horse and cared for you himself. Then he came for me to help when it got worse. I was grateful to be here when you needed me so."

Mistress Greenleaf has such a pleasant, low voice, and I recall her humming in the night, a comforting alto. There's something to her accent like her son's—more English than Colonial, as we'd call it, that I recall from first meeting her. She stirs something in a silver flagon and turns to help me sit up. "Here's some strong broth, dearest, and you shall drink it all. Then some special tea, then you shall sleep again."

With a fat bolster behind me, I am able to sip the broth, and drink it all, hungry and thirsty at once. It tastes very salty and rich with marrow. The apothecaress bids me drink her tea, which tastes of grass, but smells of lavender and valerian. I feel sleep coming on, but still my chest hurts to breathe. She helps me to make water in the China chamberpot, then back to the bed and under the cover. I want to sit up a bit longer.

I lean across my knees, coughing roughly into my hand while the kind woman straightens the woven cover and takes up her tray. At the door, voices—they come in upon Mistress Greenleaf's heel. My sister Thankfull is here with the good young doctor.

"Mistress Tacit, you live!" Dr. Greenleaf, still bantering with my silly nickname, beams down upon me. "My mother's panaceas are the true healers here."

I cannot greet them so politely, abed as I am, my loose hair too short for a bed braid and my nightcap strings untied, but I bow my head to show my respect. I grasp at my gown's neckline, a little aghast to be seen in such undress, by a gentleman not my husband.

Thankfull takes my hand and sits right next to me on the bed like a sister does, feeling my forehead, smoothing my hair aside to feel my cheeks. I turn my face away to cough, rough as a plucked fowl, unable to prevent my voice from sounding loud in the small chamber.

"Sister, you gave us such a fright," she says, her blue eyes bright with concern.

"Mistress Marsh, your fever has broken, and you're breathing well now, what a delight!" Dr. Greenleaf chuckles. "Such news, aye? How does your chest? Mother plastered you twice, once with onion and another with the mustard. You may have some blister there."

With an engaging entreaty from her son, the apothecaress smiles at me and leans forward to peek inside my nightdress, while Dr. Greenleaf gazes away out the window for my modesty.

"Looks well, that, a bit pink, but it will fade. Small price to pay for clear lungs, is it not? And you're blessed not to even remember it. We thought you'd slip away once or twice, did we not, Daniel? My son the doctor keeps me on retainer as his second, to opine when he is at a loss."

"I am never at a loss, Mother, and please, Tacit, do not listen to her. She's a curiosity—a woman dabbling in men's medicine, and she does it twice as well as any of us. She shames me with her brains and beauty." He turns from the window to laugh at her, or himself.

"Piffle! Now, Mistress, you had your valerian? Are you not sleepy? More rest will do you good, but I bid you arise as soon as you feel ready, a sennight perhaps, to begin your walks again. A green tonic will help your blood and bowels, meantime. I shall blend one for you for later." She stands by the bed, studying my face.

"Daniel did not tell me you were so improved in complexion. He said only that you were the strongest woman he had ever met." She feels the meat of my arm. "I think he meant your heart as much as your corpus. Don't sit up long now, lass. Lung fever is no laughing matter."

She takes my chin in her fingers a moment, a thing my mother used to do when I was young, and I believe she's judging me, and seems to find me acceptable. She rises from the bed.

"Your patient, Doctor. Mistress Lovejoy, let us give him the chamber?" Thankfull rises from the bed and passes through the open door, leaving us alone.

Daniel Greenleaf turns and sits in the chair, taking my wrist for a pulse and looking into my eyes. "Mouth open, if you please? Ah. Very good." He clears his throat, and proceeds. "I must listen to your breathing, I'll just—" he turns me bodily, like a stubborn child put in the corner, so I face the wall. Daniel Greenleaf leans his ear against my back, and I feel a warmth and fondness within me, as his cheek presses my back through the gown, that I haven't felt since my husband died and left me alone and grieving. I didn't know my blood could ever warm thusly again.

"Breathe normally, please, I want to listen to the lungs." His face feels warm against my body. I have not been so near a man in ages. A welter of confused emotions blooms within me, between weakness from my illness to shame over my limp appearance and a little warmth, flushing stronger, of something that feels wickedly like desire. He touches me and I flush. That is the one thing I did not expect.

"Very good. Aye, we'll leave it for the nonce. Your lungs are clearer now."

I cough again, sounding like one of Lincoln's mules, and he feels my forepate with the back of his hand like my sister had done, his skin bloodwarm to mine.

The doctor murmurs to himself, "Humph."

Waves of sleep break over me, but I so want to ask, *what happened?* I mime my hands being bound, and the see-saw action of the ducking stool, then fainting.

"Fellows should never have ducked you. He shouldn't have ducked either of you, certainly not on a cold day like that. He knows better." Dr. Greenleaf gives a grunt of disgust. "The entire trial was a sham. There's no such thing as witchcraft, any educated man would agree. It's barbaric!"

I want to lie down again but I think of Zuriel—I touch my arms where Zuriel had been burned, and I mimic her broken fingers, still minding my voice to be still.

"The girl's wounds? Oh, I tended her, no fear, good Lady Silence. My mother made her a healing salve. She used some of your beeswax—your sister Mistress Johnson brought some to give to Mother. You'll have to ask what she put into it, but the girl's arms are healing well. Any rate, her step-mother will not harm her again. She died."

I gasp, covering my mouth. My days!

"Aye, Goody Hobart has left this life. She took sick as you did, I saw her—alas, they stoned her pretty well beforehand, and a blow to the head, some pond water in her gullet, and a cold day? She sickened and died a few days ago." He scoffs, "Of course, quoth the villagers now, that she be innocent."

Aphra Hobart dead. I wag my head in wonder. What will happen now?

"I'll agree—she was innocent of witchcraft," says the doctor. "But a mother's heart she never had. Whether the Devil was in her or no, she was not a kind lady. And Hobart the minister must answer."

I'm not sorry she's dead. She was a poison to Zuriel—and to me, though I care not what happens to myself more than what betook the girl. I cough again, burying my face in my arm.

He touches my cheek again, then does an unexpected thing. He holds my chin in his fingers, as his mother has just done. He touches my tousled hair. The tenderness overwhelms me. I have missed tenderness so very much.

"Mistress—pray pardon me, I am outside of myself." He makes excuse. "Take your sleep now, and worry not."

He removes the bolster from behind me and pulls the covers over my shoulders, as if I were a child again. My eyelids are heavy. I curl between the warm linen sheets, drifting with the feel of his hand still on my crown.

"Sleep now, good lady, and I will visit you on the morrow."

The court sitteth again

"Oyer, oyer, this tribunal is in session. Oyer, oyer."
John Richardson, Esquire, a Boston magistrate newly appointed to serve Hingham, enters wearing a long white periwig and his black gown with miniver. Four ministers follow him, none that I recognize. The Old Ship meeting-house is full, congregants waiting to hear what shall become of the case of Goodwife Hobart's witchcraft and Zuriel's accusation—and the Widow Silence Marsh, penitent, in a case outstanding and held over due to illness and death.

All is a repeat of the last time we foregathered, minus the Rev. Hobart, and Zuriel at my side to witness, and the long board table before us all, ready to again sit in judgment. I am at hand as witness, again, not fighting but acquiescing to the summons. I will, however, not speak this time, no matter their methods. Perhaps I will not need to.

"Zuriel Hobart, a minor child, please come forward." Magistrate Richardson calls her forth. She leaves me at the bench and steps forward, with a confidence she did not possess just a month ago. With her blue gown and crisp collars, and her hair up under her cap, she looks older this day, although she is still the minor child they addressed.

"Miss Zuriel Hobart, you came before the tribunal in November with an accusation of witchcraft. Do you still make that charge toward your step-mother?"

Her voice is clear and true. "I do not."

"Your step-mother has died from her ducking, and some say that has proven she was not a witch. What do you say to that, girl?"

Zuriel holds her head up and speaks clearly to the panel, neither bashful nor awkward. "I do not say she is a witch. I told my father that she had worked devilment upon me, and had burnt me with the iron, and my father the parson took that to mean she had practiced witchcraft. I never meant she was a real witch."

"You are saying that your father the minister made a grievance of your cry for help? Tell us what happened."

"My step-mother used me harshly since I was a wee child. She brake my fingers when I was shielding myself from her blows," Zuriel holds out her crooked hand to prove her point. "She burned me, shook and pinched me many times. Upon that Saturday, I arrived home from my ride out upon my pony, and I had not even made visit to the Nichols house, as is my wont. My step-mother became convinced that I had visited the Nichols house and cursed me and Mistress Marsh, who is a dear friend of mine, and began to lay upon me with the red-hot poker. When my father came in, she uttered her curse again and I cried out so she wouldn't hurt me anymore. I had not told tales to my father, only taking my chastisement like a Christian child. My father had told me many times to honor and obey my new mother.

"But I confess, your worship, that I did not honor her as I should." She squares her shoulders, prepared for her penance.

"Aphra Hobart was a difficult woman, we have seen," the new magistrate says, looking at his papers. One of the elders scribbles his pen and parchment, keeping up with the testimony.

"As to the charge of witchcraft, we may drop that altogether, seeing as the accused has died. Nevertheless," Richardson removes his spectacles and addresses the congregation and villagers crowded in to hear the judgment, "I think it fitting now to admonish you, good people, to remember that there *is no thing such as witchcraft.* These are modern times, and there is no magic and devilry at play here—only God's foolish sinners, the weak in heart and mind. Let us have no more of this, shall we call it a delirium or a panic? Enough is enough. Come, good people." He brooks no rebuke.

Magistrate Richardson replaces his spectacles and clears his throat. "Now as to the other charges against Goodwife Hobart, of cursing, blasphemy and obstructionism, we shall also let those charges lapse, as there is no accused to be punished—rather, one might say she has been punished thoroughly enough." Richardson looks at his time-piece. He straightens his pages in an abrupt sharp shuffle against the tabletop.

He looks at young Zuriel again. "As to your confession of breaking the commandment against your parent, seeing that the parent in question is deceased, I will hand this over to the new minister at Hingham to discuss with you at greater length. We understand that your father has been recalled to Boston, and will be placed in a new congregation soon, elsewhere in Massachusetts Colony. If you do not speak with your minister here in Hingham, you may speak with your new minister about it in the new church where he is settled next. Or speak with your—ah, father. It is no longer a matter for this tribunal to address. But it is proper that you recognize your fault and do plan to make amends for this weakness, that's a good girl."

This gentleman has no interest in prosecuting domestic quarrels. Our congregation seems baffled by this turn of events, when they have been used to judging, accusing, and shaming all and sundry for their missteps, public and private. I am also taken by surprise and try to comprehend what I've heard.

Daniel Greenleaf, a row behind me, rises with his hand up. "Your Worship, if I may address the board?"

"Of course, Greenleaf. What have you to add?"

"I provide this knowledge, gentlemen, that my father and mother, The Rev. and Mrs. Daniel Greenleaf of Boston, would like to take Zuriel into their home for indenture—to learn apothecary, if the Rev. Dr. Hobart is amenable to such an arrangement. It will give him the opportunity to focus on his new assignment and living arrangements, and at no cost to himself." He speaks deferentially, but I know already that it isn't a request. The doctor, or rather, his mother means to have it her way.

This is a surprise to me. I would have squealed in excitement had I permission to give voice. From my bench I see Zuriel turn toward him with a look of sheer joy and excitement. In the weeks between these two trials, she and Mistress Greenleaf have become as close as kin. A chance to learn apothecary craft and live in the city of Boston were opportunities the girl would be twice blessed to receive. If I were to live in Boston, as I sometimes imagine, I could still see the girl and we could be as sisters then. I could not think of a better place for Zuriel to bloom into womanhood, far better than the indifferent household of the Rev. Hobart and whichever Separatist woman he'll choose for his next wife.

"We will advise the Rev. Dr. Hobart of this and grant our permission, if he is amenable. Anything else, doctor?"

"Only that I have treated the girl's wounds and she has healed well. She is lucky to get away without worse. Whatever your board may call it, that was *deviltry* to so abuse a child. Good day, gentlemen." He sits again, his participation complete, though I know he won't leave without bidding me farewell. I hold a small worry in my heart that I shan't see him again, once they remove to Boston with Zuriel. This thought grows bigger by the moment.

But the court has not finished on this day.

"Zuriel Hobart, we have rescinded the charge of witch-craft and thus the case is dismissed. Please be seated, child." Richardson waits while she returns to the front bench with me.

"There is one further charge in relation to this trial that needs attention. Widow Silence Marsh, born Silence Nichols, pray you come forward."

This is my moment. I squeeze Zuriel's hand gently, always mindful of her crooked fingers, and rise.

Behind me I hear the doctor utter, "Stand tall, Tacit."

"Widow Marsh, as regards the charges of witchcraft against your aggressor, we have dismissed the case and there be no further ado about it. But somehow you were entan-gled through, it seems, your friendship and kindness to young Miss Hobart. Do I understand correctly that you had seen the girl's wounds previous to the complaint, and were unable to stop the late Goodwife Hobart from harming her step-child?"

I nod.

"And you gave your testimony, such as you were able, without the use of your voice as stipulated under the decree and censure set you by magistrate Sir George Fellows in No-vember in the Year of our Lord Seventeen and Twenty-two, is that correct? Aye, and in direct opposition with the said penance of silence, you were also forced to appear to testify in the case?"

Again I agree.

"And by keeping the terms of such censure, you were charged with contempt of the proceedings and sentenced to the ducking stool, is that true and correct?"

Indeed it is.

"Aye, you were chastised for keeping your silence and in contempt if you did not." He clucks and looks over the parch-ments before him. He wags his head.

"Widow Marsh, I hereby clear the charge of contempt against you, although you were heretofore disciplined for it. I should like to rescind the judgment against you and clear you of any wrongdoing in that case. You were in a position of what the scholars call Hobson's choice—that is, on the horns of a dilemma, with no real choice at all. To your everlasting credit, you chose the more difficult path, of keeping your covenant, unfair though it be. For that, Widow Marsh, you are to be commended."

I will not say that he is wrong. I feel a deep gratitude to this magistrate for explaining my case so clearly, pressing my hand to my breast and nodding, as is my way.

"My predecessor here as magistrate, as you know, Sir Fellows, was recently recalled to England and I have undertaken to reassess his cases. And it seems to me that in your case, the adherence to a too-severe understanding of the niceties of law—well, let us say that you more than paid your portion. At this time," he looks down the board at the sitting ministers, "given the recall of the previous magistrate and the sitting minister of this congregation, I should like to nullify your sanction. Any further charges and overblown vindictive disciplines—." Richardson sighs, his blown breath fluttering his minivers. "Your censure—your silence ends today." He nods sharply, looking around the meeting-room. "It ends now."

There is not a pin's worth of rebuttal.

He looks kindly upon me, an unexpected quirk in his cheek. "And I should like to ask you one thing. Pray answer as you see fit, without prejudice, mistress. Do you accept this nullification?"

I hold my hand to my heart and nod from habit. Richardson cocks his head at me, quietly urging. He says not another word, but I trust him.

Then I cough, clearing my froggy throat, and respond. "Aye." Gasps and chuckles stir in the benches behind me.

The new magistrate smiles, as a kindly grandsire. "Very well. This case is also dismissed, and the court is adjourned." He nods sharply at his cohort as they gather their papers. "No more of this," he says to them. "It is beneath the court to hear such bygone, superstitious nonsense as this. *No more*."

I turn about and Zuriel sallies into my arms, squealing and laughing, still a child despite her new prospects. "You can talk, you can talk again!"

"I may." I am shy about my voice now, with everyone listening and gazing at me.

Father comes to put his arm about me, heedless of who can see. "I have missed your voice, daughter." He kisses the top of my head, a shameless public show of affection. "I am pleased, girl. Very pleased."

I find myself in the midst of a knot of family and friends who have helped me or held me up along the way, and, truth be told, some who have stayed in the dark edges, afraid to be tainted by my shame. I know their names. I know who has been with me, and who has shunned me. The Pilgrim fowl are always near at hand, waiting for crumbs to peck at.

But here's Prudence Henry squeezing my hand and blessing me with her own happiness, a rounded middling and her firstling child to come in spring. And Mary Reeves, her face barren of veil, her cape about her shoulders and a winter cap on her head, watches from the side of the room, her gloved hands gesturing a message of love to me, without words. My dear brothers Roger, Nathaniel and Jazaniah are near, teasing me about my voice and my silence, as brothers will, happy that the awkwardness and shame has gone at last.

"There you are, Mistress Marsh. I am so pleased for you," gushes Rebecca Lincoln, hard upon my father's left hand. "You did well to obey orders all this time. You were ever an example of blessed, silent womanhood." Ah, such a woman will be my step-mother, I can all but guarantee. I must surely move to Boston. Mayhap the good apothecaress will have me for apprentice as well.

Standing back observing all is Dr. Daniel Greenleaf, taller than most, his long blue cloak over his shoulder like some sort of knight errant, his breeches tucked into boots, arms at rest by his sides. He catches my eye and I am captured, then, utterly free at last to say how I feel, to think my own thoughts, to speak my mind, to thank him for helping me, for showing me how to be fiercely free in the world I had built for myself, and the prison inflicted upon me. His gaze holds me like a strong rope, a steady handclasp. His look seals my desire.

In this moment, I am, as it happens, speechless.

* * *

As the crowd disperses, Father goes round to get Ginger and the wain from the sheds, and Zuriel accompanies me thither, her arms around my waist.

"I don't want to let go of you in case you disappear," she keeps saying. She has been staying with Daniel's married sister Hannah Johnson, where I had recuperated, and now the arrangement is to change again. Zuriel will remove to Boston to the Greenleaf house, to abide with the doctor's youngest sisters and his mother, to take on her apprenticeship.

We return to Father's house out at Black Rock, where the Jerusalem Road jogs south, with Raven and Ginger tied in the stable, and my beloved sisters cooking up a feast. My brothers stoke the fires and pour beverage and laugh in delight, as near to a Christmas revel as we have ever had in dour old Hingham town. When the mulled wine is poured and passed round and drunk up, Daniel calls for attention.

"Everyone, please charge your cups again, prepare for a draught, because I have a pledge to offer." There is a slight bustle while Roger pours warm spiced wine and ale into cups and tankards. The scent of cinnamon and burnt orange peel fills the air.

"I should like to propose a compliment to the courage and resilience of one person in this room, someone who has been steadfast in her honor, deeply caring, fiercely independent, outrageously stubborn—," and here a cry rises as my brothers hoot at me, and I blush like Zuriel. "—and so much more than I can say in one breath. But to the woman who holds my admiration, my deepest esteem, and, I must own it—my heart. To Silence."

"Silence." The keeping room resounds with their voices, speaking out my name, my sentence, my sin, my release, my silence.

* * *

DANIEL GREENLEAF AND I MARRY IN JUNE, in Boston, with wine and cakes and ale, and a pair of old shoes dragging behind the carriage from the governance hall to our newly rented home among the fine folk of town. Rose petals from my mother's garden and grains of rice rain from the well-wishers; gold pennies fly from Daniel's fingertips, and the wharf rats and street children squeal and dive for them. My inner voice tells me I am safe now, and beloved by a man who truly sees and knows me, and that I shall bear blessed children and live long, with many songs and stories to tell.

I shall be silent no more.

Fin

Afterword

Silence Nichols Marsh Greenleaf was a real person, and so were the members of her family. Silence was my seventh great-grandmother, and the events of her life: losing her mother, her husband, and her newborn daughter in one terrible year, are true. In researching my ancestors' lives, I was much taken with what I consider the blessing/curse of names like Waitstill, Experience, Fear, Obedience, Freelove, Temperance, Charity, Thankfull—and Silence. Her name chilled me. What kind of name is that to live up to? What kind of life would you have if that were your name? The Puritans intrigued me, and I didn't want to write a book about witches, but the two phenomena go almost hand in hand.

I took Silence's life facts and her name, and put them in the Crockpot of my imagination, and let them simmer for a few years. I wrote a poem about it, I did a lot of reading, and in November 2021 I drafted a version of what became this story. What would happen if you were silenced for a year? Why would you be so punished? But it also resonated with me, because women are constantly silenced in our world, still today, not only back in Pilgrim days or pioneer days or all the days back to the beginning of writing and words. We are sick of being silenced for our thoughts, our ideas, and when we protest the crushing edicts that control our lives.

My response is that we will have our say, no matter how you try to silence us.

Although the surname of the minister Rev. Hobart is the same as a longstanding parson of Hingham, everything about him and his family and actions is fictional. There was no Zuriel or Aphra, no Mr. Henry, no Magistrate George Fellows, and no witchcraft trial.

But Daniel Greenleaf was my seventh great-grandfather, so I feel justified in making him intelligent, handsome, and loving. My eighth great-grandmother Elizabeth Greenleaf was indeed an apothecary in Boston—she is known as "the Mother of American Pharmacy." She opened a shop on Washington Street, between Court and Cornhill, near the corner of Court Street, in order to pay for her son Daniel to attend Harvard, while her husband the minister was away preaching.

Daniel and Silence went on to have eleven children, with six sons who grew up to fight in the American Revolutionary War. (Her firstborn son was named for her first husband, David). One of her daughters named a child for her, Silence Joslin, but there the name dies out in the family. I have never heard of another with this name, although I'm sure they existed, and I hope I never do. It seems a cruel attribute to put upon an infant—or a child of any age.

Like Silence, I, too, have lost a child, so I know her grief; as well, a community shunned me when I divorced my former clergyman husband. I know the feeling of being silenced, and I wanted to set that to record. I have been to Hingham, stood where the Marsh home was rolled across the frozen Straits Pond, and walked the shores of Hull. I have been to the Old Ship Church, now a beautiful Unitarian Universalist church in Hingham, the oldest church in continual use as a church in America.

I have followed Silence to the grave, as it were, to her final rest in Bolton, Mass., next to her beloved second husband Daniel, and several of her adult children. She is an enigma to me, and yet I feel I have brought her likeness to life. I hope you love her as much as I do. For those of you who have read my historical novel, *The Bereaved*, Silence Greenleaf is Martha Lozier's second great-grandmother, through her mother's side.

Enjoy more about
Silence: A Novel
Meet the Author
Check out author appearances
Explore special features

About the Author

JULIA PARK TRACEY is an award-winning journalist, editor, poet laureate, and author of several books. Inspired by a mysterious train receipt in her family's scrapbook, she researched her Orphan Train roots and wrote *The Bereaved* about her found relatives. She has ancestors—or should we say *an-sisters*? In digging through her family history, she has uncovered a trove of powerful women who break rules and stand tall against whatever dares to oppose them. One such heroine is the Puritan woman named Silence Greenleaf. Julia lives in the low Sierra of California in a carefully restored 1880 Victorian, with her family and beloved cats, bees and chickens.

Acknowledgements

Thanks to Ancestry for leading me through the arteries and capillaries of my family history, so that the story of Silence Greenleaf could be discovered.

For their companionship on my adventures through the Deep South and up into coldest New England, I must thank sister Carolyn Park Rich and cousin Amy Murch Sloan, who undertook a 1600-mile road trip in 2022 to find, see and acknowledge the slavery and plantations in our family tree, and up into the backwoods and byways of Massachusetts to find the houses and villages where Silence and Daniel met and lived. Also to my beloved in-laws, Joedy and Cindy Tracey, for their kind hospitality in Burtonsville, MD.

For their loving editorial support and occasional lash of the whip, I thank Max Wong, Suzy Vitello, Sang Kim, and Catie Gardner Giusta for steering me into the wind or into the lee, when I needed it. Thanks also to Nick Petrulakis of Newtonville Books, late of Books Inc. in California, for his long-standing friendship and that incredible dinner at the Bell in Hand Tavern, the oldest tavern in Boston, where Elizabeth Greenleaf and her family might have supped.

Thanks to the powerful women at Sibylline Press who see my work and support it with all their might: Vicki DeArmon, publisher, Alicia Feltman, art director, and Anna Termine, rights manager—you ladies rock!

And, as always, my dear husband Patrick Tracey, without whom life would be much, much harder in every way. Thank you for believing in me.

Book Group Questions

1. What do you think of the Puritan giving of names to daughters and sons to inspire a virtue, such as Mercy, Charity, Thankful or Love? What do you think of the giving of names such as Silence, Waitstill, Experience, or Fear? How do those names sound to you today? How do they differ from more recent naming trends such as Tiffany (the wealth of the 1980s); Savannah, Cheyenne, Austin (city or place names, 1990s); Sage, Mandala, Thistle or Kale (nature or spiritual names, 2000s), and other like names?

2. Do you think you could live with a year of silence? How long is the longest you have been silent, and for what purpose? How do you think you would have dealt with the punishment meted out to Silence, and what do you think of the church/magistrate's reasoning behind it?

3. Who is silenced in this novel? Besides the main character, whose voice is hushed, whose experience hidden, whose story ignored? Who does the silencing? Who holds the power?

4. Are all women witches or are none of them? The author plays with this idea by giving women certain powers that seem mysterious or magical, but are they more than just talents? Is Elizabeth Greenleaf an apothecaress or a witch? Is beekeeper Silence a witch or just good with animals? Is Huldah a witch or a midwife? Depending on your point of view, a case could be made that Silence is a witch—or not, and so might any woman.

5. Which is more powerful—the society you live in? The religious authority you subscribe to? The government you live under? Which can do more damage? Which is harder on a daily or personal level?

6. Do you think life in the country or the city is better for broader thinking, or healthful living? Which is more important—the body or the mind?

7. What are your thoughts about the medical treatments from Mr. Henry, from Mrs. Greenleaf, and from Dr. Greenleaf? What of Hulda and Jolly's midwiving?

8. Silence says, "This is how they teach us that we are worthless." Do you agree or disagree with that statement? Has that changed for women since 1723 when this story takes place?

Sibylline Press is proud to publish the brilliant work of women authors over 50. We are a woman-owned publishing company and, like our authors, represent women of a certain age.

Eleven Stolen Horses:
A Wild Horses Mystery

BY ROBIN SOMERS

MYSTERY
Trade Paper, 306 pages (5.315 x 8.465) | $17
ISBN: 9781960573865
Also available as an ebook and audiobook

News reporter Eleanor Wooley wants to start her life over in the foothills of the Sierra Nevada, but when her new best friend suddenly disappears, she combs remote landscapes searching for her friend and, ultimately, finds herself in grave danger.

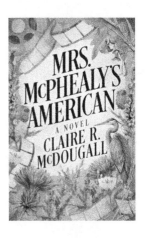

Mrs. McPhealy's American:
A Novel

BY CLAIRE R. MCDOUGALL

FICTION
Trade Paper, 344 pages (5.315 x 8.465) | $19
ISBN: 9781960573940
Also available as an ebook and audiobook

A one-way ticket to his ancestral home of Scotland lands beleaguered Hollywood director Steve McNaught at his distant relative's, Mrs. McPhealy's, in Locharbert where he's an immediate outcast and soon discovers that even love with a local can't save him.

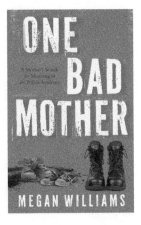

One Bad Mother: A Mother's Search for Meaning in the Police Academy

BY MEGAN WILLIAMS

MEMOIR
Trade Paper, 224 pages (5.315 x 8.465) | $17
ISBN: 9781960573858
Also available as an ebook and audiobook

A book for every mother who thinks she is failing the test of motherhood. Or thinks that challenging athletic feats or professional achievements may be easier than being a mother. That is—most of us. This is the thinking that landed the author in the police academy looking for win.

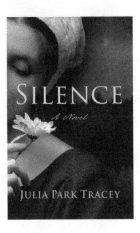

Silence: A Novel

BY JULIA PARK TRACEY

HISTORICAL FICTION
Trade Paper, 272 pages (5.315 x 8.465) | $18
ISBN: 9781736795491
Also available as an ebook and audiobook

A whiff of sulfur and witchcraft shadows this literary Puritan tale of loss and redemption, based on this best-selling historical fiction author's own ancestor, her seventh great-grandmother.

For more books from **Sibylline Press**, please visit our website at **sibyllinepress.com**

Printed in the USA
CPSIA information can be obtained
at www.ICGtesting.com
JSHW080038250824
68621JS00008B/3

9 781736 795491